SCARED STIFF

"What is it, Del Rey?"

Del Rey closed her gaping mouth; her fleshy chin rippled slightly. One puffy finger, tightly encased in a plastic glove, pointed to the withered woman on the embalming table. Not eager to follow her point, I kept my eyes fixed on the moritician.

"She's . . . not . . ."

"She's not . . . what?" I asked.

Del Rey shook her head and moved carefully toward the embalming table, where Sparkle Bodie lay lifeless.

She motioned me closer to the body. I took a reluctant step forward and peered cautiously into the dead woman's face. It was colorless and slack—and then I noticed her eyes.

They were rolling under the lids, as if she were dreaming.

One eye fluttered open, and Sparkle Bodie looked right at me. . . .

Other Connor Westphal Mysteries
by Penny Warner

DEAD BODY LANGUAGE
SIGN OF FOUL PLAY

RIGHT TO REMAIN SILENT

A CONNOR WESTPHAL MYSTERY

PENNY WARNER

BANTAM BOOKS
New York Toronto London Sydney Auckland

S

RIGHT TO REMAIN SILENT

A Bantam Crime Line Book / December 1998

CRIME LINE and the portrayal of a boxed "cl" are trademarks of Bantam Books, a division of Bantam Doubleday Dell Publishing Group, Inc.

ISBN 0-553-57962-2

Bantam Books are published by Bantam Books, a division of Bantam Doubleday Dell Publishing Group, Inc. Its trademark, consisting of the words "Bantam Books" and the portrayal of a rooster, is Registered in U.S. Patent and Trademark Office and in other countries. Marca Registrada. Bantam Books, 1540 Broadway, New York, New York 10036.

PRINTED IN THE UNITED STATES OF AMERICA

OPM   10   9   8   7   6   5   4   3   2   1

To Tom, Matt, and Rebecca
My partners in crime

ACKNOWLEDGMENTS

I very much want to thank the following experts in their fields for assistance on detail and veracity:

Dr. Linda Barde, Director of Special Education Services and Sign Language Instructor, Chabot College, Hayward, California
DCARA - Deaf Counseling and Referral Agency, San Leandro, California
E. Clampus Vitus, Calaveras County, California
Melanie Ellington, Counseling and Correctional Services, Jamestown, California
Mario Marcoli, Gold Prospector, Jamestown, California
Mother Lode Coffee Shop, Jamestown, California
Luci Zahray, Poison Expert

And many thanks to those who contributed their expertise to the manuscript: Janet Dawson, Lucy Galen, Jonnie Jacobs, Peggy Lucke, Lynn MacDonald, Betty Mc-Broom, Camille Minichino, Stacey Norris, Constance Pike, Edward Pike; Geoffrey W. Pike, Geoffrey E.C. Pike, Michelle Smythe, Shirley Stadelhofer, Sue Stadelhofer, Vicki Stadelhofer, Camille Thompson, and Diana Todd.

A special thanks to: Cassie Goddard, Amy Kossow, and Linda Allen.

"... pulseless and cold,
with a derringer by his side
and a bullet in his heart,
though still calm as in life,
beneath the snow lay he who was at once
the strongest and yet the weakest
of the outcasts of Poker Flat."

—Bret Harte
The Outcast of Poker Flat

RIGHT TO
REMAIN SILENT

She's . . . dead!"

At least, I thought that's what he said. I later learned I missed a crucial word. But Sluice Jackson, the old miner, wasn't speaking very clearly. With wisps of strawlike hair sticking out from under his Forty-Niners cap, he looked like a frightened scarecrow running down the driveway of Memory Kingdom Memorial Park, waving his bony arms as he flagged me down.

Late for work, I'd been pedaling like a frantic Margaret Hamilton from *The Wizard of Oz* when he nearly collided with me in the middle of the road. Folks nearby say he was screaming loud enough to wake the dead. Of course I couldn't hear him. But deafness didn't keep me from noticing the horrified look on his red face.

"Sluice! What is it?" I said, more angry than alarmed. His distraction had caused me to hit one of the many potholes along Flat Skunk's Main Street, and I'd nearly dumped my bike. As I straightened it up, Sluice grabbed the handlebars with two gnarled hands and tried to speak between huffs and puffs.

". . . she's not . . . her eyes . . . she . . ."

Sluice bent over with his hands on his knees and tried to get his breath. From this position, he pointed awkwardly to the mortuary.

"What, Sluice? Is Del Rey all right? Has something happened to her?" I dragged my bike over to the driveway and leaned it up against a shrub.

Sluice straightened and stared at me through rheumy eyes, his face twisted. "Sparkle Bodie . . ."

He made no sense at all, and probably wouldn't. He'd downed a few too many bottles of Yukon Jack over the years, while eking out a living as an unsuccessful gold prospector. His eighty-something wet brain was fairly fragile.

I headed toward the mortuary with Sluice wobbling on spindly legs behind me, but he stopped short at the door, reluctant to accompany me further. I left him muttering to himself in a flurry of fall leaves as I shut the door on the crisp morning air. Down the hall I located the familiar sign on the embalming room door that read NO ADMITTANCE. I pushed through boldly, semiprepared for the smell reminiscent of my high school science class. Del Rey, the new mortician, stood leaning against the wall.

I glanced over at the embalming table and wished I hadn't. Lying on the cold slab was the body of a very old woman, naked, shriveled, and still. I recognized Sparkle Bodie immediately. With a shiver I looked back at Del Rey, whose normally crimson-cheeked face now matched the color of the gray stainless steel table.

"Del Rey? Are you okay?"

She shook her head while taking short breaths.

"Do you need a doctor?" I asked again. "Are you dizzy? A heart attack? What is it, Del Rey?"

Del Rey closed her mouth and swallowed, her fleshy chin rippling slightly. One puffy finger, tightly encased in a plastic glove, pointed to the withered woman on the table. Not eager to follow her point, I kept my eyes on the mortician.

"She's . . . not . . ."

I reluctantly sneaked a quick peek back at Sparkle Bodie, lying in wait for Del Rey's expert postmortem care, then returned to Del Rey's twisted face. I'd never seen her look the least bit fazed about a postmortem client. Even when old man Penzance had practically rolled off the embalming table last month, just prior to his embalming, she didn't bat an eyelash. She said corpses twitched and wiggled all the time when they're coming out of rigor. I thought nothing bothered her. Until now.

"She's not . . . what?" I asked.

Del Rey shook her head again, and moved slowly toward the table, while I watched from a safe distance. Sparkle Bodie appeared lifeless, just as all corpses did before Del Rey worked her magic with embalming fluid, makeup, and hair design.

Del Rey motioned me closer to the body. I took a hesitant step forward and peered cautiously into the dead woman's face. It was colorless and slack—and then I noticed the eyes.

They were rolling under the lids, as if she were dreaming.

"Oh, my God. Is she . . . alive? How—?"

Del Rey cut me off.

"I. Don't. Know. How." She said the words distinctly, as if each was a self-contained sentence. Speaking so deliberately seemed to bring her back. She snatched a lab coat hanging on the wall and draped it over the body. "But she is. And she's got to be freezing in here."

"Del Rey, are you sure she's—I mean, maybe it's just like old man Penzance, you know—"

Del Rey shot me a dirty look.

"All right! All right! So what should we do? Did you call nine-one-one?"

Del Rey nodded tightly, then turned her attention to her customer—or whatever she was called—who was now covered snugly with the lab coat.

One eye fluttered open . . . and Sparkle Bodie looked right at me.

Where in God's name was that ambulance?

．　　　．　　　．　　　．

Less than a minute later the EMTs entered with a stretcher, followed by Sheriff Elvis Mercer. One of the paramedics gave the old woman oxygen, while the other covered her with a blanket and began an IV I stood on the sidelines as Sheriff Mercer asked Del Rey a few questions I couldn't lip-read clearly. By the time the ambulance and sheriff left with a blue-tinged but semirevived Sparkle Bodie, Del Rey's hands had stopped trembling enough to get us a drink.

Forever on a diet, Del Rey opted for a "lite" Sierra Nevada pale ale, which she'd stashed away in the tiny office refrigerator. She offered me the same. It took me only a second to realize and then ignore the fact that it was still morning. We downed several swallows before speaking.

"Well, this is one for *Ripley's*, isn't it?" she said, pulling her brown knit top down over her ample hips for the third time. At thirty-five, Del Rey was two years younger and probably fifty pounds heavier than I was. But she wore it well, and I couldn't imagine her thinner. Without the padding, she wouldn't have been Del Rey Montez.

"I'd say it's one for *Hard Copy*. What are you going to wear when Jerry Springer calls to inquire about your former customer?"

She shot me a nasty look—she was getting good at them—then moved into the lobby of the mortuary to find a comfortable place to recover.

Emotionally drained myself, I dropped into one of the cozy overstuffed couches in the greeting room. The decor resembled a grandmother's parlor, complete with Tiffany lamps, velveteen love seats, and flecked rose-petal wallpaper, but with an artificial, almost Disneyesque touch.

Del Rey had been employed at the Memory Kingdom Memorial Park for six months, and during that time we'd slowly become friends. We'd met at the "Memorial Park" where her Malamute, Frosty, and my Siberian husky, Casper, played chase the squirrels.

Del Rey plopped down next to me and tried to cross

a leg over her knee. She made it about half way. "Thanks for your help, Connor. Sluice is pretty useless these days. Don't know why I keep him working the grounds. Guess 'cause he reminds me of my father and the rest of the old prospectors."

"I'm glad I was nearby. I was on my way to interview the new deputy, Marca Clemens, when Sluice ran out like he'd seen a ghost. Was that the first customer you've had come back to life?"

"She's a client, not a customer. I have clients, waitresses have customers. What do newspaper publishers have?"

"Migraines. I thought you called them corpses. Or maybe Loved Ones." I usually don't engage in much irrelevant small talk. It's a strain reading lips and I don't like to waste the energy. But at the moment, the light conversation seemed soothing. And Del Rey's Betty Boop lips were easy to ready.

Del Rey smiled. "It's nearly the twenty-first century, Connor. Even here in the historically preserved Mother Lode, terms have changed with the times. Get with it."

"Hey, at least I didn't call her *deceased* when she wasn't."

Del Rey's smile faded. "That was below the belt. Or it would be, if I had one." She hiked up her sagging knee-highs through her cotton leggings.

"How could this have happened?" I asked, still puzzled. "How could a person appear to be dead—and still be alive?"

"Good question. I read about an old guy once who lived at a nursing home in a small town. When he didn't respond, the staff just sent him off to the mortuary, assuming he was dead. Turned out he wasn't."

"That's incredible!"

"You watch. Everyone's going to be passing the buck on this one real fast. Especially the members of the Bodie family. The old woman was in poor health for a long time, but if you ask me, I think the relatives have been waiting for her to die for years."

Del Rey seemed to need more prodding for details. "What makes you say that?"

"In this business, you hear a lot of stuff. Apparently her son, Esken, didn't get along with her at all, and neither did his wife, Sonora. While Sparkle had been trying to maintain Flat Skunk as a kind of historical monument, those two have been working hard to turn the town into a bunch of money-making strip malls and fast-food joints."

"Yeah, but that doesn't mean they'd actually *do* anything—"

"And what about that other one who lives there, the one nobody ever sees? What's up with him?"

"I don't know who you mean. I thought she was alone in that big old house." As a reporter for my own weekly newspaper, the *Eureka!*, I got into the gossip mode quickly. Shame on me, I thought, as I took another sip of beer.

"I heard she has another son. He's retarded or something. Don't know his name or much about him. She never talked about him, never brought him to town."

"The Bodies are an odd family, that's for sure—always bickering at town council meetings. And that Sparkle is a feisty one. But how could she be pronounced dead when she wasn't? Didn't a doctor examine her?"

Del Rey shrugged. "I'm sure he did. You can't officially die around here without a medical certificate. But Sparkle was old. And like I said, it wasn't as if they didn't expect it at any minute, with her weak heart, enlarged liver, and hemorrhoids and whatever else was wrong with her. I'll bet one of the family members found her cold and blue and just figured she was gone. They probably couldn't wait to get rid of her."

"Still, this is a pretty big mistake. Like something out of an Edgar Allan Poe story. We don't bury people today unless they're really dead—do we?" I shuddered.

"Maybe old Doc Crippen couldn't detect a heartbeat, so he just signed the papers and sent her over to me. He's half blind himself and way past retirement. Hell, I don't know. They don't tell you anything about this in mortuary college. I think there was a paragraph or two on those early coffins with bells installed on the outside, so if the deceased suddenly woke up, he could ring the bell and alert the mourners that he wasn't dead. But I never studied anything called 'Reanimation One-Oh-One—What to Do When the Dead Body Comes Back to Life.' All I know is, it scared the shit out of me."

The phone apparently rang because Del Rey pushed herself up from the couch and went over to answer it. I watched her face as she spoke, and saw her expression change from curiosity to horror. Could things be worse than they already were? Had someone else died? When Del Rey returned with a flushed face and a second beer, I asked her what was wrong.

"It was the *Mother Lode Monitor*. They want to do a story on what happened! God, what am I going to say? They're sending a photographer over in an hour. What'll I wear? Can I lose five pounds before they get here? God, my hair—"

"Traitor!" I yelped. "What about the *Eureka!*? I want an exclusive for *my* newspaper. A story like this could be good for your business," I said.

"Or not," she added quickly. "When I think I might have actually stuck that big fat trocar into her thin old thigh and—" She shivered and gulped her beer.

I thought for a moment about Sparkle Bodie, one of the many eccentric residents of Flat Skunk. You couldn't escape them, here in the heart of the California Gold Country, where towns like Bogus Thunder and Poker Flat were once as shiny as gold nuggets. Sparkle had the distinction of being the oldest. Her forefathers from the gold and copper mines had helped shape this antique mining town. The Bodies were one of the few families to strike it rich while the rest of the gold-dreamers lapsed into poverty, depression, and alcoholism. Ironic how her descendants were doing their best to bury Flat Skunk's rustic heritage along with her. For months she'd been publicly at war with her son, Esken, and daughter-in-law, Sonora, over their own dreams of turning Flat Skunk into a trendy tourist trap.

"She wasn't, I mean she isn't . . . terribly well liked in town, is she?" I asked.

Del Rey's eyes widened. Her expressive face was easy to read. "Not with me, she wasn't. Isn't. I'm all for keeping Flat Skunk historically preserved, within reason. But when she tried to stop us from upgrading the crumbling cemetery, that was too much. She's a fanatic."

"A lot of people agree with you, from what I understand," I said.

Del Rey's eyebrows peaked like the Alps. "What have you heard? Uh, I mean, what do you know?"

I smiled at her change of phrase. I say the words "hear" and "heard" all the time, but hearing people seem to feel awkward about using the terms in front of me, as if they've said something insulting.

"Oh, I learn things, too, you know, owning a newspaper," I said nonchalantly. "People tell me all kinds of dirt . . ."

"Like who?" Del Rey said, leaning in.

"I have to protect my sources, you know. Confidentiality."

"Hell, Connor, I tell you all kinds of things about my clients. And believe me, I learn plenty in this business."

"Dead men tell no tales," I said, doing my best pirate impersonation.

"Connor, they don't have to talk to tell me their secrets."

I finished my beer and stood. "I'm going to check up on Sparkle Bodie at the hospital. See if I can beat the *Monitor* to the rest of the story. After all, I was an eyewitness."

Del Rey stood, too, and moved across the room to the gilt-trimmed phone. Another call. With her back to me, I couldn't make out what she said. But when she hung up and turned around, the alcohol flush had drained from her Kewpie-doll face.

"Was that Barbara Walters?"

"No. Sheriff Mercer."

"What's the matter?"

"Looks like business is picking up."

"What do you mean?"

"Sparkle Bodie is dead—again."

Exchanging my bike for my Chevy, I made it to the Whisky Slide hospital in less time than it takes to revive a corpse. Sheriff Mercer stood questioning a woman in green pajamas when I interrupted him.

"Sheriff! What happened?"

He gave me a look that read "Not now, Connor," and returned his attention to a "Dr. Garcia," according to the name tag. I stepped back, looking for someone else to interrogate—I mean *interview*.

I spotted Russell Jacks, the Bodie family attorney, huddled in one corner with Esken Bodie, Sparkle's middle-aged son. Apparently Russell had already been alerted to the situation. He was talking vigorously, using his slender fingers to point and jab the air. Esken, looking disheveled in his suit, paced back and forth. I couldn't make out what either one was saying, but Russell seemed tense, perhaps giving legal advice. Maybe they were preparing to sue somebody. But Esken didn't appear to be paying close attention. He just kept pacing.

Esken's wife, Sonora, immaculately turned out, sat in a nearby waiting room; I could see her through a glass partition. She seemed preoccupied with her mauve nails as she talked with another woman in sweats whom I recognized from the museum preservation society, Holly Bryson. It was a surprise to see them together, since they were on opposite sides of the town development issue. From their body language, Holly seemed upset, while Sonora appeared bored.

I was about to interrupt them to see what I could find out, when I spotted Aubrey Horne, Flat Skunk's lone librarian and most sought-after bachelor. Good-looking, he was not the stereotypical bookworm. What was he doing here? I thought, then remembered the genealogy chart he'd been creating for the Bodie family. Apparently he had an interest.

At the present time his interest was in a newer branch of the family: Sonora's daughter. I guessed Devon to be around sixteen or seventeen, although it wasn't easy to tell, with her swollen legs and protruding belly. The unmarried teenager had to be seven or eight months pregnant. All in all, it was quite a large gathering. I decided to join their conversation. They turned toward me as I approached.

"Aubrey, what happened?" I asked, scanning his face for a preview of his answer.

"Hi, Connor. You here for your newspaper?"

I nodded. "Is she really dead this time?" I glanced at Devon and wished I'd phrased it differently. This was, after all, her grandmother. But she didn't react. Her attention was held by something down the hall.

Aubrey cupped his right ear and leaned in. "Sorry. I couldn't hear you above the noise. That *screaming*. What did you say?"

I gave him a blank look. He realized I didn't know what noise he was talking about.

He nodded in the direction of a closed hospital room door and overmouthed the words as he explained. "It's Sparkle's son. He's gone crazy. They have him strapped down on a gurney in the next room. Gave him something to calm him, but he's still screaming like a woman in childbirth. It's been awful." He suddenly seemed to remember who he was with and shot Devon an apologetic look. She absently massaged her protruding abdomen as if to comfort herself.

I looked over at Esken, wondering what Aubrey was talking about. Esken wasn't screaming. He wasn't lying on a gurney. He looked fine.

Aubrey followed my glance. "Not Esken. That other one. The one who lives with Sparkle."

It was the second time today that another son of Sparkle Bodie had been mentioned. A few hours ago, I hadn't even known he existed.

Out of the corner of my eye, I saw Sonora leaving the waiting room. She was headed our way. Devon also spotted her mother, but instead of waiting to talk with her, she spun around and walked off in the opposite direction. Sonora stopped abruptly, gave a small shake of her head, and returned to the waiting room.

Aubrey turned to me. "Did you see that? I was about to say Esken's brother is kind of weird, but I think they're all weird in that family. Must be something in the genes."

"What's the brother's name?"

"Damn, I just filled in that part on the genealogy chart . . . Carl? Casper? No, that's your dog. Caleb! I think that's it."

"So what happened to Sparkle?"

"Well, apparently she wasn't all that dead when they took her to the mortuary—"

"I know that part—although I still don't understand it. But what happened here?"

"Well, the ambulance took her to the hospital. I heard the sirens going down Main Street, so I called Rebecca, the dispatcher, to find out what was happening, and I drove on over. I was curious, you know, after all that work I've been doing on their history."

Aubrey was "curious" about everything. As a librarian,

he provided an unlimited source of information—not all of it from the stacks.

"Anyway, they brought her in and got her started on an IV and stuff. The guy from the *Monitor* arrived to do a story on her, 'cause of the bizarre way she came back to life, you know. I tried to see her but they wouldn't let anyone in. Then all of a sudden we hear this *horrible* scream and the nurses go running into Sparkle's room and they find her dead again. This time for real."

"How did she die?"

"They don't know yet. But Caleb—he's retarded or something—I mean, 'developmentally disabled'—anyway he was found in her room, screaming his head off, throwing things, just bouncing off the walls, you know. And that's when they discovered she was dead."

"You mean . . ."

"Sheriff Mercer thinks maybe he did something to her in there."

"How. . . ?"

"There was a pillow over her head," Aubrey said solemnly.

"Her own son! That's just too bizarre!" I said, feeling dizzy. I have a touch of tinnitus, related to my hearing disorder—which was a result of contracting meningitis at the age of four. When I'm under stress, I experience vertigo. I leaned back against the wall to steady myself.

Suddenly the door to Sparkle's hospital room opened. A large man, maybe six feet, in loose dirty jeans and a thin flannel shirt appeared, his hands behind his back. He looked disheveled, with long strands of dark hair hanging around his face. His eyes were red-rimmed, and his cheeks were stained and smudged with dirt.

With downcast eyes, he moved through the door, followed by Sheriff Mercer. The new deputy, Marca Clemens—the woman I was supposed to have interviewed that morning—followed close behind. The big man, hand-cuffed and obviously sedated, shuffled down the hall like a zombie.

As he passed by me, our eyes locked. For the briefest moment, I caught a glimmer of helplessness in his eyes.

After all the excitement, I needed a mocha break. Apparently, so did everyone else who'd been milling around at the hospital. At a little after ten A.M. the Nugget Café was full, and the only seat I could find was at the counter.

The place wasn't fancy, but the Nugget offered me the kind of respite I craved when I wanted to think, work on a story, or just relax. The diner had come a long way since the days of the forty-niners, when bacon sold for a dollar a slice and Hangtown Fry held a double meaning. It had come a long way since last month, when the owner, Mama Cody, installed an espresso machine in an effort to meet the demands of the city expatriates flocking to the slower-paced Mother Lode.

I had mixed feelings about the changes occurring in Flat Skunk. Part of the reason I'd moved here almost a year ago from San Francisco was for the authentic feeling of the Old West. But I had to admit, I missed some modern luxuries. Like a mocha with a cinnamon-raisin bagel.

As I stirred the foam into my mocha, I glanced around the café and was surprised to see Dan Smith, my next-door office neighbor and current—what? Best friend? Boyfriend? Lover? The relationship had been developing slowly but surely, and I still tingled when I caught sight of him.

But this was odd. He wasn't one to take a break so early. I was headed over until I realized he wasn't alone. A woman with messy blond hair and a too-tight top sat opposite him. I couldn't see her face, but I didn't think I knew her. I stopped, made an about-face, and resumed my seat at the counter, hoping Dan hadn't noticed.

Just as I was about to start planning this strange woman's excruciating death, Russell Jacks perched next to me at the counter and set down his leather briefcase. His look of concern distracted me from my temporary alarm at Dan's new friend. I wondered how much Russell was involved in the ever-changing Bodie saga. After a quick greeting, I eschewed the preliminary chitchat, which I abhor, and got to the point.

"Are you representing Sparkle's son?"

Russell looked taken aback for a moment. "Esken?"

"No, the other one."

"Oh. You mean Caleb."

I nodded. So did he. "Temporarily, anyway. I haven't decided to take the case."

"The case?"

"Sheriff Mercer suspects Caleb may have killed Sparkle."

"That can't be true!"

Russell nodded again. "I agree, it's ludicrous to think a son would kill his own mother. Especially this one. Caleb Bodie just isn't, well, I don't think he's smart enough to pull it off."

"It doesn't take a lot of brains to kill someone. But the sheriff's arrested him for murder? Why?"

"He says Caleb was the only person in the room when Sparkle died. And there were indications that she didn't die a natural death."

"Like what?" I thought of the pillow Aubrey mentioned earlier.

"He wouldn't say. But the attending physician, Dr. Doreen Garcia, concurred. That's really all I know so far."

"The buzz in here is that she may have suffocated."

"You've been reading people's lips again, haven't you, Connor? Isn't there some kind of Miss Manners etiquette about that?"

I shrugged. "I haven't read that chapter yet. Besides, I read people's conversations for the practice. I have to keep up my skills if I want to be a good lip-reader. And it's no worse than overhearing something. You hearies do it all the time, I understand."

Russell smiled and nodded. "Anyway, nothing's been confirmed. Sheriff Mercer's going to make a statement later today. Probably after he combs his hair for the TV cameras. This will be on all the channels tonight, that's for sure." So much for the *Eureka!* exclusive.

Russell—no one ever called him Rusty, in spite of the red hair—and I had become acquainted during a personal injury trial I'd covered for the *Eureka!* He'd represented Esken Bodie, who made his living as a land developer, when Holly Bryson, the museum curator, sued him. Esken had wanted to move the old Flat Skunk Railroad Station to the other end of town so he could build a mini-mall on the original site. But Holly, who had worked to preserve the railroad station as a museum, sued him—after she hanged him in effigy from the railroad mail post—and won a temporary restraining order. The case was still unsettled.

I sipped from the black soup-bowl-sized mug, another one of the Nugget's concessions to the times. I kind of missed the old chipped coffee cups that sported the words "Eat Here and Get Gas." But since they'd torn down the old Union 76 station next door, those cups had taken on a whole new meaning.

"Are you going to defend Caleb if he's charged with something?"

"I suppose, if it comes to that. I *am* the family attorney. Nice mustache, by the way." He pointed to the foam on my upper lip.

Russell looked more like a college professor than a lawyer. At fifty, his Levi's were still a thirty-four, his blue work shirt was always pressed and tucked in, and his tweed sports coat set off his hazel eyes. I had never seen him in anything other than Ferragamo loafers. A mocha mustache wouldn't have the nerve to appear on his lips. Lips, by the way that were easy to read, framing ivory, orthodonture-enhanced teeth.

I wiped the foamy residue from my mouth with a finger and licked my fingertip. "What's going to happen next?"

"I'm meeting with Sheriff Mercer this afternoon. I should learn more then."

"What's the guy like? This Caleb. I heard—"

Russell looked past me toward the front door and grimaced. I turned to see Aubrey Horne entering the cafe, wiping his fingers on his handkerchief while clasping a book under his arm. The librarian sat down kitty-corner to us at the counter, as if we expected him.

Stuffing the ink-stained handkerchief into his denim pocket, he placed his paperback on the counter. I checked the cover. You may not be able to judge a book by its cover but you can learn a lot about people by the books they read. Much more than a medicine cabinet. This one was titled: *Genealogy, DNA, and Biological Predictions*. I'd wait for the movie version. But only if Mel Gibson starred.

"What are you all talking about?" Aubrey said, signaling Jilda, the thirty-something waitress. Aubrey didn't look like the mousy, chicken-chested stereotype of a librarian. A product of his Chinese mother and Miwok Indian father, he could pass for the buffed construction worker in one of those ab-flab infomercials. He could star in a one-man pin-up calendar. He could model Calvin Klein—

My daydreams were interrupted.

"I'll bet it's the murder!" Aubrey said, as if he'd just solved the case.

Russell shook his head in disgust. Not a hair moved. "Hell, it's all over town already, isn't it?"

"Listen, I'm a librarian. It's my business to know all kinds of information. So are you representing him?" Aubrey pulled out a rubber band and bound his shoulder-length hair into a ponytail.

Aubrey was like me. He didn't know how to beat around the bush, speak in euphemisms, or use subtlety. He simply said what was on his mind. I liked that about him. And the tattoo of the Tasmanian Devil on his right bicep only added to his charm.

Russell suddenly stuffed a hand into his blazer pocket and pulled out a cell phone. He flipped open the lid, then turned away to talk. I sipped my mocha and watched Aubrey order a tall, low-fat decaf cappuccino with whipped cream from Jilda. She brought him what looked like a milkshake.

Russell snapped the phone shut and replaced it in his pocket. He glanced at his watch.

"I have to run. Got a few things to prepare before I meet with Elvis. Connor, you aren't going to print anything we discussed, are you?"

Although there are no legal precedents regarding "off the record," I shrugged. "There's not much to say yet. I may come by later to ask you a few questions, after you meet with Sheriff Mercer." No one called Sheriff Mercer Elvis, except Russell and the sheriff's son, Jeremiah.

Russell nodded. "I may not be able to say too much." He downed the last of his espresso and headed for the door, nodding at several of the patrons as he passed by. He seemed to know everyone in town. Legally, I wondered?

"So, what's the dirt?" Aubrey asked, recapturing my attention. He leaned in close; I guessed he was whispering, as if it mattered with me. "Does Russell think Caleb Bodie killed his own mother? There's always been something strange about that family. I didn't even know there was another brother until I started working on—"

Holly Bryson, the woman who spent most of her free time dedicated to the museum society, when she wasn't hanging people who stood in her way in effigy, rose from the booth where she'd been sitting. She whirled around, nearly decapitating the man in the seat behind her with her arm. I followed the direction of her intense attention.

Sonora Bodie had just entered the Nugget Café.

I glanced back at Holly and caught her words in mid-sentence: ". . . hell's the matter with you?!"

The two women weren't often seen together, but here they were, twice in one day. When they happened to be in the same room, flying fur was not far behind. They usually didn't speak to each other at all, except at town council meetings, and then only in flamboyant gestures with twisted faces, from opposite sides of the room—and the fence. What, I wondered, festered between them this time?

Holly's distorted expression didn't help with my lipreading, but since she was facing me, I caught the gist of her verbal onslaught.

"—you tore down my sign! You trampled on private land! And you engaged in malicious destruction of property! Don't think I don't know what you did. And don't think you'll get away with it. That museum is a historical landmark and the people of this town want it here—including your mother-in-law, dead or alive. No so-called 'growth advocate' is going to stop Sparkle's dream from being realized."

Sonora must have responded in kind, but I missed her words. I gathered by her body language that she said something just as accusatory. Holly pushed her way out of the booth so violently she dumped over the metal napkin holder and several sugar packets. Grabbing her purse, she stomped toward the door, only to trip over Aubrey's inadvertently outstretched foot. She caught herself, gave Aubrey a wilting glare, and stormed out.

Sonora took a seat at the booth with her daughter, Devon, but neither of them said anything, and I turned back to Aubrey. He shrugged as if he were an innocent bystander in a scene from *Who's Afraid of Virginia Woolf?* He twirled back around on his red leather stool, trying to look casual, but his cheeks were filled with roses.

After a sip of cappuccino, he said: "This heritage-versus-progress battle is getting on my nerves. I mean, that Jiffy Lube downtown looks like something out of the old *Gunsmoke* show. Notice how it blends so well with that *Bonanza*-looking KFC? What's next? A rodeo-style gas station? A *Wagon Train* Starbucks? The Flat Skunk Library designed like a gold mine?"

I smiled weakly. It was true. If we weren't careful the town would soon look more like Walt Disney's Adventureland than an authentic pioneer mining town. I wondered, was it just a matter of the old-timers clinging to the past? Or did they truly want to preserve the original charm of the historic Gold Rush town?

I had a feeling the battle was only just beginning to heat up.

Out of the corner of my eye, I saw Dan rise from the table where he'd been talking with the pouffy-haired blonde. Distracted by the brief catfight, I'd nearly forgotten about him—and the stranger he'd been talking with. His bearded face was obscured by his hand so I couldn't read his lips, and the woman's back was to me so I could tell nothing about their current conversation. Damn. As he headed for the door—alone—I stood up to greet him.

"Dan! Hi!" I said, stepping into his path while trying to act as though I had just noticed him. "Where did you come from?"

Dan brushed his blond-black beard nervously and glanced back at the woman, who remained at the table. He turned to me but his dark brown eyes didn't meet mine. "Hey, Connor. Uh, how's it going?" With that, he went out the door.

Brrr. Was it something I said? I thought things were going well for us lately. I gazed back at the woman seated at the booth and caught her watching Dan as he passed by the café window. From her profile she could have been attractive, but she looked tired and worn, and it was difficult to determine her age under the pantina of makeup—she could be anywhere from mid-thirties to late forties. The brown roots of her blond hair were showing, and the sculptured do was no match for the cool fall weather. She wore an expensive-looking fuzzy lavender sweater and floral silk scarf around her neck, but the sweater was wrinkled and the scarf appeared frayed. I watched her track Dan as he headed across the street and into the hotel office building.

Aubrey poked me, disturbing my dark thoughts. He looked annoyed. "Did you hear me? You're not watching my lips."

"I'm sorry, no. What did you say?"

He lifted his genealogy book. "I said, who needs books when you have live theater right here? Oh, never mind. So are you going to dig up the dirt on this Sparkle Bodie thing for your paper?"

"You think there's some dirt?" Out of the corner of my eye, I saw the unnatural blonde rise from the table, gather her enormous designer shoulder bag, and saunter over to the gum machine. Her lavender skirt hugged her hips, and even matched her CFM—loosely translated as "I'm easy"—shoes.

"I've been doing that genealogy work for the Bodies. A couple of interesting things have turned up," Aubrey said.

"Like what?"

"I really shouldn't say, you know. Not until this thing is resolved."

While I admired Aubrey's ability to come to the point when he wanted to know something, I detested his evasiveness when questioned directly. I wasn't worried. In a matter of moments I'd have him begging to spill his guts.

I shrugged a "whatever" and held up my mug. "I need a refill. Want one?"

He shook his head. I waved to Jilda and signed, "More mocha, decaf," which was literally translated to "More coffee, deaf." Curious about sign, Jilda had asked me to teach her some basic American Sign Language vocabulary. She had most of the foods and drinks in the diner down. Now she wanted to tackle the dirty words. Those would be easy. They were the first words I learned at deaf camp when I was a teenager.

While I waited for my refill, I studied the case full of bran muffins and whole-wheat bagels incongruously juxtaposed next to the glazed chocolate doughnuts and berry pies. I tried not to drool down my Dr. Seuss T-shirt.

"Connor, *chérie*. What can I get for you? More mocha?"

It was Jean-Philipe, a Frenchman who had been hired at the Nugget about the time the espresso machine had been added. More of Mama Cody's attempts to give the old diner a new café appeal.

Beer, whiskey, and rotgut had been Flat Skunk's drinks of choice for decades. Now they seemed to have met their match in espressos, mochas, and cappuccinos. Coffee drinks had suddenly become the new antidotes for all that ailed the townspeople. Although Poison, the bar on the other side of town, was still home to the few diehard prospectors who mined the area, the Nugget had become the hangout for the newly arrived ex-suburbanites and retirees.

With his heavy French accent, Jean-Philipe was difficult for me to understand. With words like "Connor" and "mocha," he stressed the second syllable instead of the first, which utterly confused me.

I usually answered him with "huh?" Luckily the French are physically expressive, using their faces, hands, and bodies, much like the deaf. Despite his receding dark hair and a strong nose, Jean-Philipe exuded an earthy sexiness that he conveyed easily with his body language. He had charmed most of the women in Flat Skunk, me included.

"Mo-*cha*?" he repeated, leaning close to me and holding up a coffee cup.

"Yes, please, Jean-Philipe." I felt myself blush and hoped my cheeks didn't clash with my top.

"Whipped *cream*? Cinna*mon*?" He pointed to each.

I nodded. He could have said "Arse*nic*?" and "Cyan-*ide*?" and I would have given him the go-ahead.

"Could I have a canbrerry ban, I mean *cranberry bran* muffin?" I added, doing my best to hold up my end of the witty repartee.

"Hea*ted*? Wis but*ter*?"

"Yes, I will marry you," I thought, and nodded ambiguously.

Jean-Philipe's eyes abruptly moved to my side. I turned to face the uniformed officer who had sidled up next to me.

"Coffee, black, please." It was Marca Clemens, the deputy who had taken the place of the unfortunate former deputy, now a part of Flat Skunk's notorious history. But that's another story.

Flat Skunk was not only becoming progressive, it was trying its damnedest to be somewhat politically correct. Marca was one of a handful of female deputies in the entire Mother Lode region.

"Hi . . . there," I said, not quite knowing what to call the new cop. Deputy? Ms. Clemens? Officer?

Marca Clemens nodded. She gave me one of those polite I-know-you-but-I-can't-remember-how looks. We'd never been introduced. Most women don't intimidate me, and most uniforms don't intimidate me, but this new deputy had a presence that I could almost feel. I stuck my hand out.

"I'm Connor Westphal. I don't think we've met. I was supposed to interview you this morning, for my newspaper, the *Eureka!*"

She shook my hand briefly, forced a brief smile, then took her coffee from Jean-Philipe. She said something facing straight ahead that I couldn't make out because of her thin lips and lack of expression. I had a feeling either she didn't understand my speech or she didn't know I was deaf.

I leaned in. "I was wondering . . . have you made an arrest in the death of Sparkle Bodie yet?" I asked boldly. I'm sure it was the mocha talking.

She didn't respond.

"I think you have Caleb Bodie at the jail—Sparkle's son? Is he being held for murder?"

Again I missed her words. I asked her to face me and repeat herself. It took her a moment to process the request and understand why I had made it. This time, looking squarely at me, she overenunciated each word.

"I'm sorry but I can't discuss the Bodie case. The sheriff will be issuing a statement later this afternoon and you reporters can get the information at that time."

"But I—"

"You'll have to excuse me. I'm on duty. I have to get back to work." Marca Clemens paid for her coffee, covered the paper cup with a plastic lid, and swaggered out. She actually swaggered. That's what a uniform does to you, I supposed. I turned back to Aubrey, who sat perched on his stool, watching the whole scenario with a smirk.

"Hell of an interview," he said sarcastically. "I'd hate to go under the hot lights with you. I'm sure I'd tell you my innermost secrets the moment you pulled out the first fingernail."

"Shut up," I said, and elbowed him so he nearly spilled his coffee milkshake. "If you don't tell me what you learned from the genealogy search, I'm going to print a story about that Vargas book of nudes you didn't return to the library for four months."

"You wouldn't."

"Headline: *'Librarian Hoards Overdue Book. Returns It Without Paying Fine.'* You'll be history," I said solemnly.

"I'll be ruined. My career destroyed. I'll be out on the street," he joked.

"You'll never work in this town again."

He hunkered down. I could tell he was dying to tell me. "Okay, okay. I didn't find out that much. Really. In fact, it's what I didn't find that's so interesting. I was halfway through the research when I hit a stumbling block. In all the family papers Sparkle gave me in preparation for the research, I noticed one of the birth certificates was missing."

"So? You can always write to the county for another one."

"That's what I thought. But the day after I told Sparkle about it, she suddenly dropped the project."

"That's odd. Whose birth certificate was missing?"

"Devon's. Esken and Sonora's kid."

I sipped my fresh mocha and thought about Esken Bodie. As a land developer, he'd been his mother's primary opponent in her efforts toward town preservation. Everyone knew Esken wanted to turn Flat Skunk into a money-making tourist attraction. He was quite outspoken in his complaints about the lack of business profits in town.

"You know, Esken dropped a bombshell at the last town council meeting," I said.

"I was there. He wanted to bring in McDonald's! Even one that served espresso, no less. That got vetoed by his mother and her historical society members in a flash."

"Maybe it all boils down to a family quarrel between Esken and his mother. Think there's any connection to her death in all this?"

Sparkle was not about to let her town change. Her family had been original settlers soon after gold was discovered in 1849. The early incorporation campaign brought on by Esken had been a small war, with incorporation the loser. Sparkle had the money and influence to back her side, and Esken did not. That meant there would be no chains, no franchises, no "golden arches," and no minimalls in the near future, even if they were built to resemble Dodge City.

"So what about Esken's brother? They say he's strange, but would he have any reason to kill his own mother?"

"I hear he's got a temper, but no one ever sees him much. Kind of like our own Boo Radley, you know, from *To Kill A Mockingbird*. There have been rumors over the years. But here in Flat Skunk, I think anything is possible."

Aubrey was right. In this historical yet burgeoning community, caught in its own adolescence, just about anything could happen. It was a time of unrest, and my newspaper had been full of related reports, aside from the usual drunk-and-disorderly. A brilliant retired chemist recently had been arrested in nearby Whisky Slide for manufacturing methamphetamine, and a popular soccer coach from Poker Flat was serving time for dealing drugs to high school students. Just last week, the former historical society chairman had been jailed for embezzling funds. Even a record number of Clampers—members of the raucous organization of E. Clampus Vitus—had been spending the night behind bars.

And now a possible murder of an old woman by her own son?

Someone tapped me on the shoulder, a little more forcefully than necessary. I jumped, then whirled around.

"Ouch! What are you trying to do? Tap me to death? Jeez—"

It was Esken Bodie, his eyes wild, his hands trembling. His usually smooth face was unshaven, his always-combed hair was windblown.

Realizing his recent loss, I flushed. "Esken! Sorry. Are you all right?" Of course he wasn't. His mother was dead and his brother had been escorted out of the hospital in the custody of the sheriff.

"Connor, I need to talk with you . . . you come outside for a moment? It's . . . urgent." He was mumbling, and I had difficulty making out every word, but I think I got the gist.

I looked at Aubrey, who gave me a raised eyebrow. I took it to mean, "Here comes your newspaper story, Connor."

Leaving some money on the counter to cover my tab, I followed as Esken moved impatiently to the door and held it open for me with his foot, one hand nervously tugging at his collar. A gust of wind blew in, riffling his hair, but he didn't seem to notice. I followed him out the door.

"Can you come to my office?" I asked. He nodded. I led him across the street and up the back stairs of the former Penzance Hotel building. Making my way down the hall, I glanced at Dan's office door. It was closed but the light was on, and I could feel rhythmic vibrations coming from the floorboards. I gathered he was listening to music.

I unlocked my office door and, plopping my backpack on my littered desk, sat down, gesturing for Esken to take the chair opposite me. He hunched down, and pulled at his tie, trying to loosen its grip.

"What's up, Esken?" I asked curiously. I knew the

middle-aged man only as a newspaper client. He'd placed ads for property several times, but I was fairly certain he hadn't come today to discuss layouts and panel rates.

"My brother, Caleb. The sheriff's got him locked up over at the jail."

"I know. Why is Sheriff Mercer holding him?"

"That's why I'm here. I want you to see him."

"The sheriff?"

"Caleb."

I'm sure my mouth dropped open. "Why me?"

"Because, I think you're the only one who can find out what really happened in my mother's hospital room."

"Esken, why do you think your brother would talk with me instead of to you or Russell or the sheriff? He's never met me. I'm not a psychologist or anything. Isn't he, uh . . . mentally challenged, or whatever they call it today? I have no experience with that kind of disability." Some people actually think all disabled people are alike.

Esken smoothed his tie down the front of his shirt and frowned. "He's not retarded, Connor—"

"Well, whatever it is, I—"

"He's deaf."

Deaf?" I repeated, thinking I'd misunderstood.

Esken frowned. "Deaf-mute, actually. He doesn't speak. At first Mother thought he was retarded, but later . . . well, it turned out he just couldn't hear."

"He's deaf!" It took me a moment to absorb this new information. "Does he have vocal cords?"

Esken blinked rapidly a few times. "What?"

"Vocal cords. Does he make sounds? Someone said he was screaming at the hospital."

"Yeah, he has vocal cords. Why?"

"Then he's not considered a deaf-mute. Mutes are usually incapable of vocalizations."

Esken stroked his tie as if it were a cat resting on his chest. "Deaf, mute, what's the difference. Just a matter of semantics, isn't it? The point is he doesn't hear and he doesn't talk."

"Does he sign?"

"Not really. He points, you know, and sometimes acts out simple stuff. We can usually understand him when he wants something, as long as it's basic, like a drink or his flashlight. But he never learned regular sign language."

"For God's sake, why not?" I asked.

Esken shifted uneasily in his chair and pulled again at his tie. "No one figured out he was deaf until he was about ten. And then—"

"What!?" My mouth dropped open again. Incredulous, I tried to repress my growing anger. "You're kidding! How could your mother not know he was deaf?"

Esken fiddled nervously with a gray sock.

"Problems like that weren't so easy to detect back then, you know. They didn't have the kind of hearing tests they have today, especially out here in these isolated old mining towns. You pretty much had to figure it out yourself with a couple of pan lids. Now I guess they've got all kinds of gizmos to test kids' hearing. But back then, it wasn't routine."

He was right. Newborn infants can be tested today—with an OAE, otoacoustic emissions test; an ABR, auditory brain stem response; and other early intervention techniques. Specialists are now able to discover a hearing loss very soon after birth. Yet surprisingly, a good number of children still slip through the cracks.

"Didn't your mother suspect anything?"

"Not for a long time."

"I just can't believe this!"

"Ms. Westphal, you've gotta understand Caleb. He was always a wild child—almost uncontrollable really. Mother knew there was something wrong, the way he'd carry on, screaming but not talking. When Dad died, she was worried that somebody'd send Caleb to an institution, and she just couldn't have handled that. Besides, there was the stigma back then . . ."

"A stigma? You mean for being deaf?" He was right, there had always been a stigma attached to deafness. Some deaf people were treated as retarded, if not downright damned. Some were pitied; others, not so fortunate, were abandoned or even killed. Luckily people had come a long way in their understanding of disabilities. But we weren't there yet.

He shook his head in frustration. "No. I told you. We didn't know he was deaf. We thought he was retarded. I think Mother was a little bit ashamed, like it was her fault or something. Maybe she thought it was some kind of punishment for some past wrong. She just couldn't accept the fact that Caleb wasn't perfect. So she sort of kept him hidden away, to protect him."

"Such backward thinking—unbelievable! What about his education? It wasn't like you didn't have any money to pay for tutoring or special schooling. And what about friends? What was his childhood like?" I stared at Esken, waiting for further explanation of this bizarre story.

He took a deep breath. "Mother tried to teach him herself for awhile, with home schooling. She didn't want anyone interfering, like I said. But Caleb wouldn't pay much attention. He was always off in his own world. He mostly played by himself, coloring, drawing pictures, copying alphabet letters, looking at books. Even though nothing seemed to have any meaning for him, I guess he was attracted to the colors and designs of books. Or maybe he knew there was something there but he couldn't grasp what it was. Hard to say."

"So your mother assumed he was retarded because he didn't behave normally," I asked incredulously.

Esken shrugged, not meeting my eyes. "He was different, you know. He didn't learn, even though sometimes he seemed smart enough, figuring out how things worked and all. He did amazing things with his hands. And he was fascinated by the mines and caves. But then he'd just get out of control."

"How did Sparkle finally figure out Caleb was deaf?"

"By accident, really. See, Caleb's real good at noticing signals. Back when we were kids, Mother'd called us to dinner, I'd look up, and he'd see me out of the corner of his eye and imitate me. If I turned to a noise, so would he. When he didn't respond to a sound, I just thought he wasn't listening because he was busy doing something. But one day, I figured it out."

"What happened?"

"Mother was in the kitchen, putting away a load of dishes. She had a stack of plates she was trying to set up in the cupboard, but she lost her balance and dropped everything. The plates came clattering down on the floor, making a horrible racket. I jumped a foot when it happened—Caleb and I were right in the next room. But this time Caleb had his back to me. And he just went on playing, as if nothing happened."

"So, after all those wasted years, that's how you discovered he was deaf." I had read one story of a deaf child being mistaken for developmentally disabled. It was still so hard for me to believe that someone could overlook a child's simple inability to hear for lack of intelligence. This wasn't the Dark Ages.

"I told Mother, but she didn't believe me at first. Then she started ringing bells, playing music at full blast, banging things behind his back, even screaming his name. Caleb didn't respond at all when his back was turned. Just kept coloring his picture. I even remember what the picture was about: his favorite subject, caves."

"So what did your mother do when she found out her son was actually deaf and not mentally retarded?"

"She hired an old classmate who had been a school-teacher. Betty McBroom, I think her name was. She came and worked with Caleb for a short while. Mother didn't trust many outsiders—it was just her way—so she picked someone she knew wouldn't spread any gossip about Caleb. She hoped he could learn some language skills if he was only deaf. But the teacher hadn't worked with disabled kids, and she had trouble with him. Since he'd had no language training while he was young, she said it had affected his mental development. She said he probably wouldn't ever learn language beyond the few made-up signs we'd already been using with him. Like 'go,' 'sit down,' 'eat.' "

Esken demonstrated the sign for "go" by first pointing

away, then mimed patting a chair seat for "sit down," then put his fingers up to his mouth for "eat." The gestures were not too dissimilar from signs used in American Sign Language for the same words.

"So Sparkle kept him at home, unstimulated, uneducated, unsocialized, and—"

"I don't think you understand, Connor. Mother was alone—our daddy died just after Caleb was born and she was on her own. She wasn't well educated, you know. Dropped out of school at fifteen to marry my daddy. She thought she could provide the best life for Caleb—away from the taunts and misunderstandings of others. People calling him 'retard' and making fun of him. She loved him. But he was . . ." Esken paused.

"What?" I urged.

"He was difficult, you know. Not being able to communicate, I think he was frustrated. It was hard to tell what he actually understood. So much of what he did was mimicry. He just kind of lived in his own world, you know."

It was almost unfathomable. A deaf child left to figure out the world without communication, without the ability to express himself, talk to other people, understand abstract concepts. Would that child be able to think, to wonder, even imagine? It was mind-boggling.

But part of me understood how it had happened. Deaf people have been misunderstood throughout history; it had apparently happened to Caleb.

"So what do you want from me, Esken? I won't be able to communicate with him, just because I'm deaf. It took me years to learn to lip-read. I still misunderstand speech a good deal of the time, and once in a while I find someone who doesn't understand my speech. I can only use sign language with those who have studied ASL. That's not a lot of people, you know. You said Caleb doesn't have speech or know sign. How am I supposed to communicate with him? I can't read his mind."

I could feel the anger rise up in me again as I spoke. It was frustrating to hear Caleb's story. I almost wished Esken hadn't told me.

Esken leaned in. "I want you to see him. I thought maybe you could, I don't know, understand him somehow, in a way that hearing people might not. You said you didn't really learn formal sign language until you were in high school. What did you do when you couldn't communicate with your friends or family? When lipreading didn't work?"

Images of the school playground came back quickly. Early on I had attended a regular hearing school, then spent some time at an oral deaf school to learn lipreading skills and speech. We were never allowed to use sign language of any kind in the classroom. In fact, we were sometimes rapped on the hands or ridiculed by the teacher if we did. But the moment we got onto the playground, there was no stopping those little fingers. They flew into motion, along with our hands, arms, our whole bodies, as we gestured, mimed, and acted to get our points across. A wink, an eyebrow lift, a twist at the mouth, a head nod—all were understood instantly by my deaf peers. We even made up our own signs that I later learned were not recognized by other deaf people outside of our little group.

"All right, I'll go see him. But I don't think it will do any good. I'm pretty sure we won't be able to communicate, if he's had no language instruction at all. We're way past that at this point. And the lack of language development could, as you mentioned, have caused him to be developmentally delayed."

Esken tightened his tie, then rose from his chair, and pulled his suit jacket together, buttoning it formally. "Thanks, Connor. I just thought it was worth a try. I don't know what else to do, aside from getting Russell Jacks to plan his defense. Only Caleb knows what went on in that hospital room. It's not looking good for him, but I'm sure he didn't have anything to do with Mother's death."

As Esken left my office, I turned toward the window and watched two young children playing on the sidewalk across the street. I couldn't hear them talking but they were definitely communicating with each other. One boy was pointing at something and punching the other boy. The boy being punched wasn't angry or crying, as expected, but was giggling and returning the punches. I looked in the direction of the point. Of course. It was a girl, about their same age, smiling sweetly at both of them. The message couldn't have been clearer.

I drove home to collect some paperwork I'd left behind, and spent an hour with Casper, playing "go-get-the-ball" and teaching her the signs for the game. She's a quick learner, and understood "ball" almost immediately, confusing it only once with "shoe." It was a nice break before tackling the added pressure of having to meet Caleb Bodie in jail.

"Hi, Sheriff," I said, after closing the door to his small office on Main Street. "Got a book for you."

I had swung by the tiny Flat Skunk Library on my way to the sheriff's office and picked up a copy of *If I'm So Lovable, Why Am I Still Single?* He'd been having difficulty meeting women lately, and I was worried he was about to give up. Since his wife left him last year, he'd been at loose ends. I hoped this book would help him with a few strategies for finding a date. I dropped it on his desk and sat in the chair opposite him.

"What's this, C.W.?"

I was getting used to Sheriff Mercer's habit of abbreviating words whenever he could. He picked up the book, flipped through the pages, and set it back down. "Think I'm getting desperate?"

"Not at all. I just thought it might offer you a few tips you haven't already thought of. You're looking good today, by the way. New haircut?"

Sheriff Mercer ran thick fingers over his buzz cut. It looked recent, and was the only thing I could think of to compliment him on, except his khakis. I didn't want him to think I had a uniform fetish.

"Yeah, but she cut it a little too short, don't you think? I'm going to let it grow out a bit this time."

"Good idea. You'd look great in a ponytail, dyed blue, shaved on the sides, and permed. But then, you'd look great in anything, Sheriff."

Sheriff Mercer raised a fuzzy eyebrow. "What do you want, C.W.?"

Oops. I had gone too far. He knew me too well.

"I'd like to see Caleb Bodie."

The sheriff rubbed his eyes, causing his thick eyebrow hairs to stick out like caterpillars. Then he leaned back and folded his hands over his broad chest. He relished the power thing.

"Why?"

"Esken asked me to. Apparently Caleb is deaf, and Esken thinks I might be able to communicate with him."

"Deaf? I thought he was . . ." Sheriff Mercer touched his temple twice.

"He may be. But he's also deaf. Esken wants me to meet him. Mind if I see him for a few minutes?"

The sheriff rose slowly from his chair. "I suppose not. But make it quick. He's a probable fifty-one fifty. I don't want him riled up and screaming again. I think my own hearing lost a couple of dBs from the last outburst. You're going to have to teach me some of that ASL." The sheriff, who preferred to speak in code whenever possible, wiggled his fingers in front of his face, imitating signs. He looked silly.

"Thanks, Sheriff. I'll be quick. I owe you a lasagna dinner for this."

Sheriff Mercer opened the door to the back part of the building and led me down the hall to one of two jail cells. Caleb was in the first cell, sitting on the bed, staring out the small barred window.

"Can't let you in. He's too unpredictable. But you can sit outside his cell and try to talk with him. There's a chair over there, if you want one." He pointed to a nearby folding chair, propped against the opposite wall.

I nodded. Sheriff Mercer gave me a last warning look and left, leaving the door open behind him.

Caleb didn't look over as I entered, his eyes still fixed

on the view from the jailhouse window. I called out "Caleb," just to see for myself if he would respond. Kind of like what folks do when they learn someone is blind, and wave a hand in front of their face to make sure.

Caleb gave no response. I tapped on the cell bars. Nothing.

I waved my arms and stamped my foot.

Caleb Bodie turned and looked directly at me.

Without warning, Caleb shot like an angry gorilla to the cell bars. He stuck his thick arms through the slots and waved them wildly. I backed up, out of reach, my heart beating double-time.

Caleb grasped the bars and pressed his tearstained face against them. At six feet, two hundred pounds, he appeared menacing, even behind the steel bars. His hands were scraped, and his nails were jagged and bitten to the quick. Unshaven whiskers sprouted on his chin, gray mixed with brown like his brother's coloring, and his dark hair hung over his lined forehead. Caleb's puffy lids made his eyes look small.

I stood frozen, waiting for his next move, but he seemed to have locked onto the bars. As I watched his callused fingers finally relax their grip, I could feel my heartbeat return to nearly normal. I smiled weakly and lifted a hand in universal greeting. Caleb reached out through the bars with one hand, as if asking for something. I shook my head in incomprehension, wondering if he was trying to communicate with me, or take hold of me. His intense eyes never left mine.

I stared at him helplessly, not knowing what to say or do. He didn't know speech. He didn't know language. What was I supposed to accomplish here?

Wanting to appear more relaxed than I felt, I looked around for the chair and started to pull it over, then realized I wanted to be on eye level with him in order to try to communicate. I shoved the chair away and sat down cross-legged on the cold linoleum floor. Caleb followed my every move. I lowered my hand and patted the floor, gesturing for him to sit down, too. He remained standing for several seconds, towering over me. Then he loosened his grip on the bars and settled on the floor.

Had he understood my gesture? Or was he just mimicking me?

I smiled and nodded, and gave him a thumbs-up, all the body language I could think of. He copied the hand gesture, but not the facial expression. As I swept my hair out of my face, he did the same. Maybe he was just easily suggestible, like yawns that spread unconsciously from one person to the next. I interlocked my two index fingers in the sign for "friend." Awkwardly, he did the same.

He was simply aping me.

Not taking my eyes off Caleb, I called for the sheriff, hoping he'd hear me. Caleb stretched his mouth in response, mimicking my call. Sheriff Mercer entered the hallway.

"Problem?" he asked, his hand on his gunbelt.

"No, I just wondered if you'd do me a favor, and bring me a pad of paper and a pencil."

I glanced back at Caleb. He was no longer imitating my speech, just watching the two of us intently. I looked back to Sheriff Mercer.

"Paper, yep, but no pencil. Could be used as a weapon."

"How about a crayon or a felt-tip pen, then?"

The sheriff disappeared for a few moments, then returned with a yellow legal pad and a wide-tipped black felt pen. The most damage it could do was to make a big black mark if you tried to stab someone with it. I thanked him and placed the pad in front of me on the floor. I began to draw.

After a quick stick-figure sketch of a man and a woman, I turned the pad around and showed it to Caleb. I pointed to the man, then pointed to Caleb. Then I wrote his name—upside-down for me, which was not an easy trick. When I was finished, I made the hand-shape of the manual letter C and touched my temple. I had just given Caleb a name sign, the letter of his first name tapped in the "male" section of the face. Caleb blankly imitated the gesture.

I pointed to the other figure, the one with more hair and a Dr. Seuss shirt and jeans. I'd thought about sketching the universal symbol for female, by adding a skirt and maybe breasts, but decided that might confuse him. I pointed to myself, then wrote my name and made the sign for Connor—the letter C on my chest. I'd been given the name sign as a kid, by a speech teacher who simply saw me as "the girl with the body aid," the bulky hearing aid that I was forced to wear strapped on my chest. Caleb copied my movement.

I had no idea if he understood what I was talking about, but I had to start somewhere. I pointed to myself again and made my name sign. I pointed to him again and made his name sign. Next I pointed to him with one index finger and to myself with the other, then linked the two fingers; once again the sign for "friends."

Caleb aped the gesture three or four times, his face serious with concentration. Did he understand the sign?

Caleb gestured for the pad.

Instead of giving it to him, I made a questioning face by raising my eyebrows and leaning my head forward, making the sign for "want"—two outstretched palm-up hands that pull back into clawed fingers. I repeated it—"want"—again, feeling like Annie Sullivan with Helen Keller. I pointed to the pad, repeating the sign, until Caleb finally imitated me. When he did, I pushed the pad under the bars of the cell door, along with the felt pen.

Caleb spun the pad around, flipped over the page, and carefully began to draw. I watched as he made a series of circles and lines. As the design began to take shape, I studied his technique. Caleb moved his hand from the bottom of the page to the top, each stroke a separate entity. A series of recognizable forms soon became apparent. In primitive, abrupt movements, he had written "C A L E B." But the name was drawn more than written.

When I recognized his name, I smiled, pointed, and repeated his name sign. He frowned for a moment, copied me, and then made my name sign. He still wasn't getting it.

Caleb flipped over another sheet of paper and drew a simple picture of a house. Next he drew two people, one very large, with little hair and big muscles, outside the house. The other person was even larger, but had no muscles, and was lying on a bed inside the house, with eyes closed, drawn as slits.

Caleb paused to look at the picture for a moment, then added a large circle encompassing the figure that stood outside the house. To the circle he added what looked like spikes all around the inside of the circle, as if the figure were being swallowed up by a large mouth with sharp teeth. The expression on the figure's face was not one of fear, however; there was a big smile.

I pointed to the figure on the bed. Caleb stared at it for a moment, then snatched the picture off the pad with an angry swipe and hurled it out of the cell.

Curious, I made the sign for "mother." Instead of imitating me, his mouth began to open and close.

The sheriff appeared at the door, grimacing and covering his ears.

"Jesus H. Christ, what is going on in here? You'll wake the dead with all that screaming! C.W., come on out of there. You've upset him again. God, what an unholy racket!"

I picked up the wadded-up drawing that lay by my foot and followed Sheriff Mercer to the door. With a glance back, I saw Caleb once again staring out the barred window.

I returned to my office disturbed by my visit with Caleb Bodie. I didn't know what was going on in that mind of his, but I had a feeling there was a lot more than what had been generally assumed. It was true that he behaved more like he was developmentally delayed than deaf, but he had also used some natural gestures that were common in the deaf community. Still, it was his facial expressions that communicated the most to me. It could have been my imagination, but I sensed someone more aware than others assumed was trapped behind those troubled eyes.

Anxious and needing a distraction, I grabbed a Cornish meat pie from DILLIGAF's deli and headed back to the office to eat in private. I stopped by Dan's office to talk with him about my visit to the jail. Or maybe I just wanted ask him about the woman he had been with at the diner. Dan's behavior at the Nugget had been uncharacteristically cool and had left me feeling unsettled. We'd been seeing each other for some time, and I thought the relationship was progressing, although still cautiously on my part. Now I'd have to think of a way to confront him on this sudden change in him—without letting him know it mattered.

I knocked, then tried the doorknob. Locked. I was about to turn away when I glimpsed movement behind the translucent glass window. Was someone there?

I knocked again, and peered through the window to see if I could make out anything, but I felt like I was looking through someone's prescription glasses—someone with severe astigmatism. Everything was blurry, but nothing moved. I had probably seen Cujo, the cat, I thought, pulling away. Or was Dan purposely avoiding me for some reason?

Jeremiah Mercer, the sheriff's son and my part-time assistant and interpreter, wasn't in his usual spot at his computer when I unlocked my office door. But the phone light was blinking on my TTY—the electronic teletypewriter used by the deaf in place of the telephone. I placed the receiver in the cradle and typed, "HELLO. CONNOR WESTPHAL HERE. GA."

"HEy Coonner sheriff here. GA."

I immediately recognized Sheriff Mercer's typing. Either too many letters or not enough letters, coupled with the fact that he held the shift key down too long so his first words often had double capitals. I'd tried to teach him to type with all caps, which is more common when using the TTY between deaf users, but old typing habits die hard. This time I switched to "hearing" typing.

"Hi, Sheriff. Sorry about Caleb but I don't think I did anything to disturb him. We were just drawing pictures. Is he still upset? GA."

"No, Now i'm upset. Caleb's gone . . ."

My arms suddenly prickled as I waited for the "Go Ahead." I gave up on the code for "Your turn to type." Half the time the sheriff forgot to use it.

"What do you mean he's gone? Is he out on bail?"

"noo. I Mean eSscaped. WHen I went to walk you out, somcone must have slipped in the back way, taken my keys off my desk, and let him out. UNlesss of course you gave him a cake with a file in it while you were in there. Anyways hes flown thee coop."

"Whoa! You're kidding! You don't know who did it? GA."

"I HAve a pretty goood idea. ESken was real upset about his brother bein in jail. DON't suppose you got any idea where they are, seeing as how ESken wanted you to talk with Caleb and all? Maybe youre in cahoots with him? GA."

"Of course not, Sheriff! I had nothing to do with Caleb's escape. So cut out the accusations or I'm going to have to come over there and smack you. What are you going to do? GA."

"IM Alerting everyone. tHis guy is dangerous and I want him back whre he belongs. I f you hear anything you let mc know, you unnderstand? GA. SK."

I swore I would, and Stoppcd Keying.

I couldn't believe Caleb was missing. I had just been there, and he'd been behind bars. He hadn't been in a frame of mind to plan his own escape. But had Esken helped free him? And where was he now?

After a halfhearted attempt at writing an article on the fall colors and trying to make metaphors out of leaves, but mostly just staring out the window at the swirling activity, I locked up my office and walked over to Russell Jack's office. The sign swinging on two small chains above the door read "Jacks and Jacks, Attorneys at Law." Although his father had died years ago, Russell kept the sign unchanged.

According to gossip at the Nugget, the source of all my best newspaper stories, James Jacks had been a well-respected attorney in Flat Skunk for four decades. He had wanted Russell to join the practice as soon as he'd graduated from law school. But Russell preferred trying his hand at his own business. He'd attempted several ventures—a Western-themed restaurant, a mail-order gold-prospecting business, and a tourist attraction at a local mine—but he'd had little success.

Eventually Russell came to his senses and returned to school. After flunking the bar three times, he'd finally passed and added his name to his father's shingle. He'd done well with his practice—albeit a small one in the town of Flat Skunk, where most of the cases lean toward smoothing ruffled feathers, defending DUIs, and drafting wills.

Russell still had plenty of time for extracurricular activities, such as serving as Noble Grand Humbug for the Clampers—E. Clampus Vitus—a rowdy brotherhood determined to preserve the town's heritage. Most of Flat Skunk's prominent blue- and white-collar men belonged, except for Sheriff Mercer. The self-deprecating group preferred Clamp-barbecues to board meetings, and plaque erections to charity balls. You could spot them at the Saturday afternoon shooting matches dressed in uniforms that harkened back to the forty-niner days—black jeans, red shirts, black vests, and pin-studded black hats. Like other fraternal organizations, they had a secret handshake, a playful initiation, and a humorous motto: *"Ensure the betterment of widders and orphans. Especially widders."*

I knocked, then opened the door to the small foyer of Russell's office, which once had been the parlor in a now-converted old Victorian. A large unoccupied reception desk stood sentry in the middle of the room, covered with documents, a phone, in/out boxes, and writing implements. The green shag carpeting was worn across the front, where many trips had apparently been made from the desk to the office at the right. The door to the office was ajar, so I peeked in. Russell sat at his large oak desk.

"Connor! Hi. I should have known it was you. I called out and no one answered." With a large grin, he gestured for me to take the seat opposite him.

I sat down and crossed my leg, guy style.

"What's up? Need some legal advice? Got a good discrimination suit I can sink my teeth into?"

"Well, I really should get to my will someday. And a nice lawsuit would be fun. Maybe we can sue the local movie theater for not showing captioned films?"

"Why not? You don't want to miss any of those first-run art films, do you? That would be criminal."

He laughed. I laughed.

He continued. "So what does bring you here? You're not going to ask me more questions about the arrest of Caleb Bodie, are you? You know that's attorney-client privilege and I can't discuss it."

Apparently he hadn't heard the latest; I decided to delay the bulletin of Caleb's escape for a few moments. I glanced at the phone and noticed the answering machine light was blinking.

"Not taking calls?"

He grinned. "The phone has been ringing off the hook ever since Sparkle's death and Caleb's arrest. I had to get some work done so I'm letting the machine take my calls. I check my messages every half hour or so. If it's important, I'll get it eventually. Why? Has something happened?" He suddenly looked alarmed.

I shook my head quickly, and got to the point of my visit.

"Russell, did Sparkle leave a will?"

"Of course."

"What did it say?"

He smiled and said nothing.

"Look, I just need to know who it benefited. It might help your client. Caleb is your client, isn't he?"

He continued smiling.

I decided to bait him with a bluff. "Russell, rumor has it Sparkle was thinking of changing her will, and that there might even be a second will. I wondered—"

"Connor, I can't say anything about that until tomorrow, when the will is read. You know that."

I nodded. "Okay. Suppose the will *was* going to be rewritten. Who do you think would benefit, if Esken and Caleb were written out? Any chance it would be the Flat Skunk Railroad Museum?"

Russell shrugged. "Sparkle was very strong in her convictions that the town should remain historically preserved. But the museum isn't the only authentic contribution to that goal."

"You mean the Clampers?"

Russell smiled that annoying smile again.

"You belong to that organization, don't you?"

"As do many of the men in this town. We care about our heritage and want to preserve it. That's one of the goals of E. Clampus Vitus."

"When the partying is over, anyway. I think beer comes first and heritage comes second, doesn't it?"

"We have a good time while we do good things. Nothing wrong with that."

"I was thinking of joining."

Russell's face went white. He must have taken me seriously. "You . . . you can't . . ."

"Why not? You're not saying they discriminate against—"

"Women . . . just aren't allowed! You know that, Connor. It's a guy thing. You wouldn't understand. Besides, it's a private group and you can't sue us for discrimination, so don't even think about it."

"It's a secretive group, too, isn't it?"

"We have our secret handshakes, yes, but they're mostly just a joke. We like to make fun of those other clubs, like the Elks, and the Moose, and those guys with the funny hats. Like I said, we mostly try to preserve our history, through monuments, plaques, and dedications."

"You got one of those black vests and hats like they all wear?"

"It's the uniform."

I relished the threat of joining the organization, even though I had no intention of following through. However, I loved the look of panic in his face. But it was time to drop the bomb.

"Well, I guess you haven't heard. You may have two clients to represent instead of just one."

"What do you mean?" Russell looked perplexed.

"Caleb's out of jail."

"Bailed so soon?"

"He escaped."

Russell rose from his chair. "What?"

"Sheriff Mercer thinks Esken let him out when his back was turned."

Russell's jaw dropped open. He glanced at the blinking light of the answering machine and I saw his lips shape the word "Shit!"

I returned to the newspapers, checking Dan's office again as I passed by. The door was still locked and light shone steadily through the frosted windowpane. I stood for a moment, staring at the door as if it might give me a clue as to what was up with Dan. But the door said nothing. No door language whatsoever.

The pile of papers waiting for me on my desk spoke volumes, however. "Write me! Fix me! Edit me!" Bite me, I responded, telepathically. The papers ignored me as usual, continuing their ceaseless demands.

I tackled an article Jeremiah had written—his first by-line, an in-depth, probing report on the rights of skateboarders. I'd indulged Miah's passion, weighing the controversy over where skaters could and could not practice their ollies and kick flips, tailslides and half-cabs. It might make an interesting contribution to the series I was running on the evolving Mother Lode. Surprisingly, the copy needed little editing, except for the occasional overuse of "stoked," "awesome," and "totally." Sheriff Mercer's son just might make a good writer some day.

I had begun the demanding second edit on a piece I was writing about the history of Clampers when the TTY flashed. I answered with my usual greeting and signaled for the caller to "Go Ahead."

"Connor. It's Esken. Is anyone there with you?"

Esken! "No—wehre are yuo?" I keyed in quickly, making errors in my haste.

"I'm at the library, where they've got one of those new pay phones with a TTY."

After much protesting, I'd finally convinced the town council to install a public TTY pay phone at the library. I wasn't the only deaf person in Flat Skunk, just the youngest. I had campaigned for our half-dozen elderly deaf who also might have use for the convertible telephone. It had taken six months to get approval, but the phone had finally been installed. I waited for the go-ahead from Esken, then realized he probably didn't know much about TTY protocol. I went ahead instead.

"Esken, did you know that Caleb escaped? Sheriff Mercer thinks either you let him out or I did. I know I didn't, so that leaves you. What were you thinking? Where is he? GA. BTW, when you're done, type GA. It means you're finished and it's my turn. GA."

"Connor, I don't know where Caleb is. I swear, I didn't let him out. But I heard about the escape over at the café. And I agree, it can only make things worse. You've got to help me find him. I don't know what they'll do to him if they catch him again . . . AG," he typed by mistake.

"Esken, you've got to call Sheriff Mercer. Or at least call Russell. Your attorney will know what to do. You have to protect yourself and your brother, but he's also got to turn himself in. If you're hiding him—"

My words were cut off by his, flashing across the small red screen. "I told you! I'm not hiding him! I don't know where he is! Look, I can't go to the sheriff or Russell, because—I've got my reasons. But I know Caleb couldn't have hurt Mother. And now—I think I'm being followed . . ."

Either he hung up on me, or we were disconnected. The screen went dead.

Three thoughts fought for space in my mind:
  —Should I call the sheriff?
  —Where was Caleb?
  —And why did Esken hang up so abruptly?

The sheriff. I should call him first, tell him I've heard from Esken, and that Esken might be in trouble. I could argue Esken's case for him, saying he swore he didn't bust his brother out of jail. But the sheriff wouldn't buy it on just my say-so. And besides, Esken said he had reasons for not calling the police himself.

I had no idea where Caleb was, so I couldn't follow through on that.

But it was Esken's sudden departure that bothered me the most.

I dialed Sheriff Mercer's TTY number. No answer, except for the standard referral, "If this call is an emergency . . ." I typed my name and a brief message to call me back ASAP. Then I picked up my backpack, locked the door to my office, and headed down the stairs. I had a hunch where Caleb might be after all.

I swung by my diner and picked up Casper for the trip. Although Casper is a working dog, entitled to free access under the disabilities act, the merchants in Flat Skunk have been reluctant to accept her presence inside their establishments. Rather than fight it, I let her run around my large backyard and play with the squirrels. I used to bring her to the office, but Miah's allergic to dog hair. This was the perfect time for an outing.

The Bodie homestead is located in a sprawling pine forest near Miwok Lake, just two miles outside of Flat Skunk. The area is destined to become tract neighborhoods and minimalls if development isn't soon halted or at least controlled.

I hated to think of this golden countryside replaced with sidewalks, streetlights, and sprinkler systems, but growth was inevitable. Adventurous retirees, disgruntled city-dwellers, and aging hippies were fleeing to the gold country faster than the miners of 'forty-nine.

The area had to make room in order to accommodate the influx of transplants, without losing its historical uniqueness and heritage. I didn't have an answer—after all, I was one of those city-dwellers who'd run for cover to the country. Who was I to say it was time to close the doors and not let anyone else in? But the thought of California's Mother Lode becoming another generic suburb scared the Hangtown Fry out of me.

I parked my '57 Chevy in front of the two-story Victorian house and let Casper out to roam the fields, while I climbed the brick steps to the front door. The name "Bodie" had been carved at the top of the pine door—craftmanship of bygone days. I knocked, hoping someone would answer and not just yell, "Come in!" Otherwise I'd be standing there for who knew how long.

After a few seconds the door opened and Sonora Bodie, daughter-in-law of the deceased, peeked out from behind it. She had pinned up her multicolored dyed-blond hair in a spray of ends. One side sported a cobweb accessory. She gave a stiff smile as she recognized me and opened the door fully. Like her husband, I'd dealt with Sonora only on a professional basis. She, too, had placed hefty display ads in the *Eureka!* for real estate sales. This time we both had different agendas.

"Hello, Connor. What are you doing out here? Come for an interview? Because I'm not giving—"

"Something's happened, Sonora."

She paused, then gestured for me to enter. I stepped inside and glanced over the foyer, trimmed with antiques. Jeweled Tiffany lamps sat on snowflake doilies that covered rosewood tables. A dark Persian rug lay framed by polished hardwood floors. Portraits of deceased Bodies filled the walls, dating back several generations.

Sparkle's likeness stood out among the collection of

Cornish ancestors. Her strong chin and nose, broad fore-head, and thin lips did not make for an attractive woman, even in her youth, but there was an air of confidence and determination in that face. Her hair, pulled back tightly, offered nothing in the way of a crowning glory, but suited her temperament and what I knew of her personality. Sensible, tidy, and controlled.

I turned to face Sonora and took a deep breath before I spoke. "Sonora, Caleb has escaped from jail. The sheriff—"

"He's escaped?" Sonora's dark complexion paled. Abruptly, she headed for an adjoining room. I followed her into an old-fashioned parlor that held still more antiques, portraits, and expensive knickknacks. But it was the large boxes sitting in the middle of the room that caught my eye. Sonora must have been in the middle of unpacking. Or packing?

She headed for a stained-glass cabinet on the far wall and pulled out a crystal decanter. After pouring herself a tumbler full of gold liquid, she downed it in three swallows. Seemingly fortified, she turned back to me and said, "Sorry. Forgot you can't . . . uh, I asked if you wanted a drink?"

I shook my head and took a seat in a velveteen chair, which was somewhat rickety and worn, but still detailed with handcrafted embroidery. Sonora sat on her knees next to a box. Missing her first comment, I leaned forward to better read her lips.

"What a mess!" she said, her shoulders sinking a good inch.

"It's not too bad. Looks like you're packing up Sparkle's things."

"I meant the family. But yes, this is a mess, too. God, that woman had so much crap. What did she plan to do with it all—save it for her burial chamber?"

As she spoke, Sonora casually stacked books, ceramic figurines, and candles into a nearby box. She paused only if an item happened to be a sheet of paper. Then she'd give it a quick scan before dropping it into the box with the other discards. Her hands revealed the first signs of aging, thin lines and a few of what I preferred to call "freckles."

She wore a diamond-studded wedding ring on her left hand, dwarfed by larger rings on the other fingers. Her porcelain nails were trimmed to a reasonable length, but they still looked artificial. She was dressed in pale blue sweats that matched her fuzzy slippers. Her skin was free of makeup.

"So what do you want, Connor?"

"Tell me about Caleb."

Her face darkened and her movements slowed. She plopped the next few items into the box, but she didn't respond to my inquiry.

"Is he prone to violence?" I probed a little more.

Sonora thought a moment, her eyes moving to the striking portrait on the wall. I recognized a younger version of Sparkle Bodie, looking very much like a feminine version of her son, Esken. I saw little of Caleb in her strong face, and even less of Devon, who obscured her looks with tattoos, piercings, and bizarre hair colors.

Sighing, Sonora replied, "Yes, he is violent." I waited for her to go on but she continued staring at the picture of her dead mother-in-law.

"How? What's he like?"

She bit her lip, then went on. "I didn't see him a lot. He kept to himself when I came to visit Mother Bodie, which wasn't often, although Esken was here a lot. Truthfully, he frightened me. Every so often he'd have these outbursts, like temper tantrums. My daughter, Devon, was scared to death of him as a child. She didn't like to come to this mausoleum of a mansion, either."

"Did you ever see him do anything vicious or brutal?"

She nodded. "One time Mother Bodie took away his art supplies because he had drawn on the table instead of on his paper. He exploded. Grabbed the paper and tore it up, threw the pens around the room. I thought he was going to hurt her, he was so enraged. But she calmed him down and took him to his room. His anger scared me."

Was it anger, I wondered? Or frustration. How would I have felt if someone had taken away my only method of expression? "You think he's capable of . . . murder?"

Sonora lifted a book out of the box and wiped the dust from the cover.

"That's hard to say. He is violent, but he loved his mother, of course. The thing is, I don't think anyone has ever really understood him. And he certainly can't understand us. His brain development wasn't normal, you know."

"I thought he was deaf."

"Yeah, but he's strange. Not like you. I'm sure he has some kind of retardation or something."

"Is Esken afraid of him?"

"No, Esken wants to protect him, but not the same way his mother did. Her idea of protection was to keep him away from other people. Esken thought he should go to school, but his mother said it wouldn't do any good. It was too late for that kind of formal education. They didn't get along very well, Esken and Sparkle. When they weren't fighting about Caleb, they were fighting about the land, the town, politics—even how to raise Devon."

"Esken wanted to develop the area and she didn't?"

"Yeah, he said he could see the future and he accused Sparkle of living in the past. She and Holly Bryson, the museum docent, and Aubrey, the librarian—they all wanted to keep things 'historically correct.' But not Esken. He knew this place was a gold mine of opportunity."

"And you?"

She paused, then measured her words as she spoke. "I'm a growth advocate. Of course I believe in progress. I wouldn't be able to make a living without it. You don't think Sparkle gave us any money while she was alive, do you? Ha! When I married Esken, I thought . . ."

She stopped, looked down at the book in her hand, and returned it to the box.

"You thought you might be getting some of the Bodie fortune?" I pressed.

She shrugged. "Well, someday, you know. That's not why I married Esken, of course," she was quick to add. "I just didn't know it would be this long. God, I really came to believe that old woman would live forever."

"You don't sound like you'll miss her much. There's no love lost between the two of you?"

"She was a manipulating, controlling Victorian. No, there was no love lost."

"Sonora, do you know anything about what's in the will? Any chance Esken was going to be cut out? Maybe she planned to leave her money to the museum or the Clampers or some other organization."

Sonora's eyes flashed. "That's ridiculous. You've been talking to Holly Bryson, I'll bet. That's just her wishful thinking, spreading rumors. She can't bear the thought that no more money will be coming to support the museum. Looks like she'll be out of a job."

"Have you seen the will?"

"No, but Sparkle promised that I'd—we'd be taken care of."

"But if you were excluded, both you and Esken would have a lot to lose, wouldn't you?"

Sonora sat up stiffly. "Just what are you implying, Connor? I've invited you into my home—I mean, the Bodie home—and you're making accusations—"

"Sorry, Sonora. I didn't mean anything. I was just asking questions, trying to find out what happened to Sparkle, whether or not Caleb was responsible. Esken called and asked—"

"Esken called you?" Sonora looked stunned.

"Well, yes, a short while ago. He asked if I could help him find Caleb. I came thinking Esken might be here."

"Listen, I have no idea where Esken is, or Caleb, but they're not here. Now I've really got to get to work packing this stuff up. The Clampers are coming to take it all away and donate it to some charity." She stood up, shakily, and tried to smooth the dust and grime from her warm-up suit. Moving to the cabinet again, she poured herself another drink.

"Sure you don't want one?" she asked, turning to face me. I shook my head, then followed her to the foyer, where I spotted Devon at the top of the stairs. She stepped down when she saw us.

"Where are you going, darling?" Sonora asked. She was becoming more difficult to read with her lips moving sloppily and her enunciation slurred.

Devon, dressed in an oversized striped shirt and baggy jeans that almost hid her protruding stomach, glanced back and gave her mother a cold stare. She sported over a half-dozen earrings on one ear, one in her eyebrow, and one through her lip. That one almost distracted me from her response:

"Out."

Sonora held back, saying nothing more. Devon slammed the door behind her as she left, swirling a layer of dust on the floor. Sonora winced.

"Sonora, is there any chance Esken—" I started to say, then stopped, catching sight of Casper jumping up and down outside the back window. "Casper . . . ?

I inhaled deeply. "Smoke!"

Sonora took a breath and turned her head, as if trying to detect where it was coming from. I only caught, "Oh, my God—" before she began running from room to room, frantically searching for the source. I started to head up the stairs and froze. Wisps of gray smoke appeared on the second-floor landing.

"Upstairs!" I cried as Sonora rushed out from another room.

"Sparkle's bedroom!" Sonora said, her face twisted in panic. "Call nine-one-one!"

I tried to grab her as she sprang past me and up the stairs, but missed. Frantically I looked for the phone, and found it in the room where she'd been packing boxes. I lifted the receiver and punched in the numbers. After a brief pause, I began repeating the words over and over:

"There's a fire at the Bodie estate out on Miwok Lake Road. There's a fire at the Bodie estate out on Miwok Lake Road . . ." I said it until I caught a glimpse of Sonora fleeing down the stairs and out the front door, smoke billowing after her.

I was right behind her.

I called Casper and she came leaping around from the

side of the house. Barking wildly, her head snapping, Casper continued her frantic behavior, as I turned to watch the old Bodie homestead, laced with flames and outlined with smoke. By the time the fire trucks arrived, five minutes later, half the house was engulfed.

As soon as the fire was under control, Sonora shrugged off my arm.

"I've got to go back!" I lunged to grab her as she sprinted back toward the still-smoking building, but again she slipped out of my reach.

"Sonora! Wait—" Before she could step into the scarred entryway, one of the fire fighters stopped her. I heaved a sigh of relief.

Fire fighters, both paid and volunteer—and a lot of them Clampers—had done their best to put out the flames, but the century-old lumber had provided a ready torch. They managed to save half the house, but the other half was in charred ruins.

As Sonora was guided back to the periphery, I caught a glimpse of the fire fighter who led the way, Casper at his side. It was Dan. I had forgotten that he had joined the volunteer force soon after he arrived in Flat Skunk. I hadn't noticed him earlier in the chaos. Besides, all those fire fighters looked alike in their yellow slickers and hard hats. Couldn't fool Casper, though.

"Sorry, Ms. Bodie, you can't go in the house yet. It's still hot. Hey, Connor, you want to look after her?" Dan was easy to read, his mouth outlined by that blond-and-black beard.

Sonora shook off Dan's grip and stood facing the half-charred home. Her arms wrapped around her body, she scanned the debris and wreckage, as if searching for something important. I'm no good at comforting people, never have been, but I rested a hand gently on her shoulder and tried to ease her back. Dan gave me a look I couldn't read, then disappeared into the skeletal remains. With his experience in construction work, I didn't worry about him reentering the damaged structure. I figured he knew where the dangers lay.

I returned my attention to Sonora and caught her talking to herself. ". . . find it . . . gone . . ."

"What is it, Sonora?"

". . . the will . . ."

"Oh, I'm sure it's at your attorney's office—"

"Don't you understand! It was upstairs! In Sparkle's room! I've got to get it! I—" She made no sense, and as she babbled on, I lost the rest of her words.

Sheriff Mercer appeared, gave me a nod, and turned his attention to Sonora. "Mrs. Bodie—Sonora—sorry about all this. Mind if I ask you a few questions?" He held a small notebook in one hand and a pencil in the other.

I stepped aside while Sheriff Mercer interviewed Sonora. I knew he'd be after me soon, so I decided to spend the next free moments doing a little investigating of my own first. I headed for my car, pulled out the camera I carry for newspaper photos, and moved around the perimeter of the damaged Bodie home, Casper following nervously. I spotted Dan slamming the side of an ax against what looked like an intact wall.

"How bad is it?" I asked. We hadn't really talked for several days, and the comfort zone between us seemed to have disappeared—along with the flames.

He glanced behind me, saw that Sonora was with the sheriff, and said, "This part of the house looks fairly sturdy.

The fire didn't get to the foundation here." He indicated the point where Sparkle Bodie had added on another wing, then waved his ax in the direction of the original half of the house. "But that area is essentially gone."

"How did the fire start?"

"The fire marshal suspects it started upstairs, maybe in the attic. He's searching for the hot spot."

"Hot spot?"

"Ignition source. The fire damage radiates from that point on out. The newer part of the house held up the best—the kitchen, dining room, and a couple of the bedrooms. But what's not burned is virtually ruined by smoke. It's going to take a lot of work to get it back into decent shape."

"I thought I'd look around, take some pictures for the newspaper."

"It's not safe, Connor."

I looked at him and said nothing. He smiled and shook his head. "But you're going to go in anyway, aren't you, one way or the other? So I'd better come along and show you where it's safe to go."

Dan moved to the staircase and gave it another once-over. Although scarred, it wasn't burned through and still looked like it could hold my weight. Dan checked the foundation underneath the stairs with his ax, then tapped the sloped ceiling overhead as he took a few test steps up the staircase. Once he reached the top, he waved me on. I gave Casper the command to stay then followed him, taking each step carefully, hoping I wouldn't suddenly find myself in the basement.

Sparkle's room was mostly intact, aside from one wall that was essentially gone. The room beyond it had been Caleb's, according to Dan, and it was demolished. I stepped hesitantly across the threshold into Sparkle's room. Glancing around the interior, I felt a sudden déjà vu. The room reminded me of the Calaveras Caverns and Moaning Caves I had toured soon after I arrived in Flat Skunk—only positive had turned negative. Instead of white crystal mineral deposits, black shirred formations filled what was once

Sparkle's bedroom. The scene was disturbingly beautiful, almost surreal.

In the center of the room stood Sparkle's bed, now nothing but a metal shell framing ribbons of shiny cinders. Two antique chairs, singed a colorless gray, seemed sculpted in ash. A vanity and wardrobe appeared to hang tenuously in the air, ready to collapse with a strong gust of wind. The rest of the room was littered with piles of black charred wood and seared cloth. The smell of wet ashes lingered in the thick air.

I walked gingerly to Sparkle's bed and examined the nightstand next to it. A few slightly melted medication bottles, their contents unrecognizable from the soot and heat, stood like tilted mushrooms. The trash can at the side of the bed had turned black, but the carved indentation of flowers gave the receptacle a sinister beauty.

Two fire fighters in full regalia entered the room, waving axes. One said something into a walkie-talkie, then moved on. Dan caught my eye. "Don't touch anything. The fire marshal and sheriff will want to be sure of what caused the fire before anyone goes messing with the residue."

I nodded. While he followed the two fire fighters into Caleb's room, I knelt beside the trash can and carefully sifted through the contents with what was once a ballpoint pen, now melted into a permanent wave and still warm. More medicine bottles—lots of them—peeked out from the ash. From the shapes and sizes, I could tell that some were prescription, while the others looked like over-the-counter medications. Poor Sparkle, I thought. She probably ingested more medication in those last weeks than she did food.

I placed the pen back on the desk and started to wipe the soot off my fingers with the edge of my T-shirt when I noticed my fingertips were blue, not black from the ash. Ink had leaked from the pen I'd been holding in my hand. I wiped my hands on my jeans. The streak blended nicely with the stone-washed denim.

I stood up and located a tiny bathroom connected to the bedroom. The medicine cabinet, usually a revealing insight into a person's personality and character, was empty, except for a couple of metal Band-Aid boxes that remained unscathed by the fire.

Nothing else in the bathroom held my interest, so I returned to the bedroom to take a few pictures. After snapping a couple of shots, I noticed something through the springs of the burned bed. Obviously once concealed underneath, a metal box lay almost completely obscured by charred bedding. With a glance around for Dan, who was currently occupied testing beams with his fellow fire fighters, I reached under the bed and pulled out the box. Still warm.

I was about to open it when someone tapped me on the shoulder. I jumped, guiltily, and whirled around.

"What are you doing, C.W.?" It was Sheriff Mercer.

"Nothing, Sheriff. I just found this box under Sparkle's bed. I was getting it for you. I thought it might contain something important, about Sparkle, you know."

He gave me a "yeah, sure" look and took the box from my hands. After a brief attempt to lift the lid, he pulled a Swiss army knife from his back pocket, stuck the tip of the blade into the charred lock, and gave it a twist. The lock broke easily.

"You sure you should be doing this?" I asked.

"Like you said, might be something important inside. Especially if it turns out this fire was set."

I nodded as Sheriff Mercer lifted the lid. We both peered in.

"What do you think all that stuff is?"

He shrugged and lifted out a handful of papers, shuffling through them quickly. From what I could determine by looking over his shoulder, a number of the pages belonged to a genealogy chart, documenting the ancestry of the Bodie family via sea voyage from Cornwall, England, to their present-day location in Flat Skunk.

"Anything else?" I asked.

Sheriff Mercer flipped through a few remaining pages, then placed them all back in the box. "Not much. Mostly personal business stuff."

Sheriff Mercer pulled one of the deeds from the pile and examined it closely, frowning.

I knew that frown. It meant something. "What?" I asked.

"This one's the deed for the Haunted Caverns and Mine, the one old Bennegar Jacks discovered way back when. Course it quickly turned out to be worthless, like so many of the mines. Says here he sold it to Evan Lee Bodie—Sparkle's husband's great-grandfather—on August 27, 1851."

"Bennegar Jacks. I know that name. It's on one of the headstones at the Pioneer Cemetery." My Cornish ancestors were buried there, too.

"Yep, he's up there, all right. 'Here lies a man,/With gold his lust./He staked a claim,/But now he's dust.' I love that one."

"Local lore says something else, too, about him being murdered, right?"

"Yep. Course, that sort of thing happened all the time back in those days. There were more murders in this town than there were saloons—and that's saying a lot."

"There's something clipped to the back of this deed. Looks like a newspaper article."

The sheriff raised an eyebrow, and pulling the yellowed paper from the rusted clip, he gently unfolded it and held it up in sausage fingers. I read aloud over his shoulder.

"Tombstone Enterpise, September 28, 1863, Flat Skunk. JACKS, BENNEGAR SAMUEL, died at the age of 54. Cause of death was gunshot wounds to the head and chest. Ruled by Marshal Jasper Mercer foul play at the hands of an unknown assailant. Funeral services today at 2 P.M. Pioneer Cemetery. Contributions to the Widders and Orphans Fund, E. Clampus Vitus."

"Wow. A century-old unsolved mystery. Was Bennegar Russell Jacks's great-grandfather?" I lifted the article from the sheriff's hands and reread it.

"Yep. Course, there are a lot of Jackses in this town."

"And your—what, great-grandfather—was marshal?"

The sheriff nodded. "Jeremiah's the first Mercer not to go into the family business of law enforcement."

"The Haunted Caverns. That's near the old Bodie Mine down the road from here, right? Isn't that where they used to guide tourists through the crystal caves connected to the mine? They'd let them prospect for nonexistent gold nuggets. Why is it closed?"

"Too risky to take people in there after that earthquake a few months ago. Something caved in."

As I was replacing the article on the pile, I noticed a folded piece of paper that had been buried by the rest of the charts, forms, and notices.

"What's that?"

Sheriff Mercer pulled it out and took a quick look.

"Can I see it?"

"I suppose. As long as all this stuff is off the record." Reluctantly, he handed it over. Scrawled in nearly illegible cursive, it looked like "church hill." The second "c" had a little curlicue at the bottom and the two "h"'s were almost worn off, but I filled in the gaps, much like I do when I'm lipreading.

"Know anybody by the name of Churchill?" I asked.

Sheriff Mercer nodded.

"Who?"

"Some guy who ran England for a while. Think he's dead now."

I rolled my eyes and replaced the article. The sheriff closed the box. "Church hill." I wondered if it had anything to do with the Pioneer Cemetery, the spot where the old church once stood on top of the hill?

"Mind if I look over the papers a little more?" I asked.

This time Sheriff Mercer shook his head. "Sorry, C.W., I gotta confiscate and bag this stuff. Then I'll have to turn it over to next of kin—that would be Esken, if I can ever find him. Got your message, by the way. What did you want to tell me?"

I thought about Esken's phone call. This would probably be a good time to tell Sheriff Mercer my news. But we were interrupted by the fire marshal, who waved the sheriff over to discuss something he'd found.

They huddled and I couldn't read their lips, so I gave up trying. Nothing would really be known about the devastating fire—whether it had been accidental, or deliberately set—until the fire marshal finished his investigation. I wondered how Esken would take the news. And Caleb. But most of all I wondered about Devon, the daughter who seemed in a big—and angry—hurry to leave the house. She had come from the stairs just before we'd smelled the smoke.

Where was she now?

By the time Casper and I left the Bodie place, Russell Jacks had arrived to look after Sonora. She'd asked the sheriff to call Russell, when he insisted she needed attention. It wasn't *her* home that had burned, it was her dead mother-in-law's, but she seemed to take the loss hard. Maybe the old house meant something to her after all. Then again, maybe she just planned to sell off all of Sparkle's things and make some money, in case the will didn't pan out the way she hoped.

As for Devon, there was still no sign of her.

Exhausted from the afternoon's events, I decided to call it a day and head home. On my way to my car I asked Dan if he wanted to stop by for a pasta dinner and a bottle of Mother Lode Merlot, but he begged off, claiming an appointment later that evening. Even a lick from Casper didn't persuade him.

I felt a floating depression as I pulled into my diner's driveway and parked the Chevy. Casper, leaping from the car like a prisoner escaping from her cell, helped to distract me. Once inside the diner, which serves as my living space, I was licked senseless by her pink tongue and got a good workout rolling around on the floor with my Siberian Husky. When we finished roughhousing, I signed to her to settle down while I prepared a bowl of Dog Food Cordon Bleu. If only she could sign back, I thought, watching her eyes track my every move in the large diner kitchen.

After a BLT dinner for me and a bottle of Sierra Nevada beer, I settled onto the sofa bed in the back room of the diner and flipped on the TV. Something was wrong with the captioning device, leaving me only with meaningless visual images. Too tired and frustrated to try to figure out meandering plots and mumbled dialogue, I flicked it off and picked up the latest Jake Page mystery novel I'd been reading. I loved the blind detective and had been following his adventures for years. It didn't take long before I was asleep, Casper at my heels, the book on my chest, and images of fire in my dreams.

The next morning I woke up early, still curious about the genealogy research that had been locked in Sparkle's metal box. After dressing quickly in jeans, my "Death Before Decaf" T-shirt, and a Gallaudet University sweatshirt, I headed for the Flat Skunk Library to talk with Aubrey Horne. I'd recognized his distinct style of calligraphy from the papers in the discovered box. He used that particular lettering on signs all over the library.

The Flat Skunk branch of the Calaveras County Library is housed in a tiny clapboard building adjacent to the sheriff's office. Like many of the other buildings along Main Street, it had been through many incarnations—once a saloon, then a town meeting hall, then a bakery. Five years ago the county bought the place for the branch library.

Aubrey looked up from a large oak desk that served as both circulation and reference departments as I came through the front door. His long artistic fingers rested over an opened book about the historic mines of the Mother Lode. He gave a half-grin when he saw me, which caused his wire-rimmed glasses to slide down his nose. He pulled the glasses off and set them on top of the book.

"Hey, Connor. Those books you ordered are in—*The History of E. Clampus Vitus* and *Gold Diggers of 1849*. That other one about placer mining and the depletion of the land seems to be lost."

From a shelf behind him, he pulled out two books bound with rubber bands. The shelf was neatly labeled "Saves" in his familiar hand.

"Thanks, Aubrey. I need to get this article finished by Thursday or I'll have to fill the space with a bunch of fall poems Mama Cody sent in. You've saved me and the *Eureka!* from literary embarrassment. Is that one for me, too?" I pointed to the book on his desk.

"Oh, yeah! Almost forgot about it—your book about mines. Glad to help keep Mama Cody's verses from seeing the light of day. Speaking of stories for your newspaper, did you hear those sirens yester—whoops. Guess you didn't hear them, huh." Aubrey gave an embarrassed grin.

"No, but I was there when the fire truck arrived. You probably know by now that the Bodie place nearly burned down."

"They were talking about it at the Nugget this morning. Find out how it happened yet?"

"I called the sheriff but he's not sure yet." I pulled up a chair, and told him what I knew.

Aubrey looked down at his book and shook his head. "I knew something like this was going to happen . . ."

"What do you mean, Aubrey?"

He glanced up from the desk and met my eyes. "Oh, nothing. It's just that . . . You know I've been doing this research for the Bodies—well, Sparkle, actually. She wanted it ready for when the railroad museum opens next month. Guess she felt she was a big part of Flat Skunk's heritage and wanted people to know. She donated practically all the money to that museum, you know. Anyway, while I was doing some checking I . . . well, I found out a few things I don't think she would have wanted on display. When I told her about them, she asked me to stop working on the family history and made me turn over what I had."

I guessed that Sparkle hadn't expected any surprises in

her background check or she wouldn't have asked him to do the genealogy work in the first place. "What did you find out? Anything important?"

"I wouldn't say it was important exactly. These things happen all the time—today, anyway. But I guess she got kind of embarrassed about it, being old-fashioned and all. Like I said, she took the stuff I'd completed and asked me not to mention it again."

"What things?"

"Huh?"

"What things happen? You said 'these things happen all the time.' "

Aubrey shifted in his seat. "I really shouldn't say, Connor."

I tried another approach. "When did she find out about your discovery?"

"Last week. I was over at her house, asking her some questions so that I could finish the part I was working on."

"What part was that?"

Aubrey fidgeted again. "I really shouldn't say, you know. I don't think Sparkle would like it if it showed up in the *Eureka!* Of course, she's gone . . ."

"I'm not going to print it in the paper. I just thought it might help me figure out who might have killed her. If she had a deep dark secret she wanted to keep hidden, maybe someone found out—besides you, of course."

Aubrey looked as if doing a little detective work never occurred to him. "Oh, yeah. Sure. It'd be kind of interesting to find out what happened to her. With your newspaper skills and my access to information, we'd make a great team."

We? "So what did you find out?"

"You sure you won't say anything to anyone? Nothing in the *Eureka!*?" The sign of a true gossip.

"Not unless it's important to solving her murder. And I won't name my source, I promise."

Aubrey looked relieved. He put on his glasses and leaned in. "Well, it's probably nothing related to Sparkle's death, but . . . rumor has it Devon was born prematurely."

I leaned in too. "Yeah. And?"

"Well, see, Sonora and Esken were married in May. Devon said she was born December twentieth."

"Don't suppose she was a premie."

"She weighed nine pounds, eleven ounces when she was born."

I sat back in my chair. "So Sonora was pregnant before she got married. Big deal."

"True, not such a big deal, today. But back then, in a small, conservative town like Flat Skunk, it wasn't as accepted as it is today. You know how much Sparkle cared about her heritage. She was proud of marrying into the Bodie line, dating it back to Cornwall, England, when her husband's great-great-grandfather came to make his fortune in gold."

Aubrey was right. Sparkle was not the type of matriarch to handle an embarrassing situation like pregnancy-before-marriage with nonchalance. She would have done everything she could to cover up the scandal, even calling Devon premature—at nine pounds, eleven ounces. But why would that cause her to stop the genealogy search?

I thanked Aubrey for the books, then had a thought and showed him Caleb's drawing to see if he could offer some insight. He didn't add anything more than I already knew. I swore to keep him informed of any developments. He likewise promised his undying loyalty to the cause, unless of course it interfered with a Clamper function. Since he was soon to take over Noble Grand Humbug of the local chapter, he had other loyalties that came first. Like beer.

I spent most of the morning working at the newspaper, trying to catch up on the Sheriff's Blotter. The Blotter numbered more fans than the front page, comics, and obituaries put together. Chief among the fans was the sheriff himself. He loved to see his name in print. Fame was the weapon I used to get information from him. Yesterday's report was full of not-quite-headliners.

"11:24 A.M. Flat Skunk—Mary Obregar reported two

men smoking and 'cussing' in front of young children. After being told to leave, they cussed her and grabbed their genitals."

"2:45 P.M. Whiskey Slide—Kennette Faulkner reported a suspicious person, possibly drunk, working on his car who began yelling, swinging a wrench, and beating on the car. Officer found the man was not drunk, only angry about some defective car parts he had received."

"4:17 P.M. Flat Skunk—Anonymous caller reported kids skateboarding around the Pioneer Cemetery park and gazebo. Caller claimed to have been 'nearly run down' by the skaters, who had 'dyed hair and weird haircuts.' "

"9:30 P.M. Twain Harte—Roberta Alexander reported a truck on fire in front of her bookstore. Officer found the driver had used a cigarette lighter to look for something under the seat of his pickup and started a fire that damaged the seat and cab interior of the 1973 Ford."

I called it a day before anything else came in that could end up on *Hard Copy*.

At lunchtime I locked up and checked Dan's office before leaving the building. No sign of him. I was really beginning to miss him. I stopped at home to see Casper and change clothes, then grabbed a half-eaten beef-and-onion pasty and ate it on the way to Memory Kingdom Memorial Park. I hadn't seen Del Rey since the excitement the day before, and wondered if she'd recovered enough to resume the initially premature embalming of Sparkle Bodie.

I tapped on the window that overlooks the sterile room—the glass was installed for special tours—causing Del Rey to jump. I guess she was still feeling a little jittery over the disturbing events. She appeared to be filling out a form instead of a body. Capping her pen, she waved and headed out to meet me.

"Connor! Come to make sure I don't skewer any live ones?" She laughed, but the tension in her face belied her humor.

"Have you, uh . . . finished . . . Sparkle yet?"

I peered in the window and spotted Sparkle reclining on a leather chair that was tilted to a forty-five-degree angle. She was dressed in a plain green jumpsuit, her hands and feet bare. One eye was closed, the other seemed to be staring at me. I shuddered. A young woman in what looked like hospital pajamas was fiddling with a tube of super glue.

"Are you sure—"

"Yes, she's deceased. Simonie's gluing her eyes shut. One of them is still open, that's all."

I nodded and looked back at the body. Sparkle's cheeks were rosier than Simonie's, her complexion glowing warmly. She didn't look at all like she had the other day, lying on that cold embalming table, still alive. With her makeup applied, she appeared almost ready to sit up. I hoped she wouldn't.

While Simonie worked on the eyelid, a man in a white lab coat fiddled with Sparkle's bird nest of hair, which went way beyond the typical bad hair day. At this point all he'd done was backcomb the whole mess out to a giant gray puffball.

"Nice 'do," I said, hoping the stylist didn't read lips.

Del Rey laughed. "I've seen worse, believe me. Overall, how does she look?"

"She looks . . ." I searched for the right word, "lifelike."

"Good. Come on, I'll make you some tea. Got some herbal cinnamon apple that's not bad."

In a matter of moments I was sitting in the parlor of the funeral home, trying to pretend my tea was a mocha. After seeing Sparkle Bodie's new look, a question occurred to me.

"Del Rey, do you ever notice things on a body that maybe the coroner has overlooked? You know, marks, or other signs that maybe would lead to some sort of, I don't know—"

"Suspicious discovery? No, sorry. I see marks, of course, but I'm sure they've been documented by the M.E. They go over the body with a fine-tooth comb. Although come to think of it, one time this client was sent over and there were marks at the bottom of the foot that the doctor hadn't noticed. The guy was elderly, you know, and old

Doc thought he'd died of complications from a fall he took at the park. Got an infection, developed pneumonia, and died. Doc didn't see the need for an autopsy, so the body was sent directly here. When I mentioned the marks, he took a look, then called the sheriff. Turned out they were teeth marks. They finally figured out a dog had attacked him at the park. They went looking for the animal and found him in the cemetery, living off squirrels and discarded picnic food. It had rabies."

"Wow. Because of that discovery, you probably kept a lot of other people from getting rabies."

Del Rey shrugged modestly.

"Was there anything on Sparkle's body that seemed, I don't know, out of the ordinary?"

"Like what? Teeth marks?"

"Scars? Scrapes? Needle marks?"

"She had the usual scars and markings of a long life and a slow death. But nothing unusual—except maybe the stains."

"Stains?"

"Yeah, there were ink stains on her fingers. Like she'd been doing some writing. But it wasn't anything that would cause her death. Unless it was poison ink and it was injected into her—"

"Cut it out. I was just asking."

I thought about the leaking pen I had found in Sparkle's trash and checked my fingers. There were still traces of blue. I guessed it was the explanation for this mystery.

Before heading back to work, I stopped by the sheriff's office. I found him at his desk, eating a tuna sandwich, while Deputy Clemens talked on the telephone.

Sheriff Mercer greeted me with his mouth full and I couldn't make out anything but bits of sandwich. I waited until he finished the bite before asking him to repeat.

"I asked if you came by to set some more prisoners free—or just to burn the place down?"

"Very funny, Sheriff. I'm here in the sincere interest of

trying to help you solve this murder and you're mocking me. How can you be so cruel and insensitive?"

"My ex-wife taught me. So what's up, C.W.?"

I saw the deputy hang up the phone and look my way. I nodded hello; she nodded and returned to her work. I still had to reschedule that interview, but she didn't look in the mood. I returned my attention to the sheriff. After asking him if he knew more about Caleb's whereabouts or the cause of the fire, and receiving only negative responses, I brought up my latest question.

"Sheriff, I was wondering something about Sparkle. Aside from the numerous aspects of old age that contributed to her eventual death—at least initially—was there anything unusual about her medical condition that would have caused her to appear dead when she wasn't?"

The sheriff stretched back in his chair and locked his hands behind his head. It gave him an extra chin I didn't think he'd like, but I said nothing.

"You mean like tetraodontoxin?"

"Huh?"

"That stuff they get from puffer fish in the jungles. Saw it in a voodoo movie once. Paralyzes you. Sorry, didn't find anything that exotic. But it seems the M.E. found traces of several meds in her blood and tissue samples."

"Could there have been an overdose of some kind?"

"Nope. There were only traces. Not enough to kill her."

"So that's normal."

"This is not for publication yet."

I nodded.

"Well, not exactly. See, we found a bunch of meds in her room, after the fire. I asked the crime lab in Sacramento to check her out for specific toxins. Just got the initial report back. It seems she had a whole bunch of meds running through her system. They just weren't very high dosages."

"But wouldn't that still be normal for a woman in poor health?"

"It would be if the drugs were related to her medical problems."

"They weren't?"

"There were traces of all kinds of drugs—both prescription and OTCs."

Over-the-counter. My heart began to race, as if I'd just had a shot of nitroglycerine. "Like what?"

"Let's see." He lifted up a report he'd been working on. "Valium, amoxicillin, Benzedrine, Norlutate—"

"Norlutate! That's birth control—not that I would know personally . . ."

The sheriff grinned. "Fluoxetine—also known as Prozac—"

"Prozac? Was she—"

"Kaopectate, Ex-Lax, Vivarin, Tylenol, ibuprofen, Nyquil—"

I thought about the empty bottles I had seen in the trash, burned beyond recognition. And the empty medicine cabinet.

"Sheriff, you mean she had all those drugs in her?"

The sheriff sat back again. "It appears that way."

"But why?"

"Don't know. Maybe someone was trying to cure her to death."

Cure her to death. The words lingered like a medicinal aftertaste. Why did Sparkle have all those drugs running through her veins? Prozac. Was she depressed? Ex-Lax. Constipated? Birth control pills? Get real.

Had she administered them herself, in an attempt to commit suicide? It seemed unlikely. Most people in Flat Skunk believed she was determined to live forever. Sonora certainly did.

Had it anything to do with the birth certificate Aubrey had discovered to be missing while tracing her genealogy? Was it enough to inspire someone to load a medicine chest full of drugs into a feeble old woman?

The fire had certainly been convenient. If it had been deliberately set—and I would have bet my diner home that it was—the person responsible probably expected it to obliterate everything. He—or she—must not have known about the hidden fireproof box.

. . .

I found Miah at my office, sketching a cartoon for the *Eureka!*

"About time you showed up," I teased, plopping my backpack on my desk. "I wondered why I was paying you ungodly amounts of money."

Truthfully, he is a godsend and if I could, I would pay double for his services, which include keying in the boring stuff, disciplining the computer when it disobeys my commands, and interpreting tight-mouthed visitors.

Miah has an interesting style of drawing—tiny bodies with big heads, small eyes with big lips—and a satirical sense of humor I enjoy, although not many of the paper's readers appreciate it as much as I do. His latest work featured two big-headed, small-bodied women yelling at each other over a fence. One yard was filled with skyscrapers, the other with trees. The caption read: *"Not in my backyard!"*

I recognized the women immediately. The one with the bobbed hair and dangling earrings in the crowded yard was pro-development Sonora Bodie. The big-haired woman in the forest was status-quo advocate Holly Bryson.

"The hair's not big enough, but I think you've made your point," I signed. Miah had taken ASL classes at the local college and we signed at the office to give him practice. He'd become quite proficient in the past year we'd been working together.

"'Got a bulletproof vest? Sonora isn't going to like the Golden Arches earrings, you know. They clash with her outfit."

"I can't get the hair any bigger. It'll be outside the frame. It's inhuman the way we artists have to put up with all these constraints."

"If you had your way, the entire paper would be filled with your cartoons. Then where would I put the news?"

"What news?" Miah signed. "Jilda Renfrew's spellbinding column on 'The Craft Boutique Roundup' and old Mama Cody's latest inedible recipe for Applesauce Meat Loaf?"

"Hey, have you tried Mama's meat loaf? It's not bad. You know we can't print that cartoon, by the way."

"Why not?"

"Might start a war. Or rather, end a war. Permanently."

While Miah pouted, I sorted through the clutter on my desk. I made piles based on how demanding each item was, then neatened the piles several times before leaning back and twirling the chair toward the window.

From my vantage point I could see Sheriff Mercer standing on the sidewalk, engaged in a heated argument with Deputy Clemens. Judging from the way his hands were gesturing and his body was slumped, I guessed he was losing.

A few yards away, Sluice Jackson sat on a chair outside the Nugget Café, trying to sell dangling beaded earrings to a tourist. From her body language, it was clear she didn't trust the old prospector, giving him a wide berth as she passed by. Not surprising. The guy could scare Wes Craven with that grizzled complexion, scarecrow hair, and grunge-before-it-was-popular clothing.

But appearances can be deceiving, as I had quickly learned in Flat Skunk. I had misjudged a few towns-people as less than quick-witted, just because they talked slowly and moved even slower than the movers and shakers in the city. They had misjudged me, too, just because I couldn't hear.

I loved watching Flat Skunkers from my office window. I'd learned so much about the townspeople by observing their body language. I read in a book once that body language and facial expressions reveal more than seventy-five percent of the messages people send, while the actual words only give twenty-five percent. From what I'd seen, I didn't doubt it.

I wondered what Caleb Bodie had been trying to say in his cell with those large rough hands and piercing dark eyes.

I had a thought. I dug through my Rolodex and located an old business card I'd saved from my reporting days in the city. It was a number for DCARA—the

Deaf Counseling and Referral Agency for Northern California. I dialed the number on my TTY and keyed in my request. The information came through in a matter of minutes, glowing on my red TTY screen in capital letters. Just as I figured. There was an organization in the Gold Country called the Silence Is Golden Deaf Club. I picked up my backpack, gave Miah a "carry on, son" pat on the back, and left him in charge of the less-than-bustling office.

I found the Silence Is Golden Deaf Club in an old clapboard house off the main street in neighboring Whiskey Slide. A hand-painted sign on the door announced the name of the club in English and underneath in finger-spelled letters. I looked for a doorbell, then saw a smaller sign hanging in the window that said, "Come in."

The tiny foyer of the small house served as a greeting room. On the right side stood a large counter where "I-Love-You" jewelry, sign language greeting cards, and other deaf-related items were sold. Behind the counter stood a man maybe in his late sixties, his face furrowed from years of vivid expression, his fingers bony, yet nimble as he saluted "Hello." His even white teeth as he grinned looked too white and even to be real. And he wore an obvious hairpiece that he'd tried to blend in with his gray thinning hair. But the welcome felt genuine.

Before I could sign a word, he held up a finger indicating for me to wait a moment, then he keyed a few numbers into a computer.

"Finished," he signed, both hands flipping outward in front of him. "I hate computers," he added, flicking his middle fingers at the glowing screen. "I'm too old for all this high-tech stuff. But today, you can't live without it, right? So, what can I do for you?"

Not knowing whether I was hearing or deaf, he simultaneously moved his mouth—I assumed he was speaking—and used Signed English, which is a word-for-word interpretation of signs and English. Instead of signing, "You—what do?" in ASL, which would have expressed the same idea in a nutshell, his signs were literal. It's common for deaf people to use Signed English with hearing people, since hearies often don't have the ASL skills or understanding of the syntax used by deaf people. Unless they're CODAs—children of deaf adults. Then it's often hard to tell the difference. But most hearing people who learn sign language still experience some difficulty using the idioms and acquiring the fluency that native signers have. I wondered if he could tell by my opening gesture that I had learned sign language later in life, as a teenager.

"Name, me, C-O-N-N-O-R W-E-S-T-P-H-A-L. Wonder, have problem, talk with someone?" I signed in ASL.

He stuck his bottom lip out and nodded with both his head and his fist. "Me. I'm director of the club. OK?"

I nodded. He indicated a hallway and I followed him into a slightly larger living area. The room was filled with comfortable-looking couches, a number of folding chairs, a large table in the middle of the room, and a big-screen TV on the far wall, showing a captioned soap opera. I briefly scanned the words that appeared at the bottom of the screen. Someone was in a coma.

Three men sat in a corner in overstuffed chairs, carrying on a vigorous conversation with their hands and bodies. I tried not to eavesdrop, but I was fascinated by their flying fingers and flexible faces. Every few seconds they would break out into laughter—open-mouthed smiles, bobbing heads—making me curious about their conversation. I'm not sure they noticed our entrance, they were so engrossed in one another's stories. I thought they were discussing a trip one of the men had taken.

My host gestured for me to sit down on the couch. He pulled up a folding chair and sat opposite me, making communication easy. Mouth closed, he signed in ASL. "My name is Lindan Barde. It's nice to meet you, Connor. I don't think I've seen you here before." He swept his arm around the place.

I shook my head. "No, I've never been here before. I live in Flat Skunk, so it's a bit of a drive. And I didn't know you were here until I called DCARA for a referral."

"Are you deaf?" he asked, eyebrows raised. He pointed to me, then his ear, then his mouth. The sign once translated to "deaf-and-dumb," meaning a person who didn't hear or speak, but it now meant "deaf." The term "deaf-and-dumb" is not accepted any more, and is offensive to most deaf people. But the sign remains.

"Yes, since I was four years old, from meningitis. But I didn't learn sign until high school deaf camp. My parents sent me to oral schools. They had a hard time accepting my deafness."

He nodded, nonjudgmentally. I knew there was a raging battle within the deaf community as to which was better, sign or speech. But most deaf people understand there are different strokes for different folks. He didn't seem at all threatened by my history.

"Where did you go to school?" he asked. This is one of the first questions deaf people ask each other. The deaf community is small and it isn't uncommon to know some of the same people a six-degrees-of-separation kind of thing, which often sets up an immediate connection. I told him the name of my school in San Francisco, The Eileen Jackson Institute, and asked him where he attended.

"California School for the Deaf in Berkeley, then Gallaudet University." CSDB had originally been established in Berkeley, but an earthquake hazard caused the school to relocate to Fremont. Gallaudet is the university for the deaf in Washington, D.C. It had recently gone through its own upheaval, with a refusal to accept a hearing person as university president. Since that time, Deaf Power has affected many areas of deaf lives, from equal employment to environmental access.

We chatted casually for a few minutes. Every now and then I had to ask Lindan Barde what a sign meant that I didn't recognize. He patiently answered my questions

and explained his terminology. His hands, fluid and po-
etic, were easy to read, and his facial expression gave his
words the nuances required. He seemed to know what
pace to use and manually enunciated each letter or sign
clearly.

"You said you have a problem?" he asked.

I nodded. "There's a man in Flat Skunk who has been
accused of murder. He was arrested and placed in jail. I
was asked to see him as a favor to his brother. The man is
deaf—"

Lindan immediately interrupted me. "Who? What's his
name?"

I shook my head. "I don't think you know him. He's . . .
been kept at home—"

"Really? Why?" He looked puzzled.

"It's a long story," I said, and proceeded to explain
Caleb's history.

When I had finished, Lindan Barde shook a hand in the
air. "Wow. Seems unbelievable, but I've heard of this happening more than once. I had a friend who was in a home
for retarded children for eight years before they realized he
was only deaf. Can you imagine? Tragic. Even when people
know you are just deaf, they still sometimes think you are
ignorant or illiterate."

I nodded. "Now Caleb's been accused of murdering his
mother. The trouble is, he can't communicate—he doesn't
know speech or sign. Only a few homemade gestures that
are very basic. I don't know how to communicate with him
in order to find out what really happened."

Lindan glanced behind me and I turned around to follow his gaze. A woman was signing to him at a rapid pace
and I missed the details. I got the gist though: He was
wanted on the phone.

Lindan stood and signed, "Excuse me for one minute. My twelve-year-old granddaughter is home sick.
Her mother and father are at work. I told her to call if
she needed anything. Let me check on her. I'll be right
back."

As Lindan Barde left the room, my eyes drifted over to the three men, still signing busily in the corner. I hated to eavesdrop but couldn't help myself. Their finger-spelling was mostly a blur, and their signs were short and rapid. I understood only one of the men clearly; he seemed to act out more of his words than the others. When he communicated, I could follow him almost perfectly.

In a few minutes Lindan Barde returned and settled into his chair across from me.

"Everything all right?" I asked.

He wrinkled his nose and nodded. "She just wants me to bring some Popsicles when I come home. I think she only wanted to make sure I was still available."

"Is she deaf?" I asked.

He nodded. "I have three children. One is deaf, one is severely hard-of-hearing, and one is moderately hard-of-hearing—she can use the telephone with an amplifier. My deaf daughter married a deaf man, and they have three children, all deaf. My hard-of-hearing daughters also married deaf men. One has deaf children, the other has hearing children."

"Interesting," I signed. I momentarily wondered what it would be like to have a hearing child. Genetically I would probably have hearing children, since deafness caused by meningitis is not hereditary. But deaf or hearing, it wouldn't really matter to me.

"So you were saying, this man cannot communicate?"

"Very little. And I don't know what to do—although that point may be moot. He's escaped from jail."

Lindan nodded slowly, as he watched the three men in the corner for a moment, then turned back to me. Frowning and wiggling his fingers at his forehead, he indicated he was thinking. Then he stood up, walked over to the men, apologized for interrupting, and asked one of them to come and meet me. It was the man who had been gesturing so clearly.

"Connor, I want you to meet Warren Matthews. Warren is a well-known storyteller in the deaf community. He's won many awards for his folk tales, anecdotes, even the deaf jokes that he tells."

"Hello," I saluted.

"Nice to meet you, Ms. Westphal."

"Connor, I'd like you to tell Warren of your problem. One thing though—you can only use gestures to talk with him."

I had been sitting posed, ready to sign, when Lindan stunned me by saying gestures only. I looked at Warren Matthews, held up my hands—and nothing happened. Gestures only? I couldn't do it. My problem was much too complicated to express as if I were playing a game of charades.

"I . . . I can't!" I signed helplessly to Lindan Barde.

He smiled, faced Warren Matthews, and explained my problem—all in mime. It was utterly fascinating to watch. Not one word of proper sign language was used, and yet he was able to communicate the entire situation. Warren Matthews immediately understood everything Lindan relayed.

Warren turned to me. I sat stiffly, waiting for his gestures with sweaty palms. I was relieved when he signed in perfect ASL. "You say this man went undiagnosed as deaf until he was ten, so he has no communication skills. Now he's accused of murdering his own mother. Yet he can't understand the charges against him and can't defend himself. On top of that, he has escaped from jail. Am I correct?"

"You do know ASL!"

"Of course. But my first priority is communication. Whatever it takes."

Lindan joined in: "Warren is amazing. He can meet a deaf, or hearing person for that matter, from any country around the world and make anything understood, just through gesture. He's extremely gifted."

Warren didn't even blush at the compliment. He stood proudly, in total agreement.

"If you find this man again, let me know. I will come and see him. Maybe I can help." He smiled, then returned to his friends who were waiting for him in the corner. Just before he turned his attention to them, he turned back to me and signed from across the room.

"In the meantime, practice talking without words. It just takes a little imagination—and a great deal of need."

Driving my Chevy back to the newspaper office, I visualized the stories Warren Matthews had told at the Deaf Club. He'd been so clear in his gestures, a prelingual baby could have understood him.

I thought back to my elementary school days on the playground, fooling around with my friends—all hearing kids except one, who was severely hard-of-hearing. None of us had trouble communicating with each other, and yet very little was said through speech or lipreading. We acted out everything, with no question as to what was being "said." We played house and school, we put on plays, we created our own newspaper, we played ball, jump rope, and hopscotch. And I always knew what was going on. Later I learned this was called "visual vernacular," a phrase coined by the deaf actor, Bernard Bragg.

Had I lost the ability to fully express myself over the years? Had my body language become less demonstrative as I spent more time with hearing people? I find so many hearies are stone-faced when they talk, that it's hard to tell from their expressions whether they're happy, sad, or mad. With deaf people you immediately know the emotion behind the statement, without a sign or word spoken. It's distinctly represented on their faces, in their hands, from their movements.

The question remained, could I ever communicate with Caleb Bodie? And would I even be given the chance, now that he was missing?

The newspaper office was locked when I returned. Miah had left a note saying he was down the hall at his own surf and comic bookshop. Fish Out Of Water, if I needed some interpreting, or if I wanted the 1956 copy of the *Hot Stuff, The Li'l Devil* comic he'd just picked up. I had a feeling I'd be paying top dollar for that comic book. The mercenary.

I had just begun work on the weekly mystery puzzle for the *Eureka!* when the TTY light flashed. I picked it up, typed in "Connor Westphal, GA," and waited for the response.

"THIS IS CRS WITH A CALL FOR CONNOR WESTPHAL. GA." It was the California Relay System operator, interpreting for the caller.

"CONNOR IT'S ESKEN," the words, via the operator, skipped across the monitor. "HAVE U FOUND CALEB YET Q GA."

Startled by Esken's call, I paused for a moment before I began my response. The operator returned with "ARE YOU THERE Q GA." Jolted, I started typing.

"ESKEN WHERE ARE U Q NO I HAVEN'T FOUND CALEB YET. I THOT HE MIGHT BE W/ U. WHAT ARE U DOING Q U HAVE TO CONTACT THE SHERIFF. GA." With the relay operator, I could fall back into the usual shortcuts and abbreviations commonly used on the TTY. The operator replied in kind.

"CONNOR PLS DON'T GO INTO ANY DETAIL ON THE PHONE. I NEED TO BE CAREFUL. I THINK I'M BEING FOLLOWED. MY LIFE MAY BE IN DANGER. I NEED U TO MEET ME AND BRING SOME OF

THE PAPERS AUBREY WAS WORKING ON FOR MY MOTHER'S GENEALOGY CHART. IT'S VITAL THAT I GET THOSE PAPERS. GA."

"ESKEN, YOU'VE GOT TO CALL THE SHERIFF! SOMETHING'S HAPPENED. GA."

"I CAN'T. NOW WILL U MEET ME W/ THE PAPERS OR NOT Q GA."

Whether I planned to meet him or not, I could at least get him to tell me where he was. Then I would decide what to do.

"WHERE Q GA."

"REMEMBER THE PLACE I WANTED TO LIST IN THE AD LAST MONTH Q GA."

I thought for a moment. He must have meant the old Bodie Mine. He'd wanted to sell the place, but Sparkle wouldn't allow it. He'd told me that he and Caleb used to go there as kids, but after the recent earthquakes, it had been sealed shut. He obviously didn't want to identify it over the phone.

"YES. I REMEMBER. GA."

"TONITE AFTER DUSK. I'LL WAIT IN MY CAR. GA."

"SORRY, SOUNDS DANGEROUS, TOO LONELY AND DESERTED, ESPECIALLY AT NIGHT, AND ESPECIALLY WHEN U THINK SOMEONE'S FOLLOWING U. I SAW THIS MOVIE ONCE—"

"CONNOR," the words interrupted my typing. "PLS. THERE'S NOT MUCH TIME. 1 MORE THING. THERE'S A BOX MY MOTHER KEPT HIDDEN SOMEWHERE IN HER ROOM. IT'S FULL OF PAPERS. I NEED THOSE PAPERS. CAN U FIND THEM AND BRING THEM ALONG Q IT'S URGENT. GA."

He must have meant the metal box I'd found buried under his mother's bed. I hadn't noticed any terribly important papers inside—My God! Did he not know about the fire?

"ESKEN, THERE WAS A FIRE AT YOUR MOTHER'S HOME. DIDN'T U HEAR ABOUT IT Q GA."

No response came for several seconds. Finally, "MY MOTHER'S HOME," a pause. "GONE Q GA."

I hated to be the one to break the news. I tried to make it sound less than devastating. "NOT COMPLETELY. IT'S STILL STANDING. MOSTLY. I DID FIND A BOX OF PAPERS UNDER YOUR MOTHER'S BED. THEY LOOK LIKE DEEDS. THERE'S A NEWSPAPER ARTICLE, AND OTHER STUFF. BUT NOTHING OF VALUE. IS THAT THE ONE QQ GA."

"OH GOD! U FOUND IT! GREAT! BRING IT TONITE. PLS. EVERYTHING DEPENDS ON IT. GA."

"FIRST OF ALL THE BOX IS W/ THE SHERIFF. SECONDLY, HOW AM I SUPPOSED TO GET AUBREY TO GIVE ME THE GENEALOGY PAPERS Q THIRD, WHO'S GOING TO BAIL ME OUT OF JAIL WHEN I'M ARRESTED FOR AIDING AND ABETTING Q AND FINALLY, HOW ABOUT I MEET U IN A PUBLIC PLACE Q IN THE DAYTIME Q WITH A BODYGUARD Q GA."

"LISTEN, U CAN BRING A FRIEND IF U LIKE, JUST NOT THE SHERIFF. U'LL BE PERFECTLY SAFE, I SWEAR. PLS CONNOR! DO WHAT U CAN TO GET ME THAT INFO. AND COME! GA."

"WHAT ABOUT CALEB Q GA."

"I THINK I KNOW WHERE HE IS. GA."

"WHERE Q GA."

"COME TONIGHT. I HAVE TO GO. SK SK."

I hung up wondering what the relay operator thought of all this. Operators are not allowed to get involved in conversations made through the relay system. And everything said must be kept confidential, except in the event of suspected child abuse. But what if an operator heard something truly menacing, like a plot to kill the President or even a murder committed over the phone? I wouldn't be too surprised to see our operator at the mine tonight.

The mine. Only I knew where Esken meant for us to meet. And there was no way I was going there without an escort. I'd stop by and see if I could interest Dan in being my bodyguard for the event. I was fairly certain Esken was harmless. And I knew the area well—I'd explored the place before the earthquake closed it down. Did a little rappelling and spelunking—on a tour, of course. But it didn't hurt to have a six-foot-three-inch, 210-pound escort with arms the size of Uzis to back you up.

Unfortunately, Dan wasn't in. Where was he spending his time these days? He'd been out of his regular construction work for several weeks, filling in as a handyman for various elderly retirees in the area, when not acting as a volunteer fire fighter. But I'd seen him in his office more than not—at least until recently. I left a note taped to the door saying I had something to ask him, hoping it sounded intriguing.

The Nugget Café was packed in the late afternoon. There were no empty tables, but I spotted a familiar highlighted blonde sitting alone at a booth and decided to take the opportunity to ask her a few questions over a mocha and a piece of Mama Cody's bread pudding.

"Hi, Sonora. Mind if I join you?"

She looked up from her datebook slowly, her mind no doubt processing some big development opportunity.

"Hi, Connor," she said, with little expression. She looked tired as she halfheartedly gestured to the seat across from her. "You can have my table. I was just about to leave, anyway." She folded up her book, stuffed with Post-it notes, receipts, brochures, and other small papers, and secured it closed with a heavy-duty rubber band.

"You doing all right?" I asked, as I signaled Jilda for service.

"Sure. Kind of in limbo, you know, what with all that's happened. Caleb's escaped, Esken's disappeared, Devon's gone God knows where, the house is in ruins. At this point, I don't know whether I'm going to have enough money to stay in my own home. Could be worse, I guess. But I don't know how."

I nodded and tried to look sympathetic. "Sparkle really ran the show, didn't she?"

"Seems that way. But she didn't run my life, even

though she tried. Of course, here she is in her grave and she's still got this whole town under her control."

"You said Esken is missing. Did he take anything with him? Is there any reason to suspect that—"

"That something happened to him? I doubt it. He just can't take stress. I'm sure this is his way of dealing with it. By disappearing."

"Are any of his clothes missing?"

Sonora stared at me blankly.

"Sonora?"

She licked her lips. "I . . . uh . . . I don't know, actually."

"What do you mean? You haven't looked in his closet?"

She pressed her lips together then said, "He . . . his clothes aren't there. . . ."

"So his clothes are missing!" I restated what I thought was the obvious.

"Look, Connor, Esken and I . . . we don't exactly live together."

I tried not to look surprised. I must have failed, because Sonora nodded as if she'd expected my reaction. Then she glanced around the café to see if anyone else had overheard her.

She lowered her head a notch as she continued. "No one knows. At least, I don't think anyone knows. He's been living in the servants' house in the back. Been there for several years, actually. We . . . didn't want Sparkle to know. Part of the condition of the will insisted that we remain together in order to inherit her estate. But we've been separated for quite some time."

"And Sparkle never knew?"

"I don't think so. We tried very hard to make it look like we were still together."

"Why did you separate? I mean, it's none of my business, but . . ." I let the sentence hang there unfinished, hoping she would fill in the rest. Jilda came by, took my order, and gave Sonora her bill. I waited for Sonora to continue. After a few more seconds of fumbling with her wallet, I tried another question—a little more outrageous. I find if you ask something shocking, you're more likely to get a response.

"Has Esken been seeing other women?"

As expected, Sonora looked stunned. "Oh, God, no! It's not that at all. You have to understand, Esken and I got married very young. And for all the wrong reasons, which I won't go into right now. We only stayed together because Sparkle insisted on it. She wouldn't hear of a divorce. She couldn't tolerate any kind of scandal, even though divorce isn't a scandal today. But it was in her mind. No one in the Bodie family tree had ever been divorced, and she let you know that."

I started to ask Sonora another question when she glanced over my shoulder. I turned to see Aubrey heading our way. Sonora quickly packed up the rest of her belongings and stood.

"Connor, please don't say anything." She mouthed the words in an exaggerated style. I wondered if she was whispering so Aubrey wouldn't hear. I was surprised at how much she'd already told me, but then again not surprised. I've found that many hearing people seem to talk to deaf people as if the information will go no further. I nodded.

"Sonora, leaving so soon?" It was Aubrey.

Sonora made a few excuses to him, then said her good-byes to both of us. Aubrey filled the vacated spot, sliding into the red Naugahyde seat with a twist of his narrow hips. He pushed his glasses back against his face and spread both hands on the table, playing it like a piano.

"Connor! How's it going?"

"Boy, you're in a good mood. Take too many Prozacs today?"

Aubrey laughed. "Naw, don't need drugs. I'm high on life."

"You're high on caffeine, and don't tell me different. I can spot an addict a mile away. Pinwheel eyes, uncontrollable grin, hyperactive fingers. It's written all over you. I'm telling Jilda you're cut off."

Aubrey's eyes widened, his mouth pulled into a taut grimace like something out of *Dorian Gray*. He reached over the table and grabbed my wrists.

"No! You can't do that, I tell you! I need my caffeine! Don't you understand?" He waved his head back and forth as if he were Ray Charles.

I laughed. Aubrey pulled his hands away, as Jilda set down the mocha for me and a latte for Aubrey. She gave us a strange look but said nothing. She had probably dealt with coffee addicts before.

"Liquid gold, with just a hint of arsenic!" He took a swallow, made a face that said, "God, that's hot!" and set the mug down.

"Serves you right." I sipped at mine sensibly while Aubrey fanned his lips.

After a few more words about coffee, the service at the Nugget, the interesting outfit Jilda was wearing today, and Jean-Philipe's new buzz cut, I got around to the topic du jour.

"Aubrey, you mentioned something about a birth certificate in your genealogy research. Was there anything else unusual in the Bodic family history? Any other odd birth certificates, divorce decrees, unexplained deaths, or anything like that?"

"No, I'm sure I would have noticed, knowing how much Sparkle cared about her perfect lineage. Why?"

"Any health problems, other than Caleb's? Anyone else deaf or disabled?"

"Not really. There was a note on Esken's health history that said something about an Rh factor. Caleb's was marked 'feebleminded.' Oh, and 'blue baby.' Maybe he was kind of blue when he was born—no oxygen—and that caused his hearing loss, huh?"

I stiffened. "You're sure it said 'blue baby'?"

Aubrey nodded and tried another sip of his latte. "Is that something special?"

"Years ago that's what they called babies who had blood incompatibilities. If the mother was Rh positive— or was it negative, I can't remember which—and the father was the opposite, then the mother would build up antibodies against the fetus growing inside. Nothing happened to the first baby, but all the babies after that were affected. They had to be given blood transfusions right after they were born. It was very dangerous. Life-threatening."

"You think that's how Caleb was deafened?"

"I don't know. There are over a hundred different ways to become deaf. Many are hereditary, the rest are from damage and disease. I don't know if the Rh factor played a part in it."

"Do they still do that—give babies blood transfusions?"

"Not anymore. They've discovered a preventive drug called RhoGAM that is injected into the mother during or after her second pregnancy. It's supposed to fool the mother's antibodies into not rejecting her fetus, so the baby is born without needing a blood transfusion."

"Where'd you learn all this, Connor? Do you have a blue baby in your family history?"

"No. Did a story on it once, for the *Chronicle*. Being a journalist, you learn a little bit about a lot of things, but not enough to do you any real good."

Jilda brought a chicken salad for Aubrey. I envied his dietary control. Maybe that's why he had a better figure than I did. I took a big bite of bread pudding, sauce dripping from the spoon, just the way the Nugget does it best. I licked a glob from the corner of my mouth and silently blessed Mama Cody.

"Aubrey, did Devon have anything written on her health form?" It was possible the Rh factor could have been passed down to her.

"Didn't notice anything. Why?"

"Just curious."

"I'll go through my notes and see what I can find out. I'm kinda curious about this whole thing. I keep wondering why Sparkle pulled the plug on the whole genealogy thing. Besides, this is fun, trying to solve a mystery."

"I'd appreciate whatever you can find out, Aubrey. Just keep it to yourself, all right? We could end up hurting a lot of people unnecessarily if we aren't careful."

"No problem."

"Oh, and Aubrey, one more thing. Could you make me a copy of your notes? I'd like to go over them myself."

"Will do. Just don't tell anyone where you got them. I'm in enough trouble with that late library book."

Dan's door was ajar when I returned to the newspaper office. I pushed it open a few more inches and peeked in, spotting him at his desk. He didn't look up; he seemed engrossed in a collection of forms that were spread over his desk. From a distance the pile looked terribly boring, but apparently it had him mesmerized.

I stood tentatively in the doorway, waiting for a sign he might be interested in company, but he didn't move. I wasn't ready to give up on him yet. I took a step in. Nothing. "Hi," I said softly. I had learned to feel my voice through speech training, but I wasn't always sure the words came out as I'd hoped. There was no response. I must have spoken too softly. A gentle throbbing emanated from the floorboards. I scanned the room and spotted the radio light on.

I elbowed the door shut, a little more forcefully than necessary. Dan started and looked up, frowning.

"Jesus. Do you have to do that?" he said, like I did it all the time.

"What?" I reopened the door so I could watch for my phone light.

"Slam the door. You made me mark up this paper."

"Sorry. Guess you didn't hear me, for a change. Music's kind of loud, isn't it?"

He looked at the radio then back at me quizzically. He started to say something, but frowned instead and punched the radio knob off.

"What are you working on?"

"Nothing. Mortgage stuff, for my mom's house back in New York."

I scanned the desk, trying to look casual. Some loan papers, a few bank statements, a property deed, and what looked like a statement from a retirement fund were piled loosely, one obscuring the other.

"Everything all right?" I sat down in the tattered leather chair opposite him, trying to look relaxed as my heart beat double-time. Why did this man have such an effect on me? And why hadn't I had that same effect on him lately?

He tapped his pencil nervously. "Yeah, fine. You?"

"I'm great. It's just that you seem—"

Dan was looking beyond me. Was I boring him? I turned around to see if anything had distracted him. Nothing there. I turned back to face him. He mumbled something I couldn't read.

"What?"

"Nothing. I thought I saw . . . never mind. What were you saying?"

"Uh . . . I was saying . . ." Suddenly I didn't feel like getting into it. I changed the subject, and kept the conversation on safe ground. "Listen, I have to meet Esken Bodie tonight, out at the old Bodie Mine. He thinks someone's following him, and he's convinced the sheriff is after him for letting his brother out of jail, so he doesn't want to meet in public—"

"You're not going, are you?"

"Well, I don't really see why not—"

"Connor!" Dan said, and then he did something strange. He pointed to his temples, then pulled out his hands and flipped them in the air.

I stared at him. "What was that?"

"What?"

"That . . . that thing you just did. You signed."

Dan frowned. "No, I didn't."

"Yes, you did. You went like this." I repeated the action. "What was that?"

"Nothing. I'm half Italian. It's just a gesture of frustration. You frustrate me."

"Dan, Esken is scared. He needs my help. He saw some papers from the genealogy workup that Sparkle had commissioned, and he thinks—"

"Connor, you can't go! His mother is dead, apparently not from natural causes. His brother is suspected of murdering his own mother. Sheriff Mercer thinks Esken broke his brother out of jail, and the sheriff's not stupid. And now someone is following him? Why don't you just meet him in the cemetery at midnight with a black cat, wearing a sign that says 'Victim!' Haven't you seen any of those Fem-Jeop movies?"

"Fem-Jeop?"

"Women in jeopardy. You know—the ones where the women go down into the cellar because they hear a strange noise—"

"I don't hear strange noises."

"That's not the point!"

"Well, that's why I'm here! I . . . was wondering if you'd come with me. As sort of a bodyguard, not that I need one. I'm not stupid either, you know. I don't go into cellars without heavy artillery. . . ." I pulled a can of pepper spray from my backpack. "I just thought, well, I haven't seen much of you lately. Maybe we could have dinner first . . ."

Dan looked uncomfortable.

"Or not. It doesn't matter—"

"No, dinner would be nice. Sorry I haven't been much company lately. Got some things on my mind. You know."

"Is it money?" You didn't have to know how to read numbers upside-down to put two and two together.

Dan began to neaten the papers. "It's not big deal. What time tonight?"

I started to say six, which would give us time to eat, talk, and drive over to the mine, but again Dan's attention was pulled away. And again, I followed his gaze.

This time there was someone in the open doorway. I recognized the maroon hair, the eyebrow ring, the lip stud, and the wrist tattoos, not to mention the watermelon stomach. Devon Bodie.

Devon's masked expression told me nothing. She was wearing a leather bomber jacket, three sizes too large, baggy jeans, four sizes too large, and black tennis shoes with a fancy lacing job. She held a long skateboard in one hand and a rolled-up magazine in the other.

"Hi, Devon," I said, moving toward her. "Are you looking for Miah? If he's not in his shop, he might be in my office next door."

Devon gave a single nod and turned toward the stairs, away from both the places I'd suggested.

"Devon! Wait!" I bolted out of Dan's office and caught her just as she'd taken the first stair. "Could you come to my office for a minute? I want to ask you something."

"What?" she asked dully.

"Can we please talk in my office? It's kind of personal."

Devon shrugged, looking ultrabored, then followed me back to the newspaper office. I indicated a chair opposite my desk and she slumped down, the way teenagers seem to do even when they're not pregnant.

"Doesn't that hurt?" I asked, touching my right eyebrow. She shook her head. "This one did, a little." She stuck out her tongue. Imbedded in the center was a silver ball. I winced. She smiled. Apparently it was the reaction she had anticipated.

Luckily the painful-looking decoration hadn't interfered with my ability to understand her speech. Maybe the nearly black-maroon lipstick helped with outlining the words. But then again, she hadn't said much to understand.

"What's the tattoo?" I indicated her left wrist, which sported a barbed wire bracelet linked in black. A single drop of red had been added to make the back of her hand look as if it were bleeding from the barbed wire.

"I dunno. Just thought it was cool. No hidden meaning, if that's what you're asking."

"What do your parents think about all this?"

She smirked and rolled her eyes. "Naturally they went postal when they saw the tattoo. Like they've never done anything outrageous before."

"Postal?"

Being deaf, I miss a lot of the slang that seems to pop up every few weeks. It takes me longer to pick up the new terms. Even abbreviations like "fridge" for refrigerator or "rad" for "radical" had me stumped the first few times I lip-read them.

"Yeah, postal. You know, like ballistic? Wigged? Crazy?"

Postal. Most of the slang terms had a familiar basis, which helped me figure them out. I had deduced that "hella" came from "hell-of-a" and "later" came from "see-ya-later." Postal? Slang for postal workers who went nuts? Made sense.

"Listen, Devon, I wanted to tell you I'm sorry about your grandmother. And your uncle . . ."

Devon glanced away, giving a single-shouldered shrug. "Whatever."

I could sense I wasn't connecting, and I wouldn't be able to get much information from her if I didn't. Her age, her language, her style—there was no real link between us. She probably saw me as the enemy, just like her parents were—and maybe the rest of the world.

"So where'd you learn to skateboard?" I asked, rising from my chair.

Another shrug.

"Miah's been trying to teach me," I said, picking up the long board she had propped against the desk. I set the board on the floor and I stood on it, getting the feel of it. "But I can't turn. I lose my balance, which isn't so great to begin with. See this?"

I held up my arm, pulling up my long sleeve to show her the bruise on my elbow.

She half grinned. At first I thought she was letting me

know I was pretty stupid for even trying to skateboard at my age. But suddenly she did something to change my mind. She pushed up the sleeves on her brown jacket to reveal scabs on both elbows. Then she hoisted her baggy black jeans and showed me her black-and-blue shins. Finally she raised the side of her jacket and shirt to expose a bruise the size of a coconut on her right hip. A hip that featured a few stretch marks as well.

"Wow!" I said, trying to sound impressed at her trophy injuries, while hiding my concern about the safety of her baby. "Well, I'd ask you to show me a couple of tricks, but you're awfully pregnant to be skating, aren't you?"

Her face changed. She frowned and looked away. Uh-oh. Had I just undone all the progress I'd made?

She turned back, her shoulders a little tighter. "I'm careful. Besides, I've been reading a lot about pregnancy. If I fall while I'm skateboarding, I'm not going to hurt the baby. She's protected. The book says I'll be the one who gets hurt, not her."

"Do you know it's a girl?"

Devon rubbed her tummy as she spoke about her child. "Yeah. Had one of those ultrasound tests. The technician said it was a girl. Ninety percent sure. Doesn't matter to me, though."

"You're not going to keep it?"

"No."

From her body language, I could tell she didn't want me to go there. Besides, it wasn't what I'd called her in for anyway. There was something else on my mind, and it was time to get to the point, before she stormed out the door.

"Devon, what was your uncle Caleb like?"

"Weird, you know. Nobody could understand him very well. I didn't see him much. Seems like every time I came over, he'd go to his room or take off somewhere."

"Was he violent? Did you ever see him hit anyone or try to hurt anyone?"

"He had temper tantrums where he'd scream and throw his arms around and stuff, like he was frustrated. He was strong, but I never saw him hurt anyone. One time my dad got into a physical thing with Uncle Caleb 'cause he was knocking things off the table. My dad held him down and Caleb tried to fight back, but Caleb never hurt him. At least, not on purpose. But when he swung his arm out, he accidentally hit my dad in the face. Gave him a black eye."

"Do you think Caleb might have hurt your grandmother in that hospital room?"

Devon thought for a moment, then looked me straight on. "Maybe." She didn't elaborate, but I detected a growing chip on her shoulder, as if she thought I might challenge her response. What the hell, then.

"Maybe?"

"I dunno. I wasn't there. At least not in the room, you know. Who knows what he's capable of? Who knows what anyone's capable of, once their buttons are pushed, you know?"

"Can you communicate with Caleb at all?"

She looked away. "Naw. I could never understand him. He was always trying to tell me stuff I couldn't figure out. It bugged me, you know, the way he kept pointing at something over and over again. I didn't have a clue what he was talking about. He's sort of retarded, you know."

"I thought he was deaf."

"Yeah, but he doesn't act like you. You're deaf, right? But you act normal. He's kind of weird, the way he's always going out to the old Bodie Mine in the middle of the night—creepy."

"You've seen him at the mine?"

She gave a half shrug and her cheeks flared with color. "Yeah, you know, that's where everyone hangs out. We don't have any movie theaters or anything around here. There's nothing to do but get loaded and get together with some guy, you know. Anyway, I've seen him out there a couple of times, creeping around. I think the kids are scared of him. But I think they kind of like being scared of him, you know?"

I tried to picture Caleb encountering the kids at the mine. Their own teenage horror film come to life.

"Did he ever try to communicate with you out there?"

"Nope. As soon as we caught him looking at us, he'd always duck into the mine. Some of the guys tried to follow him a couple of times but they never found him. He loves it in there, I guess. But you won't catch me inside that place at night. There's some animals in those mines now. I've seen their eyes." She shivered.

Miah appeared in the doorway and called to Devon. She abruptly stood up, grabbing her long board, and headed for the door. With a glance back for good-bye, she followed Miah down the hall to his store.

By the time I got back to Dan's office, he was gone again, and I felt a pang of disappointment. The next hour passed uneventfully, until Russell Jacks poked his head into my office, right in the middle of a piece I was writing on a local historic costume collection. The owner had recently acquired a dress she was especially proud of, one worn by Lotta Crabtree. The story had potential, if I worked with it a little.

"Connor! You busy?"

I checked my watch, then waved him in.

"Just wanted to drop off this press release I wrote up. It's about the Clamp-diggings we're hosting over at the Haunted Caverns Mine next weekend. The Clampers are putting up a new plaque and having a barbecue afterward. Thought you might let the folks know."

The Clampers were always erecting plaques in the Mother Lode. All it took to get a plaque hung was an old building or a memorable death.

"Is the Haunted Caverns a historical monument now? How'd you manage that?"

Russell had owned the Haunted Caverns for years, inherited from his father and grandfather. The Caverns, more of a series of caves than a mine, were situated next door to the once-productive Bodie Mine, but Russell had kept it active, in a sense, giving tours. He'd hired local high school and college kids to lead the tourists around the stalactites and stalagmites and give them a chance to pan for gold flecks in the nearby stream.

Sonora had been lobbying to turn the Bodie Mine into a full-blown amusement park, complete with small-scale train rides, a scary mine tour, and food vendors selling sugar-stalactite-on-a-stick, but Sparkle wouldn't hear of it. Sonora had even tried to buy out Russell so she could expand his mine into a park, but he'd refused to sell. He couldn't have been making much on his mine tours, but he was a Clamper, and Clampers didn't advocate change. It had been a bone of contention between Russell and Sonora lately, and their once-friendly relationship seemed to have soured. They rarely spoke to one another in public.

"Drop it off and I'll see where I can fit it in." I knew it would need a major rewrite just to be coherent—Russell tended to go on—but it wouldn't take much time if he'd included all the details.

"Thanks, Con. Hope we see you out there. Gonna be ribs and pasties and Mama Cody's Cornish rolls."

"You selling antidotes for the indigestion?"

"Always do."

Keying in Russell's announcement, I made the requisite editorial changes, and I soon had it reading more like a news article than a legal brief. Leaning back in my swivel chair, I stretched out the knots in my back.

As soon as my thoughts let go of the Clamper event, they drifted next door, to Dan. I stood up, my body begging for some exercise after all that sitting, and paced the room, bending and twisting my head, neck, shoulders, and waist. Feeling claustrophobic, I moved to the hallway and took a few laps.

When I felt the blood begin to recirculate, I paused outside Dan's door, wondering whether he was there, and considering if I should stop in once more. He'd been so distracted earlier; I didn't feel like being ignored again.

I returned to my office and slumped in my chair, pushing the puzzle of Dan's behavior away. To distract myself, I pulled out a pad of paper. I jotted down a series of names connected to Sparkle Bodie, as I contemplated the confusing collection of random facts I'd acquired since looking into her death.

Sparkle. Caleb. Esken. Sonora. Devon.

What an eclectic collection of relatives.

I'd begun scribbling notes about each one when the floor beneath me suddenly trembled. I braced myself for an earthquake but the rumble came and went before I had a chance to really panic.

I stood up and moved toward the hallway, half expecting to see a tree toppled behind the door, or an empty space where the hall had once been. Nothing.

And then it came again, a thud, beneath my feet. A scene from Jurassic Park sprang to mind—the one where the kids are watching the glass of water as it trembles under the impact of nearby dinosaur footsteps.

Dinosaurs? In Flat Skunk? I knocked on Dan's door and tried the knob. It opened; I swung the door wide.

"What was that—"

I stopped. Dan was not alone. And it was obvious what had caused the wood floors to rattle. One of the drawers of his filing cabinet had fallen to the ground. It now lay next to his microwave oven, and his portable radio.

I glanced at Dan, who sat hunched over in the chair behind his desk. After acknowledging my presence with an embarrassed nod, he turned his attention to the woman standing in the middle of the room. The same woman I had seen him with in the diner.

"Amy . . ." I watched him speak tentatively.

She turned to me, tightened her grip on her purse, and moved toward the door. "Don't believe a thing he says," she said to me as she passed by. She spoke slowly and deliberately and her lips were easy to read. With that, she stomped out of the office.

I turned back to Dan, then felt the floor vibrate once again. Dan winced, then glanced behind me. I assumed it was Amy slamming the door on her way out.

Dan stood up and began picking up the pieces. The radio was smashed beyond repair, so he gathered the remnants and tossed them into a nearby trash can. The microwave was dented; whether it still worked would have to be determined. The contents of the drawer had jumped out a few inches but remained basically intact. I helped Dan return the drawer to the cabinet, then began picking up the smaller pieces of the radio.

"Unhappy client?" I asked, trying to appear casual.

"Something like that."

I nodded, pondering the next question I could ask that might get him to tell me what was going on, without appearing overly nosy.

"Want me to pull her hair or something?"

Dan smiled for the first time. "No, thanks. She fights dirty. I wouldn't want you to lose any of your own gorgeous hair."

I dropped a few pieces of black plastic into the wastebasket. "So, what happened?"

He shrugged, then lifted the microwave, returning it to its spot on the window seat.

". . . talk about it later?" He didn't look me in the eye when he spoke, so I only caught the end.

"Sure," I said. You could bet on it.

Thirty minutes later I was dealing with the trauma by eating a Snickers bar. As I was erasing the chocolate accents from my lips with my tongue, I caught a movement in my peripheral vision. A sheet of paper came sliding under my door. Figuring it was another flyer from the Hard Wok Café, the new Asian restaurant in town, I ignored it for a few minutes, while I wiped my face, then bent down and picked it up. When I flipped the paper over, my heart began to pound. Quickly, but too late, I opened the door and peeked out. No one in the hall.

Holding the plain white paper as if it was a sheet of gold filament, I stared at the drawing. Primitive and garish, done in felt-tip pen, it featured a man, not a stick figure but a childlike rendering. A big head on a small body, bobby-pin legs, no arms. The face had large round eyes, but no mouth, no ears, and no nose. The man stood near a prone figure, this one with missing eyes. But the figure had arms, and its hands were outstretched, as if trying to reach something. Or stop something?

I got out the magnifying glass that I use for layout detail, and examined the picture closely. The standing figure's face was covered with tiny dots. No, not covered—only the bottom half of the face was dotted. A rash? A beard? Or could they be tears?

A door at the far right side of the picture stood open, with something sticking out from behind it, near the bottom. It looked like an animal of some kind, or maybe some sort of doorstop? Or it could be a foot, I thought. The drawing was not clear. I studied the figure lying on what looked like a bed. Examining the outstretched arms closely, I noticed the hands, held tightly together, almost purposefully.

If the figure was trying to demonstrate some kind of gesture, I couldn't read it. But it wasn't difficult to recognize the artist from the distinctive style I'd seen at the jail.

Caleb Bodie.

I had about an hour and a half before I was to meet Dan for dinner. Enough time to drive to the Silence Is Golden Deaf Club and get back just in time.

Lindan Barde was not at the desk, nor was anyone else, so I stepped into the recreation area. The room was crowded with several dozen busy hands waving about, accented by vivid expressions, as members of the Deaf Community socialized over a lavish buffet. I felt out of place among the group of people, who obviously knew each other well, and wondered why I hadn't gotten involved when I first arrived at Flat Skunk. It was something I'd have to consider when I had more time.

I was about to leave but someone from across the room seemed to be gesturing me. At first glance I thought it was just someone signing dramatically to make a point. But as the face came into view, I recognized Warren Matthews. I checked behind me to see if he was trying to communicate with someone else, figuring he probably didn't remember me from my earlier visit. But he continued to wave until I acknowledged his greeting.

Once I'd waved back, he signaled for me to come over. Feeling uncomfortable at having intruded on some kind of special meeting, I waved a hand that meant, "Oh, no, really, I shouldn't," but Warren Matthews wouldn't take a negative wave for an answer.

I shrugged and made my way through the animated crowd, trying not to get in any signer's line of vision. Finding that impossible, I simply signed "excuse me" every few seconds, brushing my fingertips, until I reached Warren.

"Hey, C-O-N-N-O-R W-E-S-T-P-H-A-L, right? Welcome!" he signed, his fingers moving in a space the size of a dinner plate.

He remembered my name, right down to the correct spelling.

"Hi, Warren," I signed back in ASL, using his name sign. "Nice see you again."

"You, what doing here, you? Come party with us?"

I shook my head and continued in ASL, which interpreted into spoken English read: "No, no. I wanted to talk with Lindan Barde and you about something. But I don't want to bother you now." My hands offered the words, my face expressed my sincerity.

"No bother." He signed, shaking his head and tapping his right hand between his left thumb and forefinger. Swinging his hand around the room, he then signed, "This is a going-away party for—" He spelled a name very fast and I only caught the first and last letters. I guessed it was Sharon or Susan something.

"Know her?"

I told him I didn't know her, and he filled me in on who she was, where she was going, and why. Much like Flat Skunk, I had a feeling there were no secrets in the Deaf Community. After he had offered me food and drink, which I declined, I asked if he wouldn't mind taking a look at something for a moment. He waved me over to a deserted corner of the room.

"What's up?" he signed, twisting his palms up, middle fingers leading the way.

I withdrew the drawing from my backpack and showed him the picture of the standing giant and the reclining figure.

"I think this was drawn by Caleb, the deaf man I told you about, the one with no language skills. I've been told he's somewhat retarded as well as deaf, but I'm wondering if that's not just the impact of his language deficiency. I really think he's smarter than people realize. I wondered if it meant anything to you. I thought, since you're so good at understanding nonverbal communication, maybe you could make something of it."

Warren Matthews pulled his glasses from his coat pocket, took the picture from my hand and held it up to the light of the window. He scanned the figures and detail for a few minutes before returning it to me and removing his glasses.

"I'm not an art expert or a child psychologist, but this seems much like child drawing. These symbols here are interesting. For example, see the woman—"

"You think it's a woman?" I interrupted.

He nodded both his head and his fist. "See the hair? Children usually put hair on women and leave men bald. She's lying on what looks like a hospital bed. See the crank?"

He made a gesture as if cranking up something, then pointed to a small crooked line on the drawing I had overlooked. A handle appeared to be sticking out of the bed.

"See the circles drawn on the legs of bed? They might be wheels, like many hospital beds have."

I nodded and waited for him to continue.

"If this woman is in a hospital and she has no eyes, maybe she's blind . . . or dead."

I thought of Sparkle Bodie, lying dead in her hospital bed.

I nodded. "Yes, I think you're right. Anything else?"

Warren raised a hand above his head, indicating the man in the picture. "This figure seems almost as tall as the room itself. Interesting that he has no mouth, no ears, and no arms." He raised his eyebrows. "I wonder if it means he has no way of communicating. Maybe this represents the deaf man, Caleb." He paused, then continued. "Interesting. Look at the woman's hands." He imitated the look of the woman's arms in the picture and I mimicked him.

"Do you think she's trying to say something? Or is she trying to reach something?" I asked.

"Her arms are definitely outstretched. Maybe she's trying to reach something, but I don't think so."

"What, then?"

Warren Matthews held out his arms once again, illustrating the drawing. "When a baby reaches out like this, what does it mean?"

A wave of recognition flooded me and I felt a heat rush through my body.

"Help me up!"

He arched a brow. "Or maybe just 'help.' "

Dan's door was standing open when I arrived back at the hotel a few minutes before our scheduled dinner. A flurry of activity in his office caught my eye as I stood in the hallway. The woman Dan had called Amy stood facing Dan, her arms waving dramatically.

I stood silently, surprised by her passionate gestures. She must have sensed me; she whirled around and glared, then said something I couldn't make out. Whatever it was, it caused Dan to rise from his chair. His lips, I could read clearly.

"That's enough, Amy. It's time you left." Dan was calm as he spoke, but for a moment he looked a little dangerous. I caught her midsentence when she whirled back around.

". . . she's your latest? You don't waste any time, do you?" At first I thought the woman was talking to me, but I realized the words were meant for Dan. She looked me up and down as I stood there in my "Death Before Decaf" T-shirt and jeans.

She said something else I couldn't make out. Or maybe I didn't want to. Frowning, she stepped closer and repeated herself, but I still didn't follow. It wasn't her lips that were a problem, it was her demeanor. I started to walk away, figuring I was just adding to the problem, but I felt a hand jerk my shoulder and I turned back around.

"Don't walk away from me when I'm talking to you—"

"Shut up, Amy. Leave her alone." Dan moved in, as if worried he might have to physically intervene.

"Why can't she just answer my simple question?"

Dan started to say something, but I interrupted. Meeting her eyes, I said, "I didn't hear what you said."

Startled, the woman named Amy blinked. "Oh, my God, you're deaf and dumb! I just thought you had an accent I couldn't place, or some kind of speech impediment." She turned slightly toward Dan, gave him a smile I couldn't read, then turned back to me, wiggling her fingers in the air like a bad magician. "You know that hand-talk stuff, huh?"

This was not going to be a productive conversation. I could see Dan growing more uncomfortable and embarrassed because of her. I had been ridiculed in the past for being deaf, and had learned to ignore it. Again I turned to leave, but again she yanked me around.

"So if you're deaf and dumb—"

"I'm deaf, not dumb."

She gave a condescending smile. "Right. Anyway—"

I felt my body tense. "I really have to get back to work—"

"Work? What do you do, sell those little hand-talk cards—"

That did it. I hauled off and slapped her face. Then I turned and left before she could scratch me or something.

I unlocked my office door, slammed it shut behind me, and tossed my backpack on the desk. I stood at the window, my hands trembling, as I stared out at the foothills beyond Flat Skunk, seeing little. I hadn't hit another human being since my sister "borrowed" my new dress in the fifth grade. One slap had led to another and we were soon in a catfight that ended up ruining the dress. I learned then that violence never solved anything. But revenge did—and the next day my sister's precious little black patent Mary Janes had been redesigned—with white shoe polish, glitter, and permanent felt-pen flowers.

Before I could think up some way to ruin this woman's shoes, my office door opened and I turned around to face Dan.

"Sorry about that," he said, shrugging his shoulders. "She's not herself. She's under a lot of stress. . . ."

I crossed my arms and frowned at him, wondering why he was defending this woman. "Who the hell is she, anyway?"

Dan nodded. "Come on. Let's go get some dinner at the Nugget. I'll buy you one of those chocolate coffees you like so much to wash down Mama Cody's meat loaf, and tell you the whole story."

Curiosity overpowering my anger, I pouted another thirty seconds, hit my chin with the side of my hand, then picked up my backpack.

"What was that?"

I gave him a blank look. He repeated the gesture I'd made, hitting his chin with the side of his hand.

"It's just a sign." I shrugged.

"What's it mean?"

"Nothing."

"Connor . . ."

"First of all you did it wrong. You have to use the letter 'B,' not just an open hand. And you have to sign it sharply, not slowly."

He signed it again, this time perfectly. "So what's it mean?"

"Bitch."

"Old girlfriend? Or new?" I asked, once I'd had a revitalizing swallow of mocha. It was a do-it-myself mix of coffee and chocolate milk—apparently something had happened to the espresso machine and it wasn't working. Subterfuge? Once again I'd had to create my own makeshift mocha.

"She's my wife."

I nearly choked on my drink.

"That woman is your *wife*," I said when I could speak again.

"*Was.* She's my *ex*-wife."

Was. I had misread him. With the back of my hand, I swiped at the mustache tickling my upper lip.

"You were married to that . . . that woman?"

Dan nodded. "Amy Allen. She used to be, well, not so unpleasant. I met her in high school and we dated through senior year. Married her as soon as I was out of the academy. She loved being married to a cop."

"Oh, so she's the one you were telling me about when I first met you. The one who left you when you left the police department?"

Dan nodded and took a swallow of beer. "That's the one. Married my partner as soon as the divorce was final."

"Wow. So why is she here hassling you?"

"Guess that marriage didn't work out either."

"Really. What does she want?" I asked casually.

Dan held his beer in both hands, spinning it around in his fingers. His hands were fascinating to watch, and they never left my peripheral vision.

"She says . . ." He looked away. I waited. "Nothing. She just wants money."

I nodded for him to continue, hoping he didn't notice I wasn't breathing as I waited for the other shoe to drop. But he abruptly changed the subject.

"You still going to that mine tonight?"

I nodded, wary, but also beginning to feel a little relief. "You still want to come with me, as my backup?"

Dan sat up, shifting his concern to me. "Connor, I think it's a foolish idea. If someone's following Esken, you could get caught in the line of fire."

"Dan, I have to go. I promised him I would. He thinks I'm his only chance at helping to save Caleb. Will you come or not? If not, I can ask Russell or Aubrey or even—"

"Yeah, I'll come. Of course I'll come. But we're not walking into an old bat cave without a—"

"Batmobile stocked with Batweapons?"

"Thanks, Robin."

"I'm not Robin. Why do I have to be Robin? Just 'cause I'm the girl? I wanna be Batwoman."

"All right, all right. I'll be Robin. But I'm not wearing tights."

We shared a smile and the evening began to look brighter. Picturing Dan in tights didn't hurt, either.

Dan left me at the Nugget to run some errand before we took off, so I ran home to change into warmer clothes, brush my teeth, and feed Casper. I thought about taking her with me, but decided she might make noise when I didn't want her to, and scare off Esken. I gave her an extra helping of sourdough bread, then returned to the Nugget. While waiting for Dan, I worked on an editorial about the dangers of old mines that weren't secured well enough to keep out curious kids. Twelve-year-old Brian Hurley, the town mischief-maker, had gotten himself lost in the abandoned Poverty Mine for two days last month, scaring his family, his friends, and the town council, which was liable for damages.

When I finished that, I pulled out the drawing that had been slipped under my door. I'd shown it to Dan but his only comment was a recommendation that I show it to Sheriff Mercer. So when the sheriff sauntered into the Nugget a few minutes later, I waved him over to my booth.

"Hey, C.W. How's it going?" Sheriff Mercer squeezed into the seat, adjusting his waistband and pant legs as he got himself comfortable.

"Good, Sheriff. Hot date last night? Your cheeks are awfully rosy this morning."

"Naw. Must be the Zantac. Got an upset stomach."

"Too much Nugget bread pudding?"

He rubbed his abdomen and a button popped open on his khaki uniform shirt. I was grateful he was wearing an undershirt.

"What happened to Mary-Megan? Mary-Martha? Mary-Whosits? Didn't work out?"

"Mary-Monica. She wasn't my type. She's into all that

crystal-and-astrology stuff. Kept wanting to do my chart and read my cards and massage my feet. I don't want anyone touching my feet, you know? I got bunions."

I stifled a laugh. The sheriff ordered a banana milkshake, a platter of onion rings, and a bowl of tapioca pudding. My stomach rolled as Jilda brought over the food and drink.

"Trying to commit suicide? There are easier ways," I said, sipping my nonfat mocha.

"Like what?" the sheriff said, clearing an onion ring from his mouth just in time for me to understand him. "Dating?"

I gave an agreeable nod. "I have something to show you, Sheriff." I opened my backpack and pulled out Caleb's picture. After wiping the table of residual banana milkshake, I set the picture down facing the sheriff.

"What's this?" I think he said. His mouth was full so it was tough to tell.

"Someone slipped this under the door of my office. What do you make of it?"

Sheriff Mercer started to pick it up, then wiped his greasy fingers on a paper napkin and checked his fingertips before he lifted the artwork from the table.

"Looks like a kid's drawing. You say someone slipped it under your door?"

I paused, hoping I was doing the right thing. "I think it was Caleb. I've seen his artwork and this is his style. I took it over to the Deaf Club in Whiskey Slide, and one of the men there said it looks like a woman in a hospital bed. She could be asleep. Or she could be dead."

The sheriff pulled the drawing closer and studied it while sipping on his milkshake.

"So now you think it's a picture of Sparkle Bodie in the hospital, don't you? You think Caleb is trying to communicate something to you, am I right? Like what, C.W.? Like he didn't do it? Like he didn't slip a pillow over his mother's face and press on it until she stopped breathing?"

I snatched the drawing from his hands. "I just thought you might want to see it. You're always wanting me to share any evidence I might find."

Sheriff Mercer wiped his mouth. "Well, thanks for people's exhibit A. If I need to show it to the FBI or something, I'll give you a call."

"Very funny, Sheriff. Bet Mary-Murgatroyd thought you were a laugh riot. Bet you kept her in stitches between all those psychic readings and séances and stuff."

"I never went to any séances. But you might want to try one, C.W. Maybe you could contact old Sparkle and she'll tell you who killed her."

The sheriff nearly choked to death on an onion ring, laughing at his own joke. Good thing I didn't have to apply the Heimlich. I'm not sure I would have done it at that moment.

Ever see that movie *Mine Mutants?*" Dan said, as he drove along the bumpy dirt road that wound toward the Bodie property.

"You made that up. There was no such movie. I've seen all those old sci-fi movies, and I've never heard of *Mine Mutants.*"

Looking out over the golden hills dotted with volcanic tombstones and framed by rock-stacked fences that cast long shadows in the late-afternoon sun, I found it hard to believe the area was riddled with underground tunnels. Some led to riches, but most led to nowhere.

"I think Steve McQueen was in it."

"He was in *The Blob.* Stop trying to scare me. I'm not afraid of mutant monsters and I'm not afraid of old deserted mines."

I glanced over at a carved-out opening in the hillside as we passed. All that remained of the mining operation was a large hole, propped up by wood timbers, and sealed off with roughly hewn planks. Yet another of the many Mother Lode veins that had been mined to fortune or folly.

The Mother Lode is a misnomer. I learned that soon after I arrived in the Gold Country. There is no principal lode, with branches extending every which way. The area contains a series of veins, chutes, and chimneys. Some are narrow threads, some over eight thousand feet wide; some rich, some poor or unsalvageable. But not all veins are connected to the "Mother."

"Have you explored many of the mines?" Dan asked, when I turned back to look at him.

"Took the tours at Moaning Caves and California Caverns a few weeks after I got here, for a story. Did some spelunking and some rappelling."

Dan's eyebrows raised. "Wouldn't catch me in those tight spaces with nothing but a rope between my legs."

"Really? I would have thought you'd enjoy careening down the sides of bottomless caverns, exploring the depths like James Mason in *Journey to the Center of the Earth.* You'll have to try it sometime. You're not claustrophobic, are you?"

He shifted in his seat. "No. As long as you don't put me in small tight spaces."

I suppressed a smile but he caught it.

"What? You don't have any phobias?"

Ex-wives, I wanted to say. "Just one. Avita-nila-phobia."

"What's that? Fear of spiders? Open spaces? Leading a normal life that doesn't involve chasing after murder suspects?"

"Fear of wasting my life doing nothing."

Dan slowed the car as we rounded a blind curve. As soon as the road straightened out, I could see the Bodie Mine in the dimming light ahead. Esken's late-model Jeep Cherokee was nowhere in sight.

"There's the mine," I said, as we turned off the main road onto Vulture Point Road. It was off to the side, the weatherworn sign dangling crookedly at the entrance.

After agreeing to meet Esken, I had read up on the Bodie Mine to better prepare myself. It was a pocket mine discovered in 1863, while Bennegar Jacks—the same Bennegar Jacks mentioned in Sparkle's hidden deed—was digging a posthole for his boss, Evan Lee Bodie, great-great-grandfather to the young Devon Bodie. The mine took in $4,000 in three days, and totaled $18,000 within a few months. Grateful for the discovery, Bodie sold Jacks the neighboring caverns for another $20,000, but they had pinched out soon after the sale and operations were suspended. It ended up losing as much as it had made those first few months.

I thought about Russell's great-grandfather Jacks and wondered how he had ended up mysteriously dead.

"There's Esken's car," I said, pointing to the Jeep parked on the side of the road. It had been out of view, hidden behind a manzanita bush, camouflaged by its dark green color. I leaned forward, straining to see, but couldn't make out any detail from that distance. "Can't tell if he's inside."

Dan drove his Bronco slowly, trying to avoid the rocks and potholes that bounced us up and down like pioneers in a covered wagon.

"God, you could really use some new shocks," I told him. He ignored me.

After a few more bumps and dips we pulled up behind Esken's Jeep and parked. I could tell immediately Esken wasn't inside. Armed with my pepper spray, my lead-weight Doc Martens, and a club of a flashlight, I opened the Bronco door to check things out. A quick glance back at Dan stopped me halfway out of the car.

I looked at him, stunned. "What the hell is that?"

"A precaution." Dan pulled his jacket around him and quickly stepped out of the car. I jumped out, moved over to him, peeling open his jacket, and staring at the shiny object tucked into his belt.

"You brought a gun?"

He shrugged. "You never know."

"Are you still licensed to carry?"

"You've been reading too many detective stories. We don't 'carry,' we 'pack.' Today if you're carrying, it's a cell phone."

"Whatever. Are you legal?"

Dan gave me a don't-go-there look and pulled the jacket back around him. I shivered at the thought of the thing.

And then I really wanted to touch it.

"Can I see it?"

"No."

"Why not?"

"It's not a toy."

"I know that. I've just never held a gun before. I want to see what it's like."

"Another time. Come on."

He brushed past me and headed for Esken's car, stepping over the discarded beer bottles and empty chip bags.

Dan waved me over from the other side of Esken's Jeep. He was frowning.

"What is it?" I said, tensing.

With a nod of his head, he indicated the passenger window. I stepped around and took a look. The window had been smashed.

Sweat tickled my back. I scanned the ground and peered inside the car before I said anything. When I looked up, Dan was facing the mine entrance, his hands cupped around his mouth. After a few moments he dropped his hands.

"No answer?" I asked. Dan shook his head. I started to reach for the Jeep's door handle when he stopped me.

"Better not touch anything. Just in case."

"We'd better call the sheriff." I pointed inside Esken's car. A cell phone sat undisturbed between the seats, covered with a few flecks of glass. Dan pulled up his jacket sleeve, reached in carefully through the hole in the window, and withdrew the phone.

"Yeah, let him know we're out here."

"I'm going to take a look around," I said.

Dan tugged at my arm as I started to head off. "Don't go in the mine without me, you hear?"

I tapped my ear and shook my head.

"Connor."

I gave him a dirty look, then began circling the car, examining the ground once again. Making wider and wider loops, I scanned the dirt for something, anything that might tell me what had happened. It was getting harder to see in the oncoming darkness. Nothing but broken amber glass, cigarette butts, assorted food wrappers, and an old *Penthouse* magazine.

I bent down to have a closer look at the food wrappers, wondering if an old Doritos bag might have a story to tell, and spotted a wadded up sheet of yellow paper. I picked it up and began unpeeling the wad. It was the same kind of paper that had been slipped under my door. I recognized the familiar 800 number scrawled in black ink. It was the California Relay System used by the deaf for interpreted calls.

"Dan!" I caught him as he ended his call to Sheriff Mercer.

"Sheriff will be here shortly. We're not to touch anything. Just stay put."

"Look." I held out the wrinkled paper for Dan to see.

"Yeah?" The number meant nothing to him. When I explained the significance, he still gave little reaction.

"Dan, I know Esken is here somewhere. We've got to find him. Obviously he wouldn't smash his own window. Someone did that. And he may need help." I moved toward the mine opening. Dan held me by my shoulder.

"Connor, you can't go in there. That *someone* may still be around. You said Esken was in danger. Don't you think it would be foolish to go looking for trouble?"

"Dan, Esken is the one in trouble. Come on. This is why I brought you. You've got your gun."

Flicking on my flashlight to ward off the interior darkness, I headed for the mouth of the mine, a small, unprepossessing opening that once welcomed miners, then tourists. I ducked under the distressed frame where a board had been pulled off, and entered carefully. The sudden cold was chilling, the darkness pervasive, and the beam of light did little to illuminate the damp nooks and crannies.

And it was cramped. No place for a claustrophobic, I

thought as I looked back to check on Dan. He was right behind me, his hand on his belt. I inhaled the musty, dark air and shivered. Caves like these were always cold—usually in the mid-forties, I'd read—and they were subject to powerful winds.

I caught a movement overhead.

Bats?

No. Just shadows of my flashlight playing on the rocky ceiling.

But bats were certainly a possibility. And it was almost dusk. Flying time, as I recalled.

As I moved deeper into the mine, I checked on Dan again, hoping he was still behind me. He was right on my heels, one hand on his belt, the other on his own flashlight. Was that sweat on his forehead—or lighting trickery?

Dan shone the light on his face, causing eerie shadows on his lips and brow. "Connor . . . slow down . . ." That was all I caught. Reading his lips by flashlight was more than challenging.

I moved forward into the maze of twisting passages, stepping over more beer cans and litter, shining the light over names carved in limestone walls and half-rotted wood planks that held back the earth. The place seemed an unending labyrinth of tunnels. It was difficult to decide which way to go. Occasionally a trickle of dirt seeped, a reminder of our unstable environment. Most of these old mines had been closed years ago for good reason.

I checked again for Dan. Still right behind me. I reached back and tucked his hand into the back of my jeans waistband for reassurance. Then I moved deeper into the cavern.

After an abrupt turn, the tunnel narrowed considerably. One path led to a large opening, the other to a hole the size of a small dog. I squatted and peeked into the hole, shining the light inside.

The room came alive with glittering light and color. Shades of yellows, reds, and blues sparkled where there had once been darkness. Fascinated by mines and caverns, I'd written an article on the hidden beauty soon after I'd come to the Gold Country. Jewel-like white pearls and strands of orange corkscrew straws seemed to grow from the ground. Overhead shone a glorious chandelier, made from thousands of years of dripping water and trace minerals.

Stalactites jutted from the ceiling and stalagmites rose from the ground, creating the sensation of sharp teeth in a monstrous mouth. I'd read that these limestone icicles grew only half an inch in a hundred years, and marveled at the two- and three-foot lengths in this cave.

I flashed the light around slowly, and spotted cone-shaped peaks, bony fingers of dripstone, looking fragile as they stood in clusters like spiky bushes. Along one wall sprouted colorful gypsum flowers, interspersed with intricate crystallized popcorn. Smooth flowstone draperies that looked like petrified waterfalls, and prickly helictites that resembled deep-sea coral, flourished on another wall. Cauliflower-shaped crystals curled upward from the ground, as if cultivated in an organic rock garden.

After a few moments of awestruck fascination, I stood up and let Dan have a look at the vast subterranean room. While he shined his light on the fantasy world, I moved off to the room with the wider opening. This area had obviously been visited frequently. More beer bottles, cigarette packs, and candy wrappers remained to tell the tale to future archaeologists.

The room had been stripped of most of its mineral jewels. Only large plain rocks remained, propped around as if they were furniture. The stones were carved with names, dates, slogans, and profanities. I couldn't identify the pungent smell, but it reminded me of a dead mouse I'd found in my run-down diner when I'd first moved in. After a closer inspection with the flashlight, I discovered a pile of tiny animal bones nearly hidden behind one of the larger rocks. Whatever it was, it had been dead a long time. Next to the bones was a cluster of mushrooms. How had they managed to grow in this sunless place?

I knelt down to examine the mushrooms more closely. I was about to stick my finger in the growth when I realized

what had fertilized the collection of toadstools. Guano. Just
as I pulled back I was startled by a high-pitched frequency.
Alarmed, not used to hearing anything at all, I stood up and
whisked the light around the room and over my head.
What—?

Before I could finish the thought, the ceiling came alive.
A wave of black fluttering wings swooped down on me. The
rush of movement caused me to drop my flashlight, knocking out the only source of light. And for the first time in a
long, long time, I heard what could only be called a piercing
scream. It was deafening.

Bats!

"Dan!" I yelled. Something swept past my shoulder. I
ducked to avoid it—them.

Bats! I wracked my memory for information about
bats, besides the fact that I could hear their high-frequency
sounds. Some people thought bats had a sixth sense, much
like deaf people are mistakenly believed to have. But it was
simply ultrasonic vibrations that bounced echoes off the
walls to form a kind of "sound picture." That much I knew
because I was fascinated by the fact that some deaf people,
like myself, could hear them, when they couldn't hear anything else. Even better, hearing people could not. Not without the help of a microphone.

I felt something swoop by my face.

What about that bloodsucker rumor? The book I'd
read as a child said that most bats weren't bloodsuckers.
Vampire bats maybe, but they didn't suck human blood, the
way they did in the Dracula movies.

But bats did carry disease. One bite and I could be in
line for a long painful series of rabies injections. I hate nee-
dles more than I hate bats.

Something furry flew by my face. I screamed again, and
brushed it away frantically, unable to see anything. I tried to
duck, covering my head with my arms. That sudden movement caused me to lose my balance. I reached back to brace
my fall and knocked my arm against a hard surface in the
blackness. As my hand pressed against it, the object—long
and flat—gave way.

In a matter of seconds the rocks propped by the decaying wood beam turned into an avalanche of dust and debris. The wall and ceiling caved in, leaving me alone, in total darkness.

With a bunch of bats.

Dan!" I screamed.

How far would my voice carry through the darkness? At least he knew I was in here. Didn't he? He'd been only a few yards away.

I brushed the debris and dust from my hair and clothes, and did a quick check to see if I'd injured anything. Aside from a few scared wits, nothing seemed to be damaged.

What if the whole mine had caved in? Was Dan all right? Something fluttered by. I shivered.

Then something swooped by my hair.

I let loose a howl and swiped at my head with both hands like a madwoman. A bat was caught in my hair, I was sure of it. I wasn't taking the time to think about their sonar ability to avoid crashing into things. I was too busy trying to free myself from the clutches of what I imagined was a flying rodent. Real or imaginary, more bats flew past my face, one brushing my open mouth as I screamed. I thought I tasted bat hairs. Ptew!

Dropping down to my knees to escape them, I felt around the ground for my flashlight. Instead, my hand struck a rock, then encountered a soft spongy object that broke off in my grasp. Mushroom. Growing in bat guano. The smell hit my nose and I felt sick.

I rubbed my hand on my jeans, then returned to my frantic search for the cold hard handle of the flashlight, brushing the surface of the ground lightly back and forth like a blind person. After a few seconds, I made contact with something. Thick. Leathery.

A shoe.

It was connected to a foot.

I screamed and pulled my hand away.

Someone was in the cave with me.

Dead? Or alive?

Before I could think what to do, a strong hand grabbed my arm.

"Dan?!" His hand released its tight clench and held me more gently. "Dan! Thank God!"

If there was a response, I couldn't hear it, and I still couldn't see anything. I reached over to feel the body attached to the arm, hoping for reassurance from Dan's touch. But before I could make further contact, his hand lifted me from the ground, roughly, urgently, but without hurting me. I was jerked forward by the grip that now encircled my arm. Although I couldn't hear his voice or see his face, his body language was clear: We had to get out of there, fast.

Awkwardly I stumbled along, one hand waving in the air to protect myself from overhanging rocks and other head-banging surprises, the other held firmly in Dan's grasp. I stumbled twice as he practically dragged me along, and bumped my shin on something hard enough to give me pause. Relentless, he pulled me forward—where were we going? In the darkness I had completely lost my sense of direction.

Dan made a sudden turn, nearly causing me to lose my balance again. Just as abruptly he let go of my arm. Panicked at being set free, I swung around in the darkness like Helen Keller, trying to find that all-important connection.

Nothing.

"Dan! Where are you?"

Something landed on my head. I screamed, thinking it was another bat, but quickly realized it was a hand. In another second Dan's other hand returned to grip my arm. He pushed me gently down toward the ground.

I figured I was supposed to duck. I bent over, squatting to my knees, as he inched me forward through a tight opening. The hole felt no larger than the size of an extra-large pizza. Dan's powerful hold released as I tentatively wiggled through the passageway, scraping every exposed part of my body as I squeezed through.

Once through the hole, I reached forward in the darkness again, searching for his reassuring hand, my skin stinging from the scrapes.

Nothing.

"Dan? Dan! Where are you!"

I got up slowly, hoping the tunnel was tall enough to accommodate my five-foot-eight-inch height, and bumped my head halfway up. Bending over again, I inched forward, my hands groping the sides of the rocky passageway that allowed for only one direction of movement: forward.

And then I blinked. I knew I blinked because there was a dim glow ahead.

Was it really light?

In the utter blackness of the cave, the tiny hole of incandescence shone like a distant beacon to a ship at sea.

As quickly as I could maneuver in the backbreaking position I was in, I proceeded along the underground passage, heading for the proverbial light at the end of the tunnel, still feeling my way. After stumbling over more debris, banging my elbow against a sharp stone, and hitting my head twice, I continued along the bumpy path. The opening, nearly hidden from view in the passageway, shone softly in the retreating light of dusk.

Like Winnie-the-Pooh as he squirmed to free himself from Rabbit's door, I squeezed and wriggled and willed myself through the opening, this one the size of a medium pizza. Exhaling the fresh air seeping in through the hole, I compressed my chest and abdomen, as I let out a small curse for all the pizzas I'd indulged in lately.

A glorious burst of wind lightly slapped my face as I finally broke through and reached the outside. The familiar smell of skunk and dry grass was a welcome perfume, compared to the stale, bat-stinking cave. Brushing off the dirt, sand, bat hairs, and guano, I stood up slowly, stretching out the kinks, and then checked myself for war wounds. I found scrapes on my legs, bruises on my arms, and blood on my elbows and knees.

Where was Dan? Disoriented and chilled, I scanned the area and tried to get my bearings in relation to the darkening hills. Where had I exited the mine? I recognized the outline of a water tower against the dark purple sky, then calculated the direction back to the mine's entrance.

"Dan?" I called out, as I followed the path around the cave. He was still nowhere in sight. Where was he? Had he gone back in for some reason? The hairs at the back of my neck began to prickle. Something was wrong.

Slowly, I approached the mine entrance and stepped hesitantly inside. "Dan—"

Another hand grabbed my arm.

"Dan!" I started. I wanted to hug him and slap him at the same time. "Thank God, you're all right! Why the hell did you leave me?"

Dan was also covered with dirt, but didn't seem to have the wounds I bore. He stared at me, puzzled and relieved.

"I've been looking all over for you! When that room caved in, I thought you were in real trouble," Dan said.

"Thank God you found us a way out. We could have been—"

A look of bewilderment crept over Dan's face. I had trouble reading his lips in the fading light, but his expression was clear. He was as confused as I was.

"Connor. What are you talking about? You were trapped in that room. I couldn't get to you. I tried to dig you out but the rocks wouldn't budge. I was just about to call the sheriff again when I heard you call my name."

"You mean, it wasn't you . . ."

"Me, what?"

"But there was someone . . . in the mine . . . he led me out . . ."

Dan stared at me as if he'd seen the Mutant of Bodie Mine. "Connor—"

"Someone . . . this hand grabbed my arm. He—it—led me through this tunnel. We wound around and then I saw the light, and you were gone, at least I thought it was you . . ."

I probably wasn't making much sense, but then I wasn't making much sense to myself either. If it hadn't been Dan who led me from the cave, then who . . . ?

Dan frowned. "Well, I don't know how you got out, but at least you're all right. We'll try to figure things out later. Right now there's something a little more pressing. I want to call and make sure Sheriff Mercer is on his way."

He started for Esken's car. I caught up.

"What is it?"

"I'll show you when the sheriff gets here. Come on."

I stopped walking. "You found something, didn't you?"

He turned around, looking tense. "Come on!"

There was something in there. I started back for the mine.

Dan grabbed my arm again. I winced. I had been grabbed once too often on that particular arm. "Connor, are you crazy? That mine is dangerous! You were just trapped in there. You could have been killed."

I tensed and he released my arm. "Tell me what you found."

Dan said nothing.

I darted into the mine. I knew whatever it was, it wasn't far inside.

Dan jumped in front of me, blocking my way. "Okay, okay, I'll show you. But you've got to stay with me. I don't want to lose you again. Come on, it's not far."

Dan led the way a short distance ahead, taking a different direction than we had originally gone. I tucked my fingers into the back of his belt and held on tight. I wasn't worried that the mine would cave in again. I figured it had done its damage. Kind of like lightning striking twice. But I wasn't too keen on meeting up with whoever might still be running around inside.

Dan turned into a small room we had overlooked when we'd first entered.

"What is it?" I said, nervously. The trickling dirt from the ceiling was disconcerting.

Dan stood aside from the opening and indicated something inside. He shone his flashlight forward; I peered in and caught my breath.

A man sat propped again the wall, his legs outstretched, his head resting gently on his chest, as if he were asleep.

But he wasn't sleeping.

I knew instantly that Esken Bodie was dead.

Dan and I were sitting perched on the hood of the Bronco when Sheriff Mercer and Deputy Clemens drove up in the beat-up patrol car. We'd been discussing the possible causes of Esken's demise, and had covered everything, from accidental death to innovative suicide to premeditated murder.

It was the possibility of murder that got me thinking about who. And why. And it had also caused a stomachache from hell.

I slid off the hood and brushed the back of my jeans.

Sheriff Mercer got out, leaving his door ajar and his lights on. The deputy followed, flicking on her yard-long aluminum flashlight and shining it my face. I held a hand up and squinted. I hate it when people shine lights in my face—it leaves me feeling very vulnerable. She dropped the light to the ground and began a sweeping search of the area, creating dancing shadows.

The sheriff nodded to Dan, then said something to me I couldn't make out in the dark. I moved him over into the beam of the car headlights and asked him to repeat the question. Suddenly he jerked his head around, as if searching the hills, then returned his attention to me. I thought I caught the word "coyote" before he started in on the questions.

"What happened here, C.W.?"

I shrugged, thinking I could save myself a thousand words with one shoulder movement, but apparently the sheriff didn't read as much into body language as I usually did.

"From the beginning," he added.

I took a deep breath, gave a quick glance at Dan, then started my story with the phone call from Esken. I recounted every detail, straight through to the arrival at the mine and the broken car window—but just short of the adventure in the tunnels and discovery of Esken's body. I saved that for a visual presentation.

"Got something to show you," I said, wiggling a finger and flashing Dan's light toward the mine. "It's in there."

Sheriff Mercer offered a raised eyebrow before reluctantly following me toward the mine entrance. Dan brought up the rear, while Deputy Clemens remained outside—sheriff's orders.

We ducked into the entrance, waving the flashlights back and forth across the ground. I moved slowly, worried that the whole place might cave in again at any second. When I arrived at the room that held Esken's body, I hesitated. Dan pushed past Sheriff Mercer and claimed the lead.

"In here," he said, nodding toward the tomblike chamber.

While Dan and Sheriff Mercer entered, I waited outside. The men ran their flashlight beams over the body, as I tried to hold onto my dinner. I peeked in and spotted Esken, still propped against the cave wall, his legs outstretched. More details came into focus as I stared at him, unable to look away. He wore dress pants, a white short-sleeved shirt, and no jacket against the constant cold. On his feet were expensive-looking leather shoes.

These couldn't be the shoes I'd felt in the darkness, could they?

As the light zigzagged across his slumped head, it was

clear Esken Bodie was not asleep. The beam of light stopped abruptly on Esken's right arm. Something glinted, protruding from his arm, dangling down slightly, tugging at the white skin.

A syringe.

I couldn't see the sheriff's expression or hear what he said, but from the back, I knew the sight had caught him up short. He stopped, jerked his head back, and tightened his grip on his holster. After a moment he turned to me and shined the light on his own face.

"What happened here, C.W.?"

I shrugged again and stepped into the room.

"Look here," Dan said, waving his flashlight over the ground near Esken's body.

Three syringes lay strewn about.

While Sheriff Mercer examined the area cautiously, I studied Esken Bodie's body from a distance, using the extra flashlight I'd borrowed from the sheriff. Odd. Esken looked more peaceful than I'd seen him in weeks. As he sat looking comfortable against the carved stone wall, his hands lay loosely in his lap. Only the ugly syringe sticking out from his arm broke the peaceful scene.

I shined the light around the area. There were no visible footprints on the stone floor, no signs of anything unusual other than the discarded syringes. The sheriff flashed his light on each of the cylinders, then turned one over with a stick that he had picked up from the ground. About the length of a Popsicle stick, the cylinder seemed fairly generic, with measurements indicated in black on one side. The plungers had all been pressed to the hilt.

Was Esken a drug user? I don't know much about IV drug use, but four syringes seemed a little excessive.

Maybe Esken was suicidal. I knew he was under a great deal of stress, with his mother dead, his brother missing and accused of murder, and his family split apart. Had he finally gone over the edge?

While the sheriff focused on the syringes, my attention was caught by a trickle of dirt slithering down the wall next to Esken's body. I shivered at the thought of another imminent cave-in. The movement drew my eyes to some fresh-looking scratches in the stone surface. In the beam of the flashlight, with the indentations illuminated by light and defined by shadow, I could just make out what seemed to be lettering. Some kid's initials? Graffiti? Obscene words?

I moved in closer and shined the light back and forth over the scratches. These weren't letters. They were more like a drawing. A familiar drawing, as a matter of fact. Rougher, less detailed, and not as smooth as the other one, but it was the same subject matter.

A woman lay prone on a bed, her arms clasped and reaching upward, with a figure at her side, one arm outstretched.

It looked like the drawing that had been pushed under my door.

Caleb's drawing.

I swung the light on the wall surrounding the drawing to see if there was anything else. The area appeared unaltered. I moved the light down to the floor and spotted a thin, sharp stick, much like the one the sheriff was using to flip over the syringe. Where had the sticks come from? Trees didn't grow in mines. They had obviously been brought inside. I squatted down to get a better look. The tip of the weathered stick was rough.

A hand touched my shoulder and I started, dropping my light. I retrieved the flashlight and shone it on the face.

"Don't touch that!" Sheriff Mercer said.

"I wasn't going to!" I said defensively. "I was just looking at it. Jeez!"

"What is it? Some kind of cave art?" The sheriff nodded toward the drawing.

"I don't think so." I reminded him of the drawing I'd found in my office.

"You think it's Caleb's?"

"Looks like his style."

He shined his light back on the drawing. "Know what it means?"

I shook my head. No sense in sharing unfounded theories at this point.

"I'm going to call the M.E. and get her out here to have

a look. Can I trust you two not to touch anything? I'll be right back." He gave me a long look. "I mean it, C.W."

I glared at him. He disappeared.

Dan moved over beside me. "What do you think?" He indicated the drawing.

"It looks like the same drawing that was slipped under my door. Only this one is coarser, probably because he carved it on a wall with a stick instead of drawing on paper with a felt pen."

"You think Caleb was here, then?" Dan asked.

I didn't answer.

Shining the light back on the drawing, I studied it again. The figure of the woman was nearly identical to the one in the drawing. But the figure standing next to the bed was different. This one had only one arm. It was outstretched.

Reaching? Or pointing?

To what? The woman and the door were on one side of the figure, but the gesture wasn't in that direction. There was nothing on the other side, where the arm seemed to be pointing. Unless.

I slid my flashlight along the wall, inching along slowly so as not to miss anything, scanning up and down. Then I saw it.

"Look!" I said to Dan. His eyes followed my finger. Several feet away another figure was etched into the wall. This figure was also one-handed, but this time the hand hung at the side of the body.

I shifted the light slowly down the wall, following the direction of the gesture. There was nothing at the bottom but a boulder about the shape and size of an ottoman. I flashed the light over the rock and noticed a mark I hadn't seen at first. A crude "X" had been scrawled on top, like something from a child's treasure map.

I glanced at Dan. He looked down at the rock, then back at me, then turned away. I followed his gaze.

"Connor!"

"Sheriff!"

"I said don't touch anything!" Sheriff Mercer said,

moving toward us. He spotted the rock with the primitive "X" scrawled on top. With Sheriff Mercer's permission, Dan began inching the rock to one side. In a few seconds, the rock slid from its anchored position, revealing a small pit in the ground underneath.

"Keep going! There's something there!" I called out.

"Easy for you to say. You're not getting a hernia."

The sheriff bent down and helped with the shoving, using his shoulder as leverage, but Dan did most of the work. After a few more minutes they had the boulder most of the way off the hidden pit that had apparently been dug into the rocky floor.

I shined my light on the uncovered surface. A glint of metal reflected back. We all squatted down for a closer look.

"It's some kind of box," I said, reaching for it. The sheriff grabbed my arm.

"Hold it!"

I pulled back. The sheriff picked up the stick he'd used earlier to examine the syringes, and poked it around in the hole. After a moment he managed to hook the handle of the box with the stick and carefully raised it from its burial plot. It was identical to the box we'd found under Sparkle's charred bed.

"What do you suppose is inside?" I said, but no one was listening to me. The sheriff continued his poking, trying to open the lid of the box with the stick. I assumed he was trying to prevent destroying any fingerprints. After a few false starts the lid suddenly flipped open. A piece of yellowing paper was neatly folded inside.

The sheriff picked up the paper by the corner and shook it open. Shining my flashlight over the wrinkled, slightly torn document, I could just make out most of the print.

"County: Calaveras. Place of birth: Mother Lode Memorial Hospital. Mother: Sonora Murietta. Father: Esken Bodie. Weight: 9 lbs, 11 oz. Length: 22". Sex: F. Health: Exc. Name: Devon Bodie."

"A birth certificate?" Dan asked, puzzled. The sheriff rubbed his forehead, as was his habit when he tried to think. The document was dated seventeen years ago, but the month seemed faint and smudged and nearly unreadable. As Sheriff Mercer held it up, I shined the light and tried to make out the date. It looked like the number "12" under the month column, but the top of the number had nearly eroded.

I turned the paper and shined the light from behind. The "2" looked more like an "0."

"I think this birth certificate has been altered."

By the time we emerged from the mine, Deputy Clemens had dusted the car for fingerprints and taken plaster casts of shoe prints from the ground.

"Find anything?" the sheriff asked his deputy, as she jotted notes in her notebook. I could barely read his lips in the glow of the sheriff's car headlights.

"Just these tire marks, made by his Jeep." She indicated the tracks left by the all-terrain vehicle. "I dusted, collected some samples of fiber from the seat, and pieces of the window, but didn't find anything unusual. A few food wrappers on the floor—they've been bagged. Some phone numbers. I'll check them out when I get back to the office."

I caught the flash of the M.E.'s blinking lights in the distance.

The swirling red-and-blue lights gave the hills a haunting, surreal glow, as the van approached; I felt the chill of the night air pierce my skin.

After brief greetings, Dr. Arthurlene Jackson, the Chief Medical Examiner of Calaveras County, accompanied the sheriff to Esken's body, along with two techs. She made her initial examination while Dan and I stayed outside, at her request. When she returned to question us, the sheriff led the EMTs to Esken's body.

Arthurlene and I had worked together on a recent murder. Perhaps "together" is a stretch. I asked her questions for a newspaper story and she reluctantly gave me the answers. She knew she was in for more interrogation now that another body had turned up. But she was determined to get her questions in first—the standard "who, what, when, where, how." She left out "why."

I answered the best I could, much like I had the sheriff, who'd asked the same questions. Dan offered a few more details I had forgotten. When she was finished, it was my turn.

"What about the syringes, Dr. Jackson? Do they have anything to do with street drugs?"

Arthurlene Jackson tightened the lab coat around her slim figure, as if strengthening her resolve not to reveal too much information. Then she tucked her ebony hands into the deep pockets, and met my questions head-on.

"They're not street syringes. They're for medical use. I won't know what was in them until Tox analyzes them, but the arms were covered with marks. This wasn't the first time he took an IV medication—or drug."

I was distracted momentarily by the EMTs, who appeared at the mine entrance carrying Esken's body on a hand-held stretcher. As soon as they reached the outside world, they hoisted him onto a roller-gurney and headed for the waiting ambulance.

Before I could get in another question, Dr. Jackson asked, "Connor. Any idea what really happened here?" She crossed her arms over her lab coat.

"Yeah, Connor. If you know something you haven't told me—" Sheriff Mercer added, appearing suddenly at her side.

"I told you both everything I know. Believe me, I'd like to find out what happened to Esken as much as you would. After all, he asked me to help him out with Caleb. But so far, I've got nothing."

The sheriff was quiet for a moment, rubbing his forehead. Then he spoke up. "You say someone helped you find your way out of the mine when you got caught in there? You thought it was Dan at first, right?"

"Yes. It was pitch black in there and I thought the whole place was coming down around me. I was so relieved when I thought Dan had found me, and was trying to find a new way out. But when we reached the exit, he disappeared. When I found him later, I asked him about it. But he said it wasn't him."

"So who was it?"

"I don't know."

"But you have an idea," the sheriff pressed on.

I glanced at Dan. He met my gaze. I looked back at the sheriff, then at Dr. Jackson.

"Not a clue," I said, stuffing my hands into my pockets.

In the right pocket I felt a small rock the size of a pea, and rolled it around in my fingers during the drive home. It wasn't until I got back to my diner that I pulled it out to look at it.

It was a gold nugget.

I didn't sleep well. Nocturnal visions of bats, bodies, and Bodies kept me from my usual pirate dreams. By morning I had a fierce headache, painful reminders of several bruises, and porcupine hair. I doubled the Motrin and shampooed the hair, but the bruises were there to stay—at least temporarily.

Dan had gone home for the night. I had half expected him to stay over after the traumatic experience, but he'd been distant again by the time the activity was over and declined my offer of a hot midnight treat. And I didn't mean a mocha.

To hell with him.

After a good game of capture-the-sock with Casper—Casper won and I was now down another sock—I headed for the office on my bike. Miah was sitting at his computer when I arrived after nine o'clock. He briefly acknowledged me with a head nod and wiggling fingers that meant "wait," then resumed his excited phone discussion.

I dropped my backpack onto my desk and checked my

messages. One had come in last night after I'd left with Dan for the mine. Miah had torn the printout from the TTY answering machine.

It read: "CONNOR, ARE YOU COMING Q I'LL BE WAITING. HURRY."

It was signed, "EB."

I glanced at Miah to ask him about the message, but I got another response of fluttering fingers, telling me to hold on. I watched him talk, trying to read his lips. He spoke mostly in single syllables that looked like "Whoa!" and "God!" and "Shit!"

Then he hung up.

"What?" I signed, open palm turned up and wagging back and forth.

Miah signed back in ASL. "Dad told me what happened to Esken last night. Wow! Is he really dead? Poor Devon. I wonder how she's taking the news. Oh, Dad said to tell you Esken was a diabetic. The M.E. thinks insulin shock caused death."

Diabetic. "Self-induced?"

"They don't know. Dad said maybe, or injected by someone else. Did you know he was a diabetic?"

"I had no idea. Anything else?"

"He also said he sent the birth certificate to the lab for prints. They won't know anything for awhile, though."

"Is the M.E. finished with the autopsy yet?"

Miah shook his head.

"Then how does she know about the diabetes?"

"She called Doc Crippen, Esken's doctor."

Sorting through this latest information, I knew I'd have to wait for the coroner's autopsy and the lab results. It was slow going, and I was feeling anxious, not just because Esken was dead, but because he'd known he was in danger—he'd asked for my help. There had to be something I could do to find out what happened. Miah interrupted my thoughts.

"Connor, can I write the story?"

I smiled. Poor Miah. I'd stuck him with the routine beer

brawls and ground-breaking ceremonies for too long. He wanted more. But was he ready? I guessed I'd find out.

"You can help me with it. This is going to be a big one and I don't want you turning it into a hard-boiled detective story. Keep it real. And don't be surprised if I edit it a lot when it's finished. This isn't Journalism one-oh-one."

Miah gave an I-know-that nod. Overly confident already. Not a good sign.

"You work on it this morning, while I go check a few things. Can you handle that and your advice column and the pet corner, and everything else?"

"Piece of cake." His fingers spelled so rapidly, it looked like all one word. I had only recently learned what "piece of cake" meant.

As I left the office, I walked slowly past Dan's door, peering into the frosted window. Nothing moved, not even Cujo the curmudgeon cat. I knocked, then tried the knob, but the door was locked.

Where was he, anyway?

With another quick "To hell with him," I walked down the stairs and up the street to Memory Kingdom Memorial Park. If anyone knew body language, albeit dead body language, it was Del Rey Montez. Maybe she could shed some light on this latest Bodie development.

"Hey, Connor, back so soon?"

Del Rey was at the reception desk when I entered through the dark wooden doors. Unlike her predecessor at the mortuary, who dressed like something out of a Disney movie, Del Rey kept her style simple. She wore her excess weight with pride, and dressed in bright colors and stylish designs.

"Hi, Del Rey. How's business?"

I sat on a velveteen couch, an ornately carved antique, and watched her finish a few notes in her ledger. She closed the book and looked up brightly. "Unusually brisk, even for an old forty-niner town like Flat Skunk, with all its homicidal heritage. Want a diet soda?"

I shook my head. Del Rey ducked behind the desk and reappeared with a can of diet raspberry-flavored Shasta. She joined me on the couch, facing me so I could read her lips. Her red-lined mouth was easy to understand.

"So tell me about Esken Bodie," she said, after a long pull from the can that left a red soda mustache on her upper lip. "What happened? I heard you found his body. What's this about needle marks all over him?"

Like I said, who needs a newspaper when you had a grapevine like the one in Flat Skunk.

"I didn't actually find the body. Dan did. And his body wasn't covered with needle marks. He's apparently a diabetic. He took insulin."

"Well, I also heard you were nearly buried alive in that cave. What happened?"

"I wasn't almost buried alive. The entrance to one of the rooms caved in, and . . ." I paused. And what? I didn't want to get into the story of the ghost who led me to safety. Too much the stuff of gothic novels. "And I had to find another way out."

She nodded suspiciously and returned to the pressing subject. "So what about Esken. Do you think it was an accidental overdose? Or was it deliberate?"

I shrugged. "Good question. Actually, that's why I'm here."

Del Rey looked puzzled. "I don't know anything about diabetes."

"I know. But you do know something about bodies. Remember yesterday I asked if you ever noticed something on a body while you were embalming it that puzzled you?"

"I remember, but no, Arthurlene Jackson is very thorough. Only that time I told you about, the man with the dog bites . . . except . . ." Del Rey paused, took another swig of pop, darkening her red artificial smile, and went on slowly. "There was one other time, when Shawna Lee Griggs was beaten by her husband. Remember? She eventually died as a result of that beating. Arthurlene documented all the bruises and marks. But when I got the body, I found something that didn't get much attention on the coroner's report."

"What was that?"

"Her nails were perfect."

"What do you mean?"

"I knew Shawna Lee from church, you know. She was always a nail biter, especially when the minister got real serious talking about the Commandments. Then all of a sudden, she gets these glue-on nails over at the Nail It To You Salon. Jilda put them on for her. They were still on when she arrived for the embalming. All except one, which Arthurlene had removed for analysis."

"So, what's the significance?"

"The only other time she got her nails done was when she first met that no good husband of hers, five years ago."

Del Rey made a gesture indicating the telephone, then got up and moved across to the desk to answer it. I sat and thought about Shawna Lee Griggs. I notice people's hands more than most, since hands often tell me more than words. I remembered the nails. What did it mean?

And then it dawned on me.

Del Rey returned with another can of diet Shasta soda, this time black cherry.

"Anyway, back to your question. Arthurlene is an excellent M.E.—the best, in my opinion. I rarely find anything that's not been documented by an autopsy. But that one time I did notice her nails. I'm just telling you 'cause you asked."

"You think she was fooling around, don't you?"

Del Rey cocked her jaw and nodded.

"Who was it?"

"Don't know. But Dickie Rufer, that mechanic over at Intensive Car, sure hung around her funeral a long time, looking like he'd crashed his favorite hot rod."

"Del Rey, think back once more. Did you notice

anything unusual on Sparkle Bodie's body when you were embalming it?"

Del Rey took a swig of her black cherry soda, wiping the corners of her mouth but missing most of the residue, and thought a moment.

"You mean like fake nails and stuff? No. The only thing I noticed was that she was alive the first time they brought her in. That was pretty unusual, don't you think? Why? You think she might have been fooling around with someone on the sly too? Sheriff Mercer, maybe?"

"Very funny. I just wondered if she might have had any needle marks, or anything that was overlooked by the coroner."

"Not that I recall."

"When Esken's body comes in, would you take a second look at it before you begin working on him? For the hell of it."

"Sure. What are you looking for?"

"Nothing in particular. Just thought, with your expertise, you might notice something the others could have missed."

"Well, don't expect much. Like I said, Arthurlene is excellent. I think she was too busy looking under Shawna Lee's nails, and missed the obvious by not looking *at* them."

"Del Rey, did you know Esken very well?"

"No. I only heard the gossip—that he was having money troubles, not to mention family problems. There was a rumor of a change in Sparkle's will, but talk like that isn't reliable. Nothing you could take to court."

"Do you think he was suicidal?"

"Hard to say. Suicide is a puzzle to me. I don't understand why people take their own lives. We've all got problems, but that's life. It's not supposed to cause death."

Miah was nowhere in sight when I returned to the office. Lunchtime. He was probably at the Nugget Café, tossing down one of their Hangman Burgers. Dan still wasn't in his office, either, when I passed by. Not that I noticed.

I picked up the phone, set the receiver on the couplers, and dialed the sheriff's number. In a matter of moments the screen lit up with Sheriff Mercer's familiar greeting:

"HEey, C.W. Whats up? GA."

"Hi, Sheriff. Any dirt? GA."

"Iff you're referring to the body we dicsovered at the mine last night, YOou know everything there is to know. gA."

"You're holding out on me, Sheriff. I can feel it. GA."

"WEell, you might be interrested in a note I found this morning over at Esken's place. BUt of course, it's confidential. NOT for publication. GA."

"SK SK SK," I typed quickly, and hung up without giving him a chance to respond. Grabbing my backpack, I locked the office, hustled down the stairs two at a time, and raced over to the jail. Sheriff Mercer still had his hand resting on the phone when I opened the door.

"You hung up on me!" he said, trying to look hurt.

"We were finished. I signed off. What did you find?"

"That was very impolite of you, C.W. You didn't give me a chance to say good-bye—"

"Would you stop! What did you find?" The sheriff loved to tease me when he had something he knew I'd want. He pretended to buff his nails while I stood staring at him. I had to pull out the big guns. "Okay, do you want homemade rigatoni Gorgonzola for dinner on Sunday, or are you going to have to open another can of Spaghetti-Os?"

He grinned. "I found a note lying on a table at Esken's home."

"You mean in Sonora's house—or the cottage in the back?"

The sheriff eyed me. "How did you know about the cottage?"

"I guessed. What did you find?"

Carefully pulling a marked Baggie from under a pile of papers on his desk, he opened it and lifted out a wrinkled piece of paper. Holding the paper by a corner, he turned it around to face me. I recognized the artwork immediately. A woman lay on a flat surface, her eyes X'd shut. This time there were no other figures in the picture. But underneath, someone had written in a nearly illegible, childlike scrawl:

"YOO kiLD aR MOMe. YOO Di."

I left the sheriff's office puzzling over three questions. If Esken committed suicide, why would he do it in the mine as he waited for me—and in such a bizarre way?

But if someone killed him, same question: Why in the mine? And, if someone *did* kill Esken, he must have known Esken was diabetic.

And finally, when did Caleb learn to write? It was a forgery, all right. The splintered letters Caleb had written earlier were drawn from bottom to top. These letters were a poor imitation. Not to mention the x's for eyes instead of slits.

I stopped at the office, desperate to catch up on work, and tried not to let the loose ends around Esken's death interrupt my concentration on such demanding topics as the Clampers' upcoming plaque dedication and the Historical Society's potluck fund-raiser.

Miah was at his shop down the hall, no doubt trying to sell surfboards to the ocean-impaired. After all, Flat Skunk is located a hundred miles from any significant body of water, if you don't count the Miwok Reservoir.

My stomach began begging for attention around one-thirty. I assumed it was for food, not general anxiety for the recent circumstances. A quick glance in passing: Dan's office was still empty.

I stopped in at the Nugget for a reliable if not delectable bite, but as soon as I entered the door I spotted Dan, deep in conversation with his ex-wife, Amy Allen. She appeared distraught, but because his back was to me, I couldn't see Dan's expression.

I quickly backed out of the café, opting instead for a Cornish pasty from DILLIGAF's Deli. With the moveable feast in hand, I headed down the street to the library. Ignoring the sign that read, "No food, no drinks, no pets except Seeing Eye Dogs," I pushed open the door with my elbow, my pasty in one hand and a brown-bag-wrapped Sierra Nevada in the other. I wished I had my hearing-ear dog with me, but breaking two out of three rules wasn't bad.

"Hey, Aubrey," I said, finding him hunched over a book at his heavy oak desk, which serves as the checkout counter, reference desk, book depository, and showcase for his Star Wars action figure collection.

"Hey, Connor." Aubrey turned his book over—a copy of the Physician's Desk Reference—and leaned back in his swivel chair. "What's up? Out gathering more news for the Eureka!?"

I sat on the edge of Aubrey's desk, knocking over Luke Skywalker and C3PO in the process, and turned to face him. Setting my pasty down, I took a swig of beer, then held the bottle out to Aubrey.

"No, thanks. Can't drink on the job, you know."

"Yeah, I guess you have to stay alert all the time in this library business, huh? No telling when a desperate book thief might try to steal the latest Hardy Boys adventure. What are you reading about?"

He glanced at the overturned book and patted his stomach. "I haven't been feeling too well. Stomachache or something. Had it for a couple of days now and can't seem to shake it. Thought I'd try to find some information in here to help."

"Any luck?"

"Zantac looks hopeful. Think I'll give it a try."

"Been downing too many of Mama Cody's espresso milkshakes, haven't you."

He gave his stomach another rub. "Probably. So what's up?"

"I was wondering. You know that genealogy chart you've been working on for the Bodies? Did you ever make me a copy?"

Aubrey's eyes shifted to his desk as he spoke. I couldn't make out his words at that angle and reached out to touch his chin, reminding him to lift his head so I could lip-read him.

". . . I don't think I should, you know. I mean, I'm sure Sparkle meant to keep it confidential. Of course, she's dead now, but still—"

I tried the approach that seemed to work before: co-conspiracy.

"I just thought maybe it would give me—you know, us—some idea of who might have killed Sparkle." I decided not to mention Esken.

Aubrey nodded but kept the frown as he spoke. "I suppose . . ." He pushed himself up and shuffled to the filing cabinet next to the old-fashioned card catalog behind him. If he said anything, I missed it. After a few minutes of rifling through an open file drawer, he paused, resting his arms on the folders.

I moved around to face him. "What's wrong?" I asked, reading his puzzled look.

"That's weird."

"What?"

"The genealogy chart. All my papers. They're gone. I'm sure I put the folder back when I finished working on it the other day. I always keep it right here in this filing cabinet. I wonder . . ."

He glanced around the room, searching for some sign of the chart, then shook his head. Moving to the desk, he lifted up papers, opened drawers, even got down on his knees and peered under the desk. When nothing turned up, he returned to the filing cabinet for another look.

"Nope. It's gone. It's definitely gone."

Aubrey tapped one long finger against his mouth and said something but I couldn't read his obscured lips. I reached up and pulled his hand away as he said, "That is so weird. Where on earth could it be?"

We were interrupted by two young kids who came to return books. The boy and girl said hello to Aubrey, dropped their copies of *Goosebumps* and *The Babysitter's Club* books in the bin next to the desk, and left. I turned back to Aubrey.

"Aubrey, was there anything else in the chart that seemed . . . unusual, besides the missing birth certificate?"

He shook his head.

"Anything about Sparkle or Esken or Caleb that didn't seem quite right?"

Another shake of the head.

"What about Devon? Do you remember anything about her?"

Narrowed eyes but no response.

"Sonora? What did you find out about Sonora's heritage?"

Aubrey's eyes flashed and his hand fell away from his mouth. "Yeah, there was something. God, what was it? I was just getting to her side of the family. I hadn't made much headway, but there was a gap . . . oh, yeah! Devon's birthdate. It was different from Devon's birth certificate, which I got from the county. I guess I just figured someone wrote it down wrong. I didn't think much of it at the time."

We were back to the birth certificate. I would have to get an official duplicate to find out what it all meant.

"Aubrey, who has access to the library besides you?"

"Oh, you know, the general public, that's all."

"I mean after hours."

He shook his head forcefully. "No one. I'm the only one with a key, besides Sheriff Mercer. He has an emergency key in case I forget mine. But that's it. Not even Twaina Bryson, the high school girl who works here part-time, can get in without me."

"Any idea who could have taken that genealogy file?"

"That's a very good question, Connor." He picked up the phone.

"Who are you calling?"

"Sheriff Mercer."

I left before the sheriff arrived. I'd find out from him later if he learned anything from Aubrey, but I had my doubts he'd discover much. Someone had taken the Bodies' genealogy workup. Why? No clue.

Who? I had a hunch.

And she was just entering the Nugget Café when I passed by on my way back to the office.

Time for dessert.

The place was thinning out when I entered. Dan and Amy were nowhere in sight, thank God, and only a handful of good old boys and high school students were still hanging about. Didn't these kids ever go to school?

I sat down at an empty booth where I could see Devon and her two girlfriends at the next booth. Devon barely fit into the seat with her huge stomach bulging in front of her. She looked rosy-cheeked and puffy from water retention, and her short maroon hair needed either mousse control or an artistic critique.

I could see only Devon's face. The other girls had their backs to me. I read Devon's black-outlined lips as she talked about her heartburn, indigestion, leg cramps, swollen fingers and feet, and a bunch of other unpleasant pregnancy complaints. It was about the time she started in on the stretch marks and hemorrhoids that I decided never to have children.

When Jilda brought the girls' mugs and my order, Twaina Bryson slipped Devon what looked like a Tums, then both friends got up and headed for the bathroom, leaving Devon alone to sip her steaming latte. I quickly moved over to her booth and slid into the seat opposite her.

"Hi, Devon. How are you feeling?"

She rubbed her tummy and shrugged noncommittally. "Okay, I guess."

I realized she was referring to her physical condition,

when I meant her emotional state, from the recent loss of her father and grandmother. Before I could pursue the question, her eyes darted away from mine to the front door of the Nugget. I turned to follow her glance and saw Russell Jacks entering the place, his hand on his ubiquitous briefcase. He waved to Devon and gave her a full grin, then swung by the counter and picked up a gooey pastry from the plastic serve-yourself breadbox.

"Hi, girls," he said to both of us. "Brought you a sweet, Devon. Looks like you could use a treat. Feeling okay?"

"I wish people would stop asking me if I feel all right. God!"

Russell gave me a look that said I-know-what-she's-going-through, even though he didn't have a clue. "Well, you take care of that baby. Sorry about your dad. Let me know if I can do anything. I'll see you girls later."

With that he set the pastry on the table, then settled onto a counter stool with his briefcase.

Devon glanced down at the sugary bun and the color drained from her face. She grabbed her stomach and dashed for the restroom, just as the other two girls were coming out. They giggled knowingly as they returned to the booth.

I followed her in.

"Devon, are you—" I caught myself before I said "all right." "Can I get you something?"

Devon was leaning over the toilet, the stall door open. I placed my hand on her back and felt her heave once. Patting her like a mother burping her baby, I looked away, trying to give her some privacy and comfort at the same time. After a few moments the nausea seemed to subside. She stood up looking white as a ghost. A curl of drool hung from her bottom lip.

"It's just morning sickness. It never went away for me. Anything sweet makes me puke." She leaned over the sink and splashed water in her mouth and on her face, dampening the maroon bangs that hung over her black-rimmed eyes.

She pulled out a paper towel and began blotting her face. I wondered about the nausea. For most women, the queasiness disappears by the end of the first trimester, but I said nothing. No sense in alarming her.

"Devon, have you been seeing a doctor?"

"Yeah, every month. Now every week."

"Have you got some . . . support with this baby?" I asked tentatively, wondering if it would get her to talk or clam her up.

"You mean the father?" She eyed me suspiciously.

"Well, yes. Shouldn't he be in on this?"

She said nothing. I decided to give it another try.

"Devon, do you mind if I ask you a personal question?" She shrugged.

"Are you still planning to give up the baby?"

"There's no way I'm keeping this kid. I'm too young to have kids, and I don't even know if I like them." She turned and fluffed her damp bangs in the mirror and I read her last words in the image. "Definitely not."

I decided to push the envelope. "What about the father? Shouldn't you—"

Devon whirled around and glared at me. "Excuse me, lady, but you have no right to tell me what I should or shouldn't do. And besides, you don't have a clue what you're talking about, so why don't you just mind your own business."

With a last glance at her reflection, she left me alone in the bathroom.

When I left the bathroom a few minutes later, the girls were gone. But someone familiar sat in my booth.

"I'm sorry. This booth is taken." I slipped into the seat and pulled my homemade mocha territorially over to my side, gripping it with cold fingers.

"Thought you wouldn't mind some company," Dan said.

"How did you know I was sitting here?"

He looked pointedly at the mocha. I unwrapped my fingers from the mug. "Oh. God, I hate being so predictable. Jilda!" I called out. "Bring me a margarita."

Jilda gave me a funny look, and went back to flirting with Russell at the counter.

"How you been?" Dan asked, drumming his fingertips on the black-and-gray Formica tabletop.

Pissed. "Fine." Wondering about you. "Too busy to think. You know the newspaper business. Never a dull headline in Flat Skunk. You?" Not that I cared. I took a sip of mocha and tried to act nonchalant.

"Listen, Connor. I have something more to tell you."
He glanced around the diner, which was now empty except
for Russell and Jilda. The hairs on the back of my neck rose.
Uh-oh.

"You remember Amy?"

I nodded and braced myself with another sip of tepid
chocolate coffee. "Your ex-wife." God, she wants him
back. She's come to her senses and realized the mistake she
made in letting him go. She's—

"She's pregnant."

It didn't compute. "She's . . . pregnant?"

Dan nodded, watching me intently.

"My God! What . . . what does she want from
you?"

"She says it's mine."

My mouth dropped open. I felt a heat rush to my face,
and it wasn't the coffee. I tried to speak but couldn't find the
words.

"It's not what you think."

I raised an eyebrow. Was all that coffee causing
my upset stomach? "Oh, really? I think it's pretty clear."
I started to gather my backpack but Dan grabbed my
arm.

"Wait, Connor. Let me finish."

I sat back, poised to fly at the next sign of betrayal.
"Okay. So finish."

Dan picked up his beer and downed half of it. Taking a
deep breath, he rubbed his forehead, then took my hand as
he began to speak. "When we were married, five years ago,
Amy was paranoid about my getting killed in the line of
duty. She . . . she even had me donate a sperm sample at the
A.I. Clinic."

"A.I.?"

"Artificial Insemination Clinic. It's in Manhattan. I did
it to reassure her. She wanted to have kids but not right
away. But she was afraid I might not be around forever. She
took out insurance, so to speak."

"So you froze your sperm."

He nodded. I was trying not to visualize the donation process. Luckily Dan broke in on my thoughts.

"When I left the police force, she started seeing Geoff, my former partner. It wasn't long before she traded me in for him. We divorced, went our separate ways, and I forgot about the sperm donation."

"What about Geoff? Couldn't he take on the job of fatherhood?"

"The marriage didn't last. They divorced six months later. I didn't know about it until she told me when she arrived the other day. We haven't exactly kept in touch over the past few years."

"And the baby? It isn't what's-his-name's?"

"Apparently not. I guess they tried, but it didn't happen. After a while they ran some tests, and found out that Geoff is sterile."

I picked up my now-cold cup of coffee and sipped it. "So your ex-wife decided to go to the bank and withdraw your donation."

"Apparently. I never notified them we were divorced."

"And now she's pregnant."

"Uh-huh."

"With your child."

Dan looked down at his fingers resting on the tabletop.

"Wow." I sat back against the chair and tried to think as I watched his fingers move restlessly. We said nothing for several minutes. Dan motioned Jilda for another beer, and when it arrived, drank half of it before setting the bottle on the table. I didn't need a beer; I was already feeling a bit numb.

"What are you going to do?"

Dan wiped the foam from his lips. "I don't know. But I've been wanting to talk with you about it. It just never seemed like the right time."

I felt something inside soften.

"What does she want? Money for child support?" I hoped that was all.

"Basically, enough to take care of her and the baby for as long as necessary. I don't think she has any legal claim, but if it's my child, I want to help."

"Is money a problem?" Aside from occasional construction jobs, Dan hadn't been working steadily since he arrived in Flat Skunk.

"Big time. I guess I could sell my mother's house. I own it now, and it's my only asset. But Mom's lived there since she was born. I can't kick her out."

I sipped the cold drink, feeling a little dizzy at this new revelation. Dan has a child? And with it the financial obligations of fatherhood.

"Wait a minute. Are you sure the child is yours?"

"I was planning to have a paternity test, just to make sure. It wouldn't be the first time she's lied to me."

"Yes, get the test. Then we'll worry about the money."

So Amy Allen wanted money for the baby, huh. I wondered if that was all she wanted from Dan Smith.

I made a date to meet with Dan that night to talk some more. I felt guilty indulging in the recent wave of self-pity, thinking Dan was losing interest and seeing someone else. Sympathetic to his problem, I was still troubled about Amy's sudden appearance. Something didn't make sense, but I couldn't put my finger on what.

While Dan headed for the clinic, I got my bike and rode to my diner to pick up the Chevy. It was time for a trip to the big city, such as it is: Whiskey Slide.

The Office of Public Records is housed in an old brick building that has recently become a national monument, thanks to the Clampers. The thick, mocha-colored bricks give the structure a feeling of permanence and strength. The building has stood since 1889, having survived two fires, one major earthquake, and eight resales. It began as an impenetrable jail for the large number of Mother Lode claim-jumpers, deadbeats, drunks, and murderers, eventually giving way to a blacksmith shop, a newspaper building, an assay office, a mercantile store, a hotel, a bank, and finally a local government agency.

I found the office of Births and Deaths, and asked for a copy of Devon Bodie's birth certificate. The woman behind the chipped wood counter led me back to a well-used computer, where all the records had been transferred to disk. All I had to do was key in the name of the person I was searching for and the record would appear. I could even take home a printout for a ten-dollar processing fee.

So much for rights of privacy.

The only trouble was, Devon Bodie wasn't listed under the county birth records. Now how could that be?

I checked for Sparkle's birth certificate, remembering her maiden name—Smiley—and located it with no problem. Esken and Caleb were both on record, and I made printouts of all three family members, as well as Sparkle's husband, Dakota, who'd died shortly after Caleb was born. But Sonora was not in the records either. I left with thirty dollars' worth of birth certificates that I hadn't really come for.

When I returned to the office, I took a few moments to read the information on each certificate. Sparkle Smiley's birth had been recorded in Poker Flat, a small mining camp outside of Whiskey Slide, on April 11, 1907.

Esken and Caleb were born at the Mother Lode Memorial Hospital in Whiskey Slide. Esken entered the world first, with no complications. Caleb, however, was also the product of an Rh incompatibility. He had undergone a blood transfusion.

I set the copies down and thought about the Rh factor, whether or not they were significant to the death of Sparkle and Esken. What about Devon? Had she inherited the Rh problem? As a firstborn, she wouldn't have been affected by the blood disorder. But if she had been a later-born child, and Sonora and Esken's blood were incompatible, Sonora might have had to undergo the RhoGAM injection to ensure the health of her baby.

Where was Devon's original birth certificate recorded? And where was Sonora's?

It was time to seek some legal advice.

I entered the foyer of Russell Jacks's office, knocked on his inner office door, then let myself in. Sonora Bodie sat opposite Russell, who was behind his desk. When she turned to face me, I caught a trace of recent tears that had been wiped from her slightly streaked face.

"Oh, sorry! I just wanted to ask you a question, Russell. I can come back later."

I started to pull the door shut when Sonora stood up and headed over.

"No, that's all right. I was just leaving." She turned to Russell, said something I missed, then gave me a tight smile as she passed by. I watched her leave, closing the outer office door behind her.

I stood hesitantly in the doorway. "Sorry about that. Didn't mean to interrupt."

"You didn't. She was finished. We were just going over a few details of Esken's estate, such as it was. She's upset about his death, you know. Sit down. What can I do for you, Connor?"

I slid into the recently vacated chair and folded my hands on Russell's desk. "I wanted to ask you about Esken's will."

Russell shook his head. "You know I can't say anything about it yet. The reading has been postponed until tomorrow. Everything will be made public then."

I pressed on. "Can you at least tell me if there was anything unusual in it?"

"Sorry."

"All right. Then, off the record, do you think Esken killed himself?"

"I don't know, Connor. He had been awfully distraught

lately. But I'll tell you this. I was shocked to hear he was dead. At first I thought . . . well, never mind . . ."

"What? Tell me."

Russell paused, his face looking tired and worn. When he finally spoke, the words came slowly, with little energy.

"Frankly, Connor, I was having a hard time representing him. Conflict of interest really; he didn't like his mother. He suspected there were changes in the will. I thought maybe he . . ." He didn't finish the sentence, so I did it for him.

"You think he might have killed his own mother?"

Russell looked at me. "Truthfully, I just don't know. In this business you find out people are capable of anything."

"Even if they're related?"

Russell shrugged and struggled with his words. "But then there's Caleb, who's so odd. Whether he's capable of murder . . . I just don't know. He may have known what his mother was up to. And he knows that mine like the back of his hand. He could have met his brother inside, but . . . the whole thing just doesn't seem likely."

"What was she planning to do? Sell the mine?"

"No, she'd never sell the mine. I meant . . . she was getting ready to . . . well, to put Caleb in an institution. She said she couldn't handle him anymore. And she knew he'd be lost without her when she died."

"You think Caleb knew about it?"

"I think he did. There were brochures on the dining table at the Bodie home last time I was there. She'd been trying to communicate it to him, to prepare him, but she said he'd just become wild every time she showed him the pictures."

"But do you think he'd actually kill his mother—and his brother? He's never done anything violent before, has he? I know he gets upset sometimes when he's frustrated. But that's just because he can't communicate. I remember becoming so irritated when I was a kid, when no one could understand me. But it doesn't seem likely that he'd plot a murder, let alone carry it out."

The attorney met my gaze, took a deep breath, and pressed his palms on the desk.

"I know he's capable of murder, Connor."

"How?"

"I know, because he tried to kill me once."

Sorry, Russell. I misread your lips. I thought you said—"

"I did," he interrupted. "But I'll say it again more clearly, as long as you understand this is strictly off the record."

I hate when people say that. I nodded reluctantly and said, "What happened?" I leaned toward him, not wanting to miss a word.

Russell squirmed in his seat, his eyes darting around the office as if searching for some assistance in telling his story. I gave him a moment before prodding him again.

"It was some time ago. And I can't prove that Caleb actually tried to . . . to harm me. I mean, I didn't see him do anything. But I suspect he was trying to kill me."

Stunned, I sat back. "What makes you think that?"

"Because of what happened."

"Well, tell me!"

Russell made a face. Getting information from him was like pulling gold from placer.

"A few months ago I was out hiking in the hills. I do a lot of hiking, you know. Anyway, I was coming down over the ridge and found myself near the old Bodie Mine. Not the front entrance, but on the side. I sat down to enjoy the view and drink some water when I saw Caleb coming out of some thistles near the side of the mine."

I remembered seeing the bushes after I'd left the mine with . . . with whoever it was that had led me out. They were large and thick, and in fact I had scratched my arm as I crawled through them.

"Well, he startled me, appearing from nowhere like that. I waved at him, and he started waving back, kind of franticlike. I thought maybe he was in trouble, so I headed down the hill, sliding on the dry grass."

"What was wrong?"

"That's just it. Nothing that I could tell. When I got down there, he started pointing at the bushes and making these weird noises. Naturally I went looking around the bushes, thinking there might be a dead animal or a snake. But it was nothing."

"Then what did he want?"

"I'm getting to that. It turns out he wasn't trying to show me something in the bushes, but *behind* the bushes."

"What?"

"An opening."

My escape hatch? I sat up. "Caleb showed you a hidden exit? Did you go inside?"

Russell glared at me. "Connor, this isn't some Tom Sawyer adventure story with a cave full of secret passageways. I should never have followed that lunatic." He caught himself. "Sorry."

I pulled back a few inches. "Go on."

"Well, after he got me to go in, he ditched me. Took his damn flashlight and left me in pitch darkness. I couldn't keep up. He was moving too fast."

"Maybe he was excited about showing you something. I mean, maybe he didn't mean to leave you—"

"Oh, he ditched me, all right. I never saw him again. I almost never saw anything again."

"What do you mean?"

"After a few minutes of trying to feel my way out, I

heard this pounding, and then rumbling. The noise seemed to be coming from all around me. All of a sudden, the whole ceiling caved in. Dirt, rocks, stones, wood, all kinds of crap just fell on top of me. I couldn't move at first. I was practically buried under all that debris."

Another cave-in? Odd. Did they happen all the time? Or only when someone was inside . . .

"How did you get out?"

"Damn lucky, that's how. It took me a while to dig out from under the rubble. Then I had to feel my way back in the pitch darkness. Ran into a couple of dead ends before I located the exit again. It took me hours."

"But you never saw Caleb?"

"No. Not until I went to the Bodie house the next day to get some papers signed. Sparkle was too ill to come to the office by then, you know. She noticed one of the bruises I'd picked up trying to get out and asked about it. That's when I told her what had happened. Right then Caleb came stomping out of his room, acting like nothing had happened. When Sparkle tried to question him, he pretended he didn't know what she was talking about. But he didn't fool me. I know he understood. And I know he was up to something in that cave. I'll bet he's got all kinds of secret hideaways in there. The guy's—"

Russell abruptly looked behind me. I turned to see Aubrey Horne standing in the doorway.

"Sorry, didn't mean to disturb you."

I rose to leave, allowing Aubrey to have my seat.

"Overheard you talking about your near-death experience, Russell. You gotta be careful around that guy. His omelet is missing a few eggs."

Russell said something but I didn't turn around in time to catch it. I headed for the door.

"Thanks for your time, Russell. I'll see you after the reading. Later, Aubrey."

I closed the door behind me, wondering what the two of them had to talk about. Sparkle Bodie, no doubt.

·   ·   ·

I dragged myself into my office, feeling drained by the visit with Russell. I'd had a hunch, based solely on intuition, that Caleb wasn't the hair-trigger maniac everyone thought. But there was definitely something going on in that unfathomable brain of his. Was it enough to make him a killer?

I sat down at my desk and had just switched on my computer when a reflection on the screen caused me to freeze.

Someone was behind me. Moving slowly. Creeping . . . toward me. I tried to turn around but couldn't move, my shoulders tight as boards, my feet stuck to the floor. I could feel the sweat tickle my chest.

As a blurred face came into fuzzy view on the screen, I saw a hand raised high over my head. Shaking off the paralysis, I whirled around and let out a scream.

Caleb Bodie towered over me, a bunch of wildflowers held tightly in his fist.

He jumped back and dropped the bouquet on the floor. No doubt I had scared him, too, by whirling around and screwing up my face. Half expecting Dan or Miah to come rushing through the door in response to my scream, I remembered they were both out. I spun the chair back around, then stood up, legs apart, ready to fight or run.

Neither of us said anything.

After a moment, I could feel my racing heart slowing. Caleb hadn't moved. He stood stock-still, as if waiting for a cue. I took a deep breath and inched forward.

Caleb tensed and took a step back. I stopped, raised a calming hand, and greeted him with the universal gesture for "Hi." Caleb didn't move. I glanced around for some idea as to what to do next. Call the sheriff? Find a weapon?

I leaned down without taking my eyes off him and picked up the scattered bouquet, collecting it back into a slightly skewed bunch. I raised my hand again, then signaled for Caleb to sit down on Miah's nearby chair. At least we'd be on an equal level and he wouldn't be so intimidating. Caleb blinked, and I repeated the gesture, this time pointing to the chair. Without looking, he eased slowly into the seat, and placed his hands on his knees. Never once did he take his eyes off me, either.

I smiled, but it felt forced. In an attempt to ease the tension, I started to sign—it was second nature when I was around a deaf person—but I quickly realized nothing I could say would make any sense to a man without language.

Except maybe the basic human needs. I pulled open my desk drawer and held up a Snickers bar. Caleb blinked, then bent forward slightly. His body language was clear. He wanted that candy bar. I leaned closer and held the candy in midair, waiting until he tentatively reached forward. After a moment, he gently took the candy.

I held my fingertips at my mouth—the sign for "food."

Caleb, his eyes still on me, blinked those long lashes as he wolfed the candy. It was gone before I had lowered my hand.

"Drink?" I signed, holding an imaginary cup to my mouth.

He nodded, licking his lips, understanding the obvious gesture. I got up and retrieved a bottle of water from the minirefrigerator in the corner. He took it carefully, but once it was in his hand, he twisted open the cap and drank the entire bottle. This was the first time he had looked away from me.

I examined his appearance as he wiped his mouth with the back of his hand. His cuffs were dirty and there were smudges of dirt on his pant legs and flannel shirtsleeves.

"Drink," I signed again. Caleb stared at me.

I tried "food" again. Nothing. I repeated the sign.

Caleb took his eyes off me long enough to quickly glance at my desk drawer.

Did he know what I meant?

"Food," I signed again, after handing over another Snickers bar. Then I added the sign for "candy," by twisting my index fingertip into my cheek. I handed over one more—my last. The dark chocolate kind. My favorite. I don't share my stash with just anybody. I don't think Miah even knows about my little gold mine.

Caleb watched me as he chewed. I signed the word again, but he made no attempt to copy me. When he was finished, he sat staring at me, as if expecting me to say something more.

I gave him a questioning look.

He raised his hand slowly and gave the sign for "drink."

I grinned and nodded, hoping the positive reinforcement would be effective. I stood to retrieve another bottled water, but Caleb rose and beat me to the refrigerator, helping himself. He returned to his chair and drank the contents down in seconds.

The man was thirsty. Not to mention hungry. I thought about taking him over to the Nugget for a meal, but he was technically an escaped murder suspect.

And I was technically aiding and abetting.

Caleb wiped the moisture from his lips and set the bottle down on Miah's desk. We stared at each other for a few minutes, not quite knowing where to go next. I tried a few basic, concrete signs—"mother," "home," "deaf,"— but Caleb showed no recognition. When I repeated the signs, and tried to act them out, he began to mimic me. This time I could tell there was no connection of the concept to the sign.

I pulled out some blank paper and set it on Miah's desk.

"Paper," I signed, brushing my palms together, then pointing to the white sheet.

"Paper," he aped awkwardly, blankly nodding his head.

"Pencil." I made the gesture of licking a pencil tip and writing on my hand. He copied my movements, again nodding up and down.

I set the pencil next to the paper and Caleb reached for it.

Pressing his hand down so he couldn't lift the pencil, I shook my head. He pulled back, looking confused.

I paused, meeting his intense gaze, then signed "paper." Nothing.

"Paper," I repeated and pointed to the paper.

Caleb reached for the pencil.

"Pencil," I signed, taking the object from his hand and setting it back down on the desk. I signed "pencil" again and pointed to the pencil, then signed "paper" and pointed to the paper.

Caleb sat still, watching my every move.

Once again I made the sign for "paper."

Without taking his eyes off mine, he slowly reached over and set his palm down on the paper.

"Yes! Paper!" I signed, grinning.

Caleb smiled slightly, still looking a little confused but seeming to know he'd done something he was supposed to.

After a moment I signed, "pencil."

This time Caleb glanced at the two items on the desk. He lifted his hand from the paper and placed it on the pencil.

"Yes! Yes! Pencil!" I screamed with my hands, feeling like Annie Sullivan in *The Miracle Worker*.

Caleb repeated my signs. "Yes. Yes. Pencil."

Then he picked up the pencil and began to draw.

I watched, mesmerized by Caleb's complete immersion into his two-dimensional world, where pictures became language.

He was drawing the figure of a man.

I instantly recognized his style from his earlier drawings. It wasn't the classic stick figure, but the childlike balloon head with a teardrop body, spindly arms and legs jutting from the trunk. As Caleb sketched in the details of the face—the eyes, the nose, the mouth, the hair—one feature was absent.

The figure had no ears. But this time there was a mouth.

The drawing was primitive and I couldn't tell if it was male or female. I pointed to the figure to catch his attention, then drew my index finger to my mouth, making a circle around my lips, the sign for "who?" All I got back was a blank stare.

Caleb returned to the paper, this time drawing the large circle around the figure, with jagged teeth on top and bottom, as if the figure had been swallowed by a huge shark head. Inside he added another figure, lying prone on the floor. The eyes were closed, the mouth was a stiff short line on the face, but this figure had ears. I glanced up at Caleb, trying to read his mind as he drew, and noticed the tears in his eyes.

What was he trying to tell me?

Caleb had just added a square in one corner of the shark's mouth when suddenly he stopped, his pencil frozen in midair. He had felt what I had felt—something heavy had shaken the floorboards under our feet. I turned to the door to see the knob twist. The door flung open.

Miah stood in the doorway, a hefty bundle of comic books at his feet. He looked startled to see the large disheveled man at my desk.

Before I could sign anything to Miah, Caleb fled the room.

"Sorry. Didn't mean to scare him," Miah signed. I explained what had happened and showed him the drawing. "What's that supposed to be?"

"Good question," I signed back, frustrated at the interruption, frustrated at the cryptic drawing, frustrated at how things were not coming together. "Where have you been? Comic book trading?"

Miah nodded. "Stopped off at my dad's first. He had some news about Esken's death he wanted me to tell you."

I was lucky the sheriff loved seeing his name in print. Otherwise I might not get half the information I did. I stared at Miah expectantly, waiting for him to go on.

"Dad said the M.E. doesn't think Esken deliberately overdosed."

"Why does he say that?"

"Esken was right-handed. The injection was made into the right arm—not something a right-handed person would do. Dad had thought maybe he committed suicide, you know, because of his financial problems and stuff, but now he thinks—"

I cut him off and made the sign for "murder" by twisting an imaginary knife into the air. "Does he really think so? I mean—"

This time he cut me off. "There's more."

"What?"

"Someone sent Dad a copy of a birth certificate. Slipped it into the mail slot . . ." He tried to finger-spell "anonymously" and gave up.

"Whose birth certificate?"

"Devon Bodie's."

I gave my hand a "wow" shake. "What did it say?"

"It was a photocopy. Said she weighed nine pounds, eleven ounces when she was born. But the health form attached said she was two months premature."

"Health form?" I sat back, slowly taking it all in. As I had suspected, someone had falsified information on her birth certificate. But why? By the time Devon was born, being pregnant before getting married wasn't such a disgrace.

"That's not all . . ."

I slammed my left hand down on the desk and signed with the right.

"God, Miah! Would you give it to me? You're driving me crazy with this episode stuff! What else?"

"There was no evidence of an Rh blood-type incompatibility on the health record."

Late in the afternoon, I left Miah in charge of the office while I ran a few errands.

My first stop was the mortuary, where I found Del Rey Montez hunched over her embalming table, cutting open something pale and puffy, that oozed red stuff.

"That's not on your diet, is it?" I pointed to the raspberry pastry. "And how can you eat that in here?"

"You get used to it. This is the only place I can eat

where no one will nag me about my diet. Except you, of course."

I pulled up a stool and picked some raspberry off the top of the dessert roll. "Seen any good bodies lately?"

"Saw one last night. On a book jacket. It belonged to Fabio. Now *that's* what I call a body."

"I meant dead ones, not prefabricated, oiled, and buffed."

"You mean like Esken's?"

I popped another bite of her sweet roll into my mouth and nodded.

"It's coming over this afternoon. Want to assist in the embalming? You seem to have an unusual interest in bodies lately."

"Thanks, but no. I think I'll go embalm my own with a couple of bottles of Sierra Nevada while you do your magic. It's just not natural the way you turn what should be mulch into the Living Dead. Easy on the rouge with him, will you?"

I left Del Rey to finish what I'd left of her pastry and headed for the Nugget. It was time for a cold beer and a quiet break.

Dan was sitting in a booth reading one of Harlan Coben's sports mysteries when I slid into the seat across from him.

"Hey," he said, turning the book over on the table. He took a swig of his beer and set it down, absently fondling the neck of the bottle, as was his habit. I found it disconcerting. "Missed you. You must be keeping busy."

"You, too," I said, then signaled Jilda for a beer. She read my sign language fluently and within minutes I had an ice-cold Pale Ale in front of me.

"Actually, I found out a few things that might help you with Sparkle Bodie's death."

"Oh, yeah? What?"

"I've been doing some research at the library."

I was puzzled. I'd thought Dan had forgotten about me these past few days, distracted by the drama of his ex-wife's appearance. I waited for him to go on, trying not to seem overly eager to hear his news. After all, it wasn't his research I really wanted.

"Anyway, I was at the Library last night, having a beer and—"

"The bar? I thought you meant the real library! So that's what you call research?" We Skunkers often get the Library, a popular new bar, and the library, Aubrey's haunt, mixed up when someone refers to one or the other.

"Wait a minute! First I went to the bar, and I got to talking to this guy. He was all dressed up in his Clamper uniform and telling me I should join up. He started talking about all the good things the Clampers do, like collect toys for Christmas, donate wheelchairs—"

" 'Protect widders and orphans,' " I finished his sentence. I knew all about the Clampers, their good deeds and fun-loving mottoes.

"Well, that, too, but he was telling me about all these plaques they put up to commemorate historical buildings and famous people and big events in the Mother Lode."

"Yeah, I know."

"Okay, but what you might not know is how well these guys keep records. He told me they've got names, dates, and places written down that go back to the mid-1800s, when the organization was first formed."

"Where are those so-called records?"

"At the library."

"The bar?"

"No, the real library. Aubrey showed me the whole collection."

I took a long pull from my beer and finished it. I debated about having another but couldn't catch Jilda's eye so I turned back to Dan.

"Well, that's fascinating, and I'm sure all the wild parties and pointless parades they've held make compelling reading, but what has this got to do with Sparkle Bodie?"

"In one of the record books there was an excerpt about a mine that turned out to be a major gold stake. It was discovered by a man named Bennegar Jacks."

"The great-grandfather of Russell Jacks. Did it say what happened to the mine?"

"No. But something happened to Bennegar Jacks. He was shot and killed."

"I know. And his murderer was never caught."

I wondered if the record book had explained what had happened to the claim. Dan seemed to read my mind, an irritating habit he was getting good at.

"Sparkle's grandfather-by-marriage, Evan Lee Bodie, eventually claimed the property. Although, how he did it isn't exactly made clear."

"Hmmm. So Bodie got the mine, made a fortune from it, and left it all to his grandson—and Sparkle." If all this was true, Russell must know it.

"Have you got a copy of this information?"

Dan nodded. "Aubrey let me make photocopies."

"Did you ask him if he knew anything about all this?"

"Aubrey said the Jacks family had a bunch of other mines and Russell had inherited one himself."

"Yeah, the one he keeps wanting to turn into a tourist attraction."

"The Bodie family took in Mrs. Jacks and her kids after Bennegar Jacks was killed. The Jacks were grateful for their care, but the old Jacks mine eventually produced a lot of gold for the Bodie family."

"I wonder—"

At that moment, the door to the Nugget Café burst open, and Deputy Marca Clemens entered, once more reminding me of that interview I'd postponed. Instead of taking a seat, she stood with her legs apart, and her hand on her gunbelt, commanding instant attention.

"Don't anybody eat or drink anything! If anyone is feeling sick, you should go to the hospital immediately. Mama Cody, I need to talk with you and Jilda about what you served one of your customers a little while ago."

"Why, what's happened?" Jilda asked, the pot of coffee in her hand shaking as she spoke.

"Aubrey Horne is in the hospital. Sheriff thinks he may have been poisoned."

I spat out my mouthful of beer.

"Connor!" Dan shook his wet hand like a rain-soaked dog. "Jesus! The beer isn't poisoned. It was in a bottle!"

"Sorry," I said.

Dan wiped the residue on the front of his shirt while I jumped up to question Deputy Clemens.

"What happened? Is Aubrey all right? Can I—"

Deputy Clemens held a hand up to shush me. "I have no comment to make at this time. You'll have to wait until Sheriff Mercer—"

I have no idea what she said after that. I was outta there.

I made a quick stop at the sheriff's office and managed to get a few more details from the dispatcher, Rebecca Matthews. She told me Aubrey was at the Mother Lode Memorial Hospital in Whiskey Slide. She didn't have much else except that Sheriff Mercer had gone there, too.

I hate the smell of hospitals. Spent too much time in

them as a kid, trying to get my ears "fixed." My parents tried several operations and "new" techniques for me, but nothing worked. If they'd had cochlear implants back then—those new gizmos doctors stick in your head to help deaf people with nerve damage—I'm sure I would be sporting one now, whether it did me any good or not. My parents meant well, but I wish they'd accepted my deafness a little sooner than they had.

I found Sheriff Mercer outside Aubrey's room. He stood talking with a thin, dark-haired doctor, looking very intense, his eyebrows nearly connected in the middle of his scowling face. I held back and tried to read the sheriff's lips. I couldn't see the doctor's mouth from my vantage point.

"When will you know—"the sheriff began. I missed the rest when he brushed his mouth with his hand. I caught a few more words—". . . pumped his stomach . . . Nugget Café . . . coffee . . . poison . . ."—but gave up when I read something that looked like "Rush Limbaugh is a big fat idiot." He really needed to learn to keep his hands off his face.

While I waited for Sheriff Mercer to finish with the doctor, I thought about who had been at the café while I was there. Aubrey had already left by the time I'd arrived, so I hadn't had the opportunity to see who he might have interacted with. But I remembered seeing Sonora and Devon leaving with a doggie bag as I entered. Russell had come in and sat at the counter, then talked on his cell phone. Even Holly Bryson had been there with her daughter, Twaina.

The only one missing from the lineup was Caleb.

"Hey, C.W., what took you so long?" It was Sheriff Mercer, startling me from my "Most Wanted" daydream.

"Sheriff! What happened? Your deputy said Aubrey had been poisoned at the Nugget Café! Is he all right?"

The sheriff waved me over to a worn leatherette seat and sat down. I perched at an angle to him so I could read his lips clearly.

"Listen, C.W., I didn't say he was poisoned. I said he might have been poisoned. There's a big difference. He might'a just had some bad meat loaf. But none of this goes into your newspaper yet. Not until we know for sure what happened. And we won't know that until Tox comes back with results of the pump."

"They pumped his stomach?" I massaged my own sympathetically.

Sheriff Mercer nodded. "Doc Garcia pumped him. Seems Aubrey doubled over in the library a few minutes after he returned from his coffee break. There were two kids in there when it happened—that was lucky, or he might not have made it. Brian Hurley made the call, while Matt Warner tried to do CPR on him."

"Smart kids."

"Yeah, Aubrey was pretty bad off. Kids said he was breathing funny, looked like a ghost. When I got there, he was in respiratory distress, so I took over until the EMTs arrived a few minutes later. They bagged him and gave him an IV, then drove like a bat out of hell to the hospital. We were right behind them, Code three."

"You took the boys with you?"

"They wanted to go, and after all, they practically saved his life. I figured they'd enjoy the ride, all those sirens and lights. Woke up the town, I'll tell ya. You could hear them clear across—" He stopped and looked at me. "Anyways, Doc took over when we got there. Now they're checking the contents. I should hear something soon." He patted his cell phone.

"You really think he was poisoned?"

"Don't know for sure. Marca's over at the Nugget looking for his coffee cup, talking to anyone who might have noticed anything out of the ordinary. Aubrey said something that sounded significant to the boys just before he collapsed."

"What was that?"

"He said '. . . in the drink . . .' and then he keeled over."

"Any idea what it could have been?"

"No telling, until the crit comes back from Tox. Arsenic is a local favorite, what with the gold refuse all over the place. But it could have been anything."

I thought about Sparkle Bodie and the collection of medications that had ravaged her weak body.

"But why would someone try to poison Aubrey?"

"Now that's the real question, isn't it?"

"Can I see him?" I asked Dr. Doreen Garcia, while the sheriff was occupied with Deputy Clemens, who had arrived moments ago. The two of them had gone off in a corner for a private discussion. Naturally I was excluded, so I took the opportunity to try to visit Aubrey.

"Who are you?" Dr. Garcia asked as I approached Aubrey's door.

"I'm Connor, uh, Horne. Aubrey's sister."

She eyed me suspiciously, but after a moment's hesitation, nodded once. "All right. But keep it short. He's resting comfortably now and I don't want his blood pressure elevated."

I thanked the doctor and slowly pushed open the door. Inside sat a security guard from the hospital. They weren't taking any chances. Good thing. Look what had happened to Sparkle Bodie when she had been left alone in her hospital room.

"Aubrey?" I hoped I said it softly. His eyes opened and a small half-smile appeared on his face. Was it from pain— or was he happy to see me?

"Connor. Hi," I managed to make out. His lips barely moved.

"How are you feeling?" I stood over him and hesitantly touched his shoulder. I'm not good at comforting people, but I felt a need to express something. A shoulder touch seemed to do the trick.

He licked his lips and spoke slowly, breathing with difficulty. "Aside from a stomachache . . . a sore throat . . . a dry mouth . . . a headache . . . and a hangnail . . . I'm great. I guess you heard what happened."

"Not really." I tend to get more information when I pled ignorance. "Just that you collapsed at the library."

He spoke dreamily, pausing between breaths. "Yeah . . .

I remember talking to a couple of kids . . . about the old *Hardy Boys* series. All of a sudden my stomach started acting up . . . and I felt really light-headed . . . and then . . . I guess I just blacked out."

"It's a good thing Brian and Matt were there."

"Yeah . . . I owe them, big time. Guess I'll order those hint books to go with the *Magic* cards they're always playing with. They're addicted to that game."

"Well, I'm glad you're all right. Sheriff Mercer sent the deputy over to check things out at the Nugget. You said you drank some coffee there, and then became sick?"

"Yeah . . . I know Mama Cody isn't the best coffee-maker in the world . . . but this stuff really must have been poison."

"You don't think it might have just been old milk or something? That new espresso machine has really got Mama Cody confused."

"It's possible. But according to the doctor, I'm the only one who's gotten sick."

"Aubrey, do you remember anyone stopping by your table? Anyone who might have had the opportunity to put something in your coffee?"

"You know I've been racking my brains about that . . . but I can't think of anyone who might have done this on purpose. And no one sat with me . . . I was by myself."

"You didn't leave the table?"

"No, I—" Aubrey stopped, his eyes narrowed. "Wait a second, I guess I did leave . . . to use the restroom. But I was only gone a few minutes—"

Aubrey suddenly stopped talking and glanced behind me. I whirled around to see Sheriff Mercer and Deputy Clemens standing officially in the doorway.

"Hi, Sheriff. I was just—"

"C.W., what the hell are you doing in here? I said no visitors except family. I should'a known. What'd you do? Tell them you're his sister or something?"

I smiled and headed for the door. "I was just checking on him, Sheriff, to see if he needed anything. That's all."

Sheriff Mercer shook his head, while by-the-book

Deputy Clemens began listing the violations I was racking up. I pushed through the door without looking back to see if they were getting out the cuffs.

Dan was in his office when I arrived. When I peeked in, he seemed to be working furiously on something terribly engaging. He jumped when I said "Hi," and dropped the weekly *Eureka!* mystery puzzle.

"Solve it yet?" I noticed his scribbles around the edges of the puzzle. The answer hadn't been filled in.

"No. You didn't give enough clues. You left something out. I've been over it ten times and still can't figure out how the dentist died of laughing gas when there are no signs of a struggle. You goofed somewhere."

I smiled as if Sylvester had just swallowed Tweety. Dan was usually so smug about figuring out my mystery puzzles. This time I had him stumped.

"Want a hint?"

"No!"

I shrugged and sat on the corner of his desk.

He put down his pen. "So, what did you find out at the hospital?"

"How did you know I was at the hospital?"

"Gee, let me see. Deputy comes into Nugget Café. Says Aubrey was in the hospital due to possible poisoning. You disappear before she can say 'Nobody leave town.' Ergo—you're at the hospital."

"Ergo? Yeah, well, he's all right, in case you care. I think he drank a bad latte at the Nugget, then felt sick back at the library and keeled over."

"Somebody spike it?"

"Dunno, but he did leave the drink unattended for a few minutes when he went to the bathroom. Anyone could have doctored it."

"You don't think the Nugget coffee is enough to bring down the weaker members of the species?"

"I've always suspected it could, but I've never been able to prove it. Here's my chance, I guess."

My eye caught a light flash from the hallway, reflecting off the door's glass window.

"Oops. TTY. Gotta run."

I hopped off the desk and skidded into the hallway, made an abrupt turn by grabbing onto the doorjamb, and flung open my door. I grabbed the phone just as the flashing light went dark.

"Damn phone," I said out loud, then dropped my backpack on the floor next to my messy desk. On top of the pile lay the drawing Caleb had made before being frightened from the room. I picked it up and studied it.

The picture looked similar to the one he'd drawn two days ago, but there was something new I hadn't noticed before. Parallel lines ran along the front of the roughly sketched building, as if underscored twice for emphasis. What were those small perpendicular lines that intersected it every half inch or so? And what was the square that Caleb had drawn in the upper left-hand corner, covered with random lines as if made by a toddler holding a pencil for the first time?

This drawing was trying to tell me something, but I couldn't read it. I needed an interpreter.

"Dan," I said, stopping by his office on the way out. "Want to take a drive to Whiskey Slide? I've got to get an art appraisal. The place should still be open at this hour. And there's a man I want you to meet."

Dan's eyes narrowed. "You've got a man in Whiskey Slide? Who is he? I'll tear him limb from limb. I'll crush his—"

I tried to look serious. "Are you coming or not?"

Dan unhooked his jacket from the back of the chair, and glanced around a last time as if looking for something. He found it—a note of some kind, which he stuffed into his pocket—then he followed me out the door.

The Silence Is Golden Deaf Club door was open when we arrived. Dan hadn't said much during the drive, which was better for me since it's not easy to read him while I try to watch the road. But he looked puzzled when we pulled up to the building.

Lindan Barde had his back to us at the counter, busily typing away on the office TTY. Dan leaned in trying to read the glowing letters over Lindan's shoulder, but I pulled him back and shook my head. It is rude to read other people's phone calls unless invited.

Lindan noticed us and waved. While we waited, Dan checked out all the gadgets for the deaf that were displayed on the opposite wall. Before I could stop him, he had three door lights flashing, two vibrator alarms jumping, and a captioned film running in the VCR. It was like taking a two-year-old to a toy store.

I had everything under control by the time Lindan hung up the phone.

"Connor! Good to see you! How are you?" Lindan signed in ASL.

"Fine, fine. Busy." I realized I wasn't speaking and filled in with a voice interpretation, switching to Signed English. "I'd like you to meet my friend—"

Dan raised a hand. The sudden movement drew my attention. With a quick glance at me, he turned to Lindan Barde and finger-spelled the letters, "D-A-N-S-M-I-T-H."

Stunned, my open mouth finally shut to a smile. When had Dan learned to finger-spell?!

When I'd composed myself, I spoke and signed, "Dan, this is Lindan Barde."

They shook hands, then Lindan invited us over to the recreation area to sit down. Lindan and I sat opposite each other, with Dan next to me. I pulled the drawing from my backpack and handed it to the deaf man.

I spoke and signed simultaneously. "That man I was telling you about, Caleb Bodie? He drew me this picture. It looks a lot like the other one, but he seems to have added something more. I wondered what you thought of it?"

Lindan held the picture close, then at a distance, studying it. He finger-spelled something to himself, then wiggled his fingers at his forehead, as if stimulating his mind. It was a common deaf gesture.

"It looks much like the other picture. But these lines don't look like the ground to me. They're parallel, with crossbars."

"What do you think they mean?"

He studied the picture another few minutes. "Could be railroad tracks."

Railroad tracks? I searched my mind for a connection. The only building I could think of that was linked to the tracks was the Flat Skunk Railroad Museum.

Had Caleb drawn a picture of the museum?

A better question: Why?

I don't like anyone else driving my '57 Chevy, but I let Dan drive it home so we could talk more easily. Twisting around in my seatbelt, I leaned against the dashboard so I could see his lips, and held the drawing.

"You really think there's something at the museum?" Dan asked.

"I think it's worth checking out. That square he drew up in the corner? Could be a box, or a paper or a sign or something. I'll bet those are the rafters with all that hay, and it looks like something is hidden underneath. He seems to enjoy hiding things."

Dan massaged the steering wheel with his hands. I think he was falling in love. With my car, of course. It wouldn't be the first time I'd lost a boyfriend to a car. But this time I was prepared to do battle.

"What are you thinking about?" Dan asked, when I hadn't said anything for several minutes.

I couldn't tell him what I'd been fantasizing about. I had to think fast. "I was wondering if the key to all this is in the genealogy chart that Aubrey was working on."

"What do you mean?"

"I mean. Aubrey must have found something in the family history. Something that the Bodies—or someone else—didn't want known."

"Like what?"

"I don't know. But if someone tried to poison Aubrey, it must have been important." I studied the picture in my hands. "Dan, what if Aubrey was using that information in some way?"

"You mean like blackmail?" Dan asked.

"It's possible. Maybe what he found out was just too tempting to ignore. Sparkle Bodie was rich. She was from the old school that keeps family secrets hidden—just look at the way she kept her son hidden away all these years."

"Maybe Aubrey was going to expose her in some way," Dan added.

I nodded. I wasn't terribly convinced of this new theory, but the feeling that Aubrey might know something meant to be kept secret was growing stronger. With Sparkle dead, and now Esken, the only Bodies left with secrets were Sonora and Devon. And they were the only two who could gain from Sparkle's death—unless there was a new will. Would they also gain something from Aubrey's death?

How did Caleb figure into all this?

I thought about the Bodie home, how it had nearly burned to the ground, leaving only a few odds and ends that didn't add up. What was the fire supposed to destroy?

"Dan, can we swing by the library before going to the museum? I want to check something."

Dan looked at his watch. "I've got an appointment in a few minutes to get those test results, but I guess we have time. The place is probably locked up, though. You won't be able to get in."

I smiled, humoring him. I wasn't going to let a lock stop me from breaking and entering. Briefly I wondered how the test results would come out, but I stuffed the thought away and tried to concentrate on the matter at hand.

Dan pulled up to the library and parked the Chevy. We both headed for the front door, which I found unlocked. I wasn't surprised, because of the panic situation in which Aubrey was discovered. People don't think about locking doors when they're rushing off to the hospital.

There were a couple of overturned *Hardy Boys* books on the floor next to the old-fashioned card catalog, but the rest of the library looked orderly—sorted, cataloged, and shelved.

"Check his desk, see if there's anything unusual in it," I told Dan, while I headed for the filing cabinet. I pulled open the drawer Aubrey had checked earlier, and rummaged through the files until the one I was looking for caught my eye.

Bodie. The missing file was here!

I pulled the file from the overstuffed drawer, thinking I'd have to tug, but it came easily. That's because there was nothing in it. No genealogy chart. No birth certificates. No references. Not even any notes.

Where were the guts of the file?

"Find anything?" I asked Dan.

"A dirty book. That's about all."

I watched him pocket a copy of Nancy Friday's *My Secret Garden*.

"Put that back!"

He replaced the book. "Jeez, Mom, you never let me have any fun."

I closed up the library on the way out, locking the door behind me. I turned to face Dan. He looked hesitant.

"I'm going over to the museum. Want to come?"

Dan checked his watch again. "You sure that's a good idea?"

"It's broad daylight. The museum is on the main street. I really don't think there's any danger, if that's what you mean."

He glanced at his watch again. "Connor, I'd love to join you on this Nancy Drew adventure, but I've got to go. Catch up with you at dinner?"

I started to touch his arm, then pulled back self-consciously. I still didn't know what was happening with him exactly, but I wasn't ready to let it go.

"All right. I'll fix something at my diner. Bring your best bottle of wine—one with a cork in it."

He leaned over and gave me a quick peck on the lips.

"You know, the museum is probably deserted . . ." I said coyly.

Dan grinned. "Boy, you're getting bold. Now you want to do it in the old train depot? Next you'll be wanting to do it in the cemetery, on the sheriff's desk, in the Nugget Café . . ."

I could feel the heat of a full-body flush. I tried to cover. "That's not what I meant. What I meant was . . . there's probably no one in there . . . and maybe it's not safe for me to go in alone. You know those horror movies where the girl wanders in by herself and never comes out again. I just thought . . ."

"I thought you said it was broad daylight." He grinned, seeing right through me.

"Oh, never mind! You're giving me a headache. I'll see you later. If I'm not at the diner, look for me at the sheriff's office. I'll be lying on his desk in a pink negligee."

He raised his index finger to his eye, then shot it toward me. Did he just sign "See you later"?

I headed for the Flat Skunk Railroad Museum.

The museum stood deserted, as I suspected. Aside from having been raised on cement blocks, the building reconstruction had not seen much progress. Architectural plans with curled edges were stuck to the distressed wood walls with pushpins, and the dirt floor had been smoothed, ready for a foundation pour. But it hardly looked like much of a future museum at this point.

The door stood slightly ajar. Nothing inside worth stealing yet. Construction workers probably came and went throughout the day, but it was now after five and I guessed they were off. I noticed a large pile of bricks stacked along one wall, each imprinted with a personalized inscription. It was one of the many ways Holly Bryson had devised to raise money for the museum: selling off bricks for a piece of immortality. I spotted Sheriff Mercer's name, Russell Jacks with his attorney logo, and Sparkle Bodie—hers etched in gold.

While I scanned the rest of the bricks looking for other familiar names, a wisp of hay tumbled down past my eyes. Looking up toward the rafters overhead, I got a sudden chill. I wondered if I was alone after all.

I backed up and located a ladder that was propped against the edge of the rafters. I was somewhat familiar with the building, having done a story on it when the renovations first began. Holly had asked for the article to help raise money. Now, carefully scanning the upstairs for movement, I waited several moments, and when nothing happened, headed slowly up the steps.

The hay was sparse over the rafters, and I had to be careful where I stepped. Every other board seemed to be loose, weak, or missing. I moved cautiously, heading for the corner indicated in Caleb's drawing. I could see the area from where I stood; the hay had been piled high at that spot.

I made my way over, testing every step before putting my full weight on each foot, and scanning the area for any movement. Surely animals couldn't climb to the top of this loft, could they? Well, squirrels. Maybe cats. And rats.

The pile was thick, as if the hay had been deliberately collected and stacked into a mound. I looked it over, then knelt down and began digging through, shuffling the coarse straw to either side as I felt my way into the heap. After several minutes of searching for a needle in a haystack, I found nothing. "Damn!"

I stood up, stepped back, and put my foot through a board.

"Ahhh!" I screamed, bracing myself on the remaining floorboards as my right leg shot through the opening. The rest of me collapsed to the floor. Reflexively I grabbed hold of a board, hoping the whole thing wouldn't give way. My left leg dangled in midair, and I could feel scrapes on either side, hot and fiery.

"Shit!"

Placing my arms flat on the boards, I hoisted myself up and gently withdrew my leg from the jagged-edged break. As soon as I was free, I scooted back and took a survey of the bodily damage. Funny thing about injuries. Two rituals seem to help: swearing, and examining the wound in detail. After that I could move on.

I stood slowly, favoring my left leg, and glanced down the hole to get a firm grasp on where I had been headed. As I peeked through the opening, I saw something white, surrounded by sprinkles of hay, lying directly beneath me. I hadn't noticed it before.

It looked like a sheet of paper.

Curious, I was about to head for the ladder when I stopped. And sniffed. A familiar smell. I inhaled deeply. It was the same distinct smell I had encountered only two days ago.

Smoke.

Smoke! Wafting up from a far corner of the loft!

Right next to where I'd climbed up.

The old place would probably burst into flames before I could even panic, I thought, standing frozen to the spot.

If I hurried I still had a chance to make it down the ladder before the flames engulfed the old building like a tinderbox. I managed to take two steps, then peered over the edge—and stopped.

No ladder.

"Shit! What's going on?" I said out loud. I could feel the beads of sweat on my forehead, down my back, even on my legs. Fear? Or heat from the nearing fire?

Being deaf, I've always had a fear of fires. Unlike hearing people, who can probably hear a fire coming as well as smell it, deaf people get no auditory warning. I'd often asked my parents what fire sounded like but they were never able to explain it to me. I imagined it was some kind of piercing scream, one of the few sounds I remembered from my childhood. It made sense that fire screamed.

I began to scream.

The flames shot up waist high in the corner, spreading fast. I glanced around, frantically looking for something to use to climb down. With the ladder gone, I saw nothing.

And the drop was at least fifteen feet.

If I fell the wrong way and broke something, I might not be able to get myself out of the building in time. Or I might be knocked unconscious.

I took short breaths, but the smoke burned my lungs and I felt my eyes water.

Fifteen feet looked like an abyss from where I stood, sweating from the heat of the growing flames.

"Jump!" I told myself. I glanced back and saw the flames taunt me. "Jump! You have no choice!"

I placed my toes on the edge of the loft. The smoke sent me into a coughing jag just as I about to take the plunge. For a moment, I wavered, almost losing my balance. As I stepped back to catch myself, I kicked some hay to the floor. Through blurry eyes I watched the tufts float lazily down, covering the paper that still lay on the ground.

Hay!

I raced for the pile I had been searching through only moments ago. Using a football player's tackling stance, with a fury ignited by adrenaline, I began shoving mounds of hay over the side to the floor.

I pushed and threw and shoved and swiped until I'd cleared out the area of most of the hay. Every few seconds I caught glimpses of the nearing, rising fire. The flames had grown taller. Intense heat prickled my sweat-covered body. Shooting sparks reminded me that there was no time for delay.

As I was about to shove one more armful of hay over the edge, the floor jerked beneath my feet. I spun around toward the fire. The upper foundation of the loft, only a few feet away, suddenly collapsed. The planks where I stood cracked from the strain, and began to bend downward.

It was as if the floor was trying to drag me toward the oncoming flames.

I had to jump.

Now.

I took a deep breath in preparation, and broke into another coughing jag. There was no time to think, no time to recover. Remembering what the guy had said when I'd tried bungee-jumping—"This is not a thinking sport"—I leaped into thick, gray air. The room had become so smoky, I couldn't see where I was heading—but I knew it was down. I just hoped there would be enough hay to cushion my fall.

I landed on my butt, right in the middle of the pile. I couldn't take a breath for a few seconds. Had smoke inhalation damaged my lungs? I began to panic, certain I would never breathe again, when the air came rushing back into my chest.

Thank God! I had just knocked the air out of my lungs when I hit the ground.

I felt around and moved a few body parts, but the hay had done its job. I didn't feel any broken bones. Hacking and wheezing, I stood up, ready to hurl myself out of the blazing barn. When I spotted the sheet of paper under my feet, I snatched it up and fled.

The fire trucks pulled up as I staggered onto the walk, gasping for air. When I turned back to survey the flames, the entire roof of the Flat Skunk Railroad Museum caved in where I'd been standing only seconds before.

"That's the second fire around here in less than a week," Sheriff Mercer said, as an EMT checked me over for damage. "And you were at both of them, C.W."

I gave an incredulous laugh, which turned into another coughing attack. When I could speak again, I managed to say, "What? Now you're accusing me . . . of being a firebug?" It hurt to talk.

"I'm not saying you're an arsonist, C.W., but my hunch

is these fires are related. And I have a sneaking suspicion you have some connection with all this. I just want to know what's going on."

"Well, so do I," I insisted. The EMT touched a sore spot and I winced. My arms and legs were bruised, scraped, and bloody.

Sheriff Mercer wandered away to talk to the fire chief, leaving me alone with the EMT, who had missed his calling as a butcher, the way he handled the meat. I told him I was fine, yes, yes, I'd go get checked, and waved him off to find some other injured victim to pulverize.

As the commotion died down, the townspeople gathered to point, rub their chins, and shake their heads. I sneaked off to my newspaper office to take stock, and avoid more questions I couldn't answer.

Passing Dan's office, I peeked in to see if he'd returned from the clinic. Sitting in his chair with his boots propped up on the desk and his baseball cap over his face, he'd slept through the whole thing. He probably hadn't been sleeping all that well lately.

I pulled the door closed slowly—no point in waking him now—and went to my own office. My eyes burned. I could feel them tearing up. After halfheartedly brushing off the debris of hay, dirt, and ash, I sat down at my desk, propped my sore elbows, and let the tears fall. I wanted someone to talk to, but I was too proud to let Dan know I needed him. It was easier crying alone.

When I thought I'd lost enough bodily fluid, I wiped my face with some paper towels I kept in a drawer, avoiding the mirror. It even hurt to cry, but it also felt good. I longed to go home and let Casper lick me back to health.

Reaching into my pocket for tissue to blow my nose, I pulled out the sheet of paper. The paper I'd snatched from the burning building.

Unfolding it, I recognized it immediately. It was a page from the Bodie genealogy chart.

I read it over quickly, scanning for some kind of significant information. It must have contained something important, otherwise why would it have been hidden in the museum? But there didn't appear to be anything relevant to the deaths of Sparkle and Esken Bodie. I read it a second time, then a third.

And then I saw what had been obscured by the plethora of family details. Misdirection at its best. A note had been written in pencil—on the back of the paper. I recognized Aubrey's handwriting. It said simply:

"Blood Type?"

I swung by my remodeled diner/home and got cleaned up, fed Casper an extra helping of dog food parmigiano and checked for messages. Nothing. I headed out for the mortuary, this time my dog at my side. I wasn't quite ready to let go of my security blanket and she could use the exercise.

Casper stayed dutifully outside, while I hunted for Del Rey. I found her just leaving the embalming room, and felt temporarily relieved I wouldn't have to go after her. But Del Rey, who takes great pride in her work, insisted on showing me Esken Bodie. She dragged me, whining and grimacing, if not kicking and screaming, into the room. The embalming process had been completed, and Esken lay resting for the upcoming services.

I mumbled something like, "He looks ready for the wax museum," before fleeing for the front room.

Del Rey followed me, then headed for the small refrigerator and pulled out a Shasta Vanilla Cream and a grape soda. I took the grape.

"Del Rey, did you notice anything unusual this time?" I said, checking for a purple mustache in the reflection of a smoky-mirror-tiled wall.

"Sorry, Con. He looked normal to me. As normal as the dead can look, that is."

"Nothing at all?"

"Well, aside from the needle marks, a few bruises on his arms, and an old appendix scar, nothing."

Del Rey pulled out his file and flipped open the chart. "Arthurlene Jackson did a thorough job, as usual. See, every little needle prick is accounted for. The dosage of insulin, what he had for breakfast—even his appendix scar is included."

"Could I see the chart?"

Del Rey hesitated. "I don't know. No one's ever asked to see a chart before. There's probably something unethical about it."

I rolled my eyes and held out my hand. She handed it over. I skimmed the information, turning the pages that listed the results of the autopsy and Esken's most recent medical history.

I stopped abruptly at his blood type. It was type O. Negative.

"Is this blood type correct?"

Del Rey shrugged. "Should be. Why?"

"It says here, type O negative."

"Yeah, so what? Some of us are negative, some of us are positive."

I nodded. "But his daughter is Rh positive."

Del Rey blinked. "That can't be," she said simply.

"Not if she was an Rh baby. She would have had to have a negative mother and a positive father. But if this is really his blood type, and Devon is Rh positive, that means . . ."

Del Rey smiled. "Uh-oh."

Sonora answered my knock after I'd repeated it several times. The door to her home opened a foot.

"Yes?"

"May I come in?" I asked, fully aware that Sonora's body language, as well as her door language, were not inviting.

Sonora looked at me for a moment, then listlessly pulled open the door. I moved past her, into the living area where the boxes from Sparkle Bodie's—the ones that had missed the fire—were now stacked. Some of the nicer knick-knacks sat on tables, counters, and the mantelpiece; the rest remained in the opened cartons.

Sonora stood watching me in her gilded sweats, her hair bound loosely behind her with a red scrunchy. She wore full makeup, but it had faded and smeared with the day. She sat on a needlepoint-embroidered otto-man; I pulled up a nearby chair so I could see her face clearly.

"What can I do for you, Connor? I don't have much time today. As you can see, I'm pretty busy." Her hand swept the room.

"Then I'll get to point. Sonora, were you pregnant be-fore you got married?"

Sonora's mouth dropped open. It took her a few sec-onds to make it work again. "I beg your pardon. I don't think—"

"I'm not trying to pry into your personal secrets, be-lieve me. I'm just trying to find out what happened to your mother-in-law and your husband. I should think you'd want that, too."

"I do, but—"

I kept talking. It was kind of a Muhammed Ali trick. Keep moving and confuse your opponent, then hit them with your best punch.

"I found a missing page from the genealogy chart that gave some information about your daughter. I think there may be a connection between what I found and the two deaths."

Sonora's face reddened. "What are you talking about?"

"Devon. I think she may be the key to all this. She wasn't born prematurely, was she? She was full term. But you lied about it, and changed the information on her birth records. Why?"

"I don't know what you're talking about. I think you'd better—"

"Devon wasn't Esken's daughter, was she, Sonora?"

Sonora seemed to have lockjaw again. I pressed on.

"And someone found out about that."

Sonora finally shut her gaping mouth. I could almost see her brain searching for something logical to say, but no words came.

I waited a few more moments, then asked more gently, "Sonora, were you being blackmailed?" It wouldn't be the first time in Flat Skunk a woman was blackmailed.

Sonora tensed and her eyes narrowed. The body language was clear. I had hit a nerve.

"You've got to tell Sheriff Mercer, Sonora. He can help you. If you—"

"You have no idea what you're talking about, Connor. No idea at all. And I certainly wasn't being blackmailed." She forced a laugh.

"No? Then what was all this secret stuff about Devon's birth?"

Sonora shook her head. "It's none of your business."

"Then I'll just have to print what I know in my newspaper, and see if anyone else can help me—"

"No!" Sonora looked horrified. The color had drained from her face. "No, please. If . . . if I tell you, will you leave it alone? Will you stop all this snooping into my affairs? No one has done anything criminal. Embarrassing maybe, but not illegal. It's not something I'm proud of. But it doesn't concern anyone else. Will you please let it go, once you've heard the truth?"

I paused. "I will, if I feel it has nothing to do with the death of Sparkle and Esken. Agreed?"

It was her turn to hesitate. She didn't trust me any more than I trusted her. "Agreed. And nothing in the newspaper."

I nodded, remembering the loophole I'd just stated a moment ago.

"All right. But you have to understand, this happened a long time ago, when things were . . . different. Especially for the people involved. People who live in a small town abhor a scandal of any kind."

I nodded.

"Yes, I was pregnant before I married Esken."

I thought about how times had changed for so many

social issues. Sonora had been pregnant out of wedlock; not something you talked about in those days. In fact, it was much the same as having a disability back then. Not exactly something to be proud of, when your child was deaf. Both of these social issues had come out of the closet, so to speak.

Sonora went on. "I realize it's no big deal now. But seventeen years ago, it wasn't accepted. Especially in a small town like Flat Skunk."

Looking worn, she continued.

"But there were further complications. You're right. Esken was not the father."

I shrugged. "So? It's not that uncommon. Apparently Esken loved you enough to marry you even though you were pregnant with someone else's child. Did he know who the real father was?"

I knew I was pushing it, but I needed to know who that man was, in order to solve this Rh blood factor issue. Sonora naturally looked reluctant to go on.

"Not . . . exactly. I was . . . raped."

I was shocked. I hadn't suspected anything like this. Suddenly I felt a wave of empathy for Sonora, having to carry that secret for all these years.

"My God. I'm so sorry." I couldn't stop myself. "Who . . . was it?"

She said nothing. Maybe she didn't know. But she had to have known! She knew the father was Rh positive and that Devon needed the RhoGAM treatment.

"You did know, didn't you?"

She nodded.

I waited, breathlessly. Was it someone I knew?

"Sonora, can you tell me who it was? It may be important."

Sonora spoke distantly, as if she had memorized the words, and told them too many times.

"I grew up here, you know. Went to the local high school, worked at the movie theater over in Whiskey Slide. One night, late, when I got off work, I headed home, as usual. But when I got to the door, I could hear my parents inside, screaming at each other, also as usual. My dad was drunk again, and my mother was taking another beating. Most of the time I just sneaked into my room, closed the door, and turned on music so I couldn't hear anything. But this time, for some reason, I couldn't stand it. So I turned around and walked away. I just had to get away from the noise."

I watched her eyes for signs of emotion, but they were dead.

"I'm sorry about your parents. That must have been awful."

She waved a hand. "Mostly I was used to it. As used to it as you can be as a kid. But I still hated being around them. Anyway, on that night I walked into the hills behind our house, so I could be alone and think. I thought it was safe. Nothing much ever happened back then, except the occasional DUI or wife-beating. I remember there was a full moon. It was light enough to see, so I just kept walking, not much caring where I was going."

Sonora stood up, got a cigarette from the mantel, lit it, and inhaled deeply. Then she continued speaking with bits of smoke illustrating her words. I had never seen her smoke before.

"I must have walked a long time, out by the old mines. It was a favorite place for us kids back then. We used to get drunk and make out and play music. Suddenly this guy seemed to come right out of the bushes. Before I could think, he grabbed me, and held me down . . . and . . . raped me."

"Oh, God."

Sonora nodded, still emotionless. "I didn't know what to do. We didn't have rape counseling back then. In fact, they used to blame the victim in those days. I was so terrified. I tried to forget about it, but a couple of weeks later I started feeling nauseated, and didn't have a period. I knew I was pregnant."

"Did you tell your parents?"

She took another drag off her cigarette, exhaling before she continued. "I couldn't tell my parents. They would have killed me—I truly believe that. Instead, I went to the guy's mother and told her."

I sat back, surprised. "Wow. So you did know the guy. It must have taken a lot of courage to tell his mother."

"You bet it did. But at the time, I didn't know what else to do. I thought maybe she'd call me a liar or a slut, kick me out of their house, maybe even tell my parents. But she didn't. She calmed me down, took control, and arranged everything."

"What do you mean, arranged everything?"

"She insisted I marry her son."

"My God!"

"I was horrified at first, too. But then she explained it all to me and it made sense. If I was married, it would suppress the scandal. It would keep the baby in the family, which was very important to her because she didn't have any other grandchildren. And my baby and I would be taken care of for the rest of our lives."

"But to marry a rapist! I could never—"

"Neither could I."

"But you said—"

"That's not what she meant. She wanted me to marry her other son."

"What?" I was getting more confused by the moment.

"The man who raped me . . . his mother claimed he didn't know what he was doing."

"What do you mean?"

"She said he was retarded."

Oh, my God. She was talking about Caleb Bodie.

She must have seen the look of recognition in my eyes. "Yes. Caleb. Sparkle convinced Esken to marry me, by offering him a huge sum of money and by holding his inheritance over his head. Naturally, being weak and money-hungry, Esken took it, figuring we could get divorced later on."

"Whoa. So Devon Bodie is actually Caleb's child, not Esken's. And that's where the Rh blood factor comes in."

Sonora stood. I followed suit.

"You said you'd keep this between us. I don't want

Devon hurt. She doesn't know any of this, and I don't want her to. You've got to understand, I love my daughter very much."

I nodded. Sonora walked over to the front door and opened it. I picked up my backpack and left the house, only pausing for a second to glance back. The door had already shut behind me.

After dropping off Casper, I drove back to town, trying to imagine what it must have been like for Sonora, marrying the brother of the man who raped her. The thought gave me a chill, not only because the idea seemed so incestuous, but also because I had spent time with a supposed rapist.

And that was another problem. After meeting him, I just couldn't see Caleb doing such a thing. He had been so gentle, so tentative, at my office. Yes, he had a temper. But wasn't that due more to frustration than rage? For him to assault Sonora just didn't ring true.

Still, there were some out there who did just that. Wasn't Ted Bundy supposed to have been such a nice guy—when he wasn't raping and murdering women? At least Ted Bundy could defend himself in court. He was brilliant. Caleb didn't have the communication skills to defend himself, nor had he shown that he had the cognitive skills to outwit so many people.

Caleb was an easy target.

I pulled up to my office, parked the Chevy in front, and crossed the street, heading straight for the Nugget. I needed a caffeine jolt to clear my mind. A makeshift mocha would do the trick. Or was I stalling about returning to my office again—worried I might find Caleb waiting for me?

The place was packed. Nothing like the scene of an attempted poisoning to bring in the customers. Once again, I found Devon nestled in one of the booths, sipping Nugget-brewed coffee. If the stuff didn't kill her, it would no doubt put her in labor, it was that potent. I slid into the booth next to hers and watched her stare into her mug, as if mesmerized by the curling steam.

I signaled Jilda for a coffee and hot chocolate. The ingredients for my do-it-yourself mocha appeared moments later.

"Where's Jean-Philipe?" I asked her, after realizing the Frenchman hadn't been around for a couple of days.

"He quit. He and Mama Cody didn't get along."

I nodded, not surprised. It was a wonder Jilda put up with the woman. I guessed I'd be making my own mochas again for awhile, until someone learned how to use the new espresso machine properly. Right now it sported a "Nugget Café" hat, hung on one of the two handles.

After an initial sip of coffee I tried to catch Devon's eye, but she still sat gazing into her drink. I thought about blowing a straw wrapper at her when I realized she was breathing funny. She almost appeared in a trance.

The sharp rhythmic breaths seemed to require her full concentration. I watched a few more seconds, fascinated, until at last she took a long, shuddering breath. Her entire body seemed to sink into the leatherette seat as her muscles relaxed.

"Devon?" I called out. She looked up. Mocha in hand, I slid out of my booth and into hers. "Are you okay?"

She rubbed her tummy underneath the rim of the table, grimacing. "Yeah, just a little contraction. I get them all the time now."

I pulled back. Contractions? Already? Was that normal? "Have you seen your doctor?"

"Yeah. They said it'd be a few more weeks. No biggie. I just—"

She stopped, midsentence, and caught her breath. The hand on her abdomen began to move in a circle double-time. Again her breaths came in short, staccato puffs. It had been less than a minute since the last contraction.

"Is there anything I—"

She waved me quiet. I sat there, breathing short, staccato breaths right along with her, until I felt dizzy and had to stop before I hyperventilated. I hoped I wouldn't faint right there in the middle of the Nugget Café. They'd probably drag me off to the hospital and pump my stomach, thinking I was another victim of the questionable coffee.

I tensed. Was that it? Could Devon be another victim of poisoning? After what seemed hours but was probably only another minute, she again took a slow, deep breath and relaxed.

"Another one?"

She nodded. Beads of sweat on her forehead sparkled through her maroon bangs.

"Maybe I should call someone? Your mother?"

"No!" She spoke sharply, then softened. "No, it's nothing. Please, just—"

She suddenly doubled up over the table.

I jumped up and yelled to Jilda. "Call an ambulance! I think it's labor. Hurry!" I moved beside Devon and tried to massage her back, not knowing what else to do. She seemed to wince in pain at my touch, so I withdrew my hands. She sat in the booth, clutching her belly and rocking back and forth. I couldn't make out her words.

"Hurry!" I called to Jilda again. The rest of the patrons in the café sat frozen in their seats, apparently waiting to see what would happen next. Nobody drank anything, I noticed. I felt helpless standing over Devon, seeing her wracked with pain.

I suddenly remembered a story I had done for the *Chronicle* on a woman in labor. She had taken Lamaze classes and it had helped her with the pain. Quickly, I took Devon's face in my hands and spoke directly at her.

"Devon, breathe! Breathe with me! Come on!"

I started in with the short breaths, puffing in her face.

She tried to focus on my mouth but her eyes kept darting in circles.

"Breathe!" I said, taking in sharper, faster breaths, as if I were breathing for her. "In, out, in, out." I blew the mouthfuls at her, and watched her bangs fly in rhythm to the breaths.

Through gritted teeth, she began to follow my lead. Tiny breaths that looked like hiccups escaped from her bouncing head as she tried to concentrate on my mouth. She licked her lips and kept it going, rubbing her abdomen until I thought she'd get skin burns.

"It's coming . . . it's coming . . . it's coming . . ." I think is what she said between puffs. I didn't want to know what she meant.

"Devon, breeeaaatheeee . . ."

I didn't see the EMTs behind me until they shoved me out of the way.

What I thought the nurse said, when I took Devon's hand as she rode into the labor ward on the gurney, was "You want a Coke?"

I thought a drink sounded good, albeit an odd offer at a time like that, but what the hell. I was thirsty from all that breathing. I said yes.

Next thing I knew, they slapped some plus-sized green cotton pajamas on me, tied a mask around my face, and shoved me into the delivery room.

Apparently what she had really said was, "You want to coach?" As in, be the labor coach.

The answer to that would have been: No!

But it was too late. One nurse sat me down on a stool near Devon's head, while another adjusted the gadgets in the delivery room. The mirror was angled so the mother-to-be could see all the gory details in living color. The delivery bed was cranked into something akin to a La-Z-Boy Recliner. And the doctor was prepped for a very fast delivery.

Most of it was a blur of busy hands, gushing fluids, and

scary-looking instruments. Everything but the screaming was over in less than five minutes.

I stopped screaming after a nurse waved the universal sign for "calm down." I couldn't read anyone's lips with all those masks—except Devon's. Her expression was clear. But instead of asking, "Is it a girl or a boy?" or "Does it have all its fingers and toes?" the first thing she asked was—

"Where's Russell?"

And she repeated it over and over again.

Russell Jacks? Why would she want to see him?

Surely he wasn't the father of her baby? I shuddered to think of the older man and the young girl together. But it happened all the time.

I glanced at the doctor, trying to read his eyebrows in case they had something important to say about the sex of the child or anything else. Even with the mask covering most of the face, I could read those eyebrows loud and clear. I glanced at the nurses for verification. They all looked the same.

Something was seriously wrong.

At that point, a nurse whisked me out of the room. I looked back just in time to see Devon receive a large injection.

"Connor! What's going on in there?"

Russell Jacks had miraculously appeared at the hospital. How had he known Devon was in labor? How does anyone know anything in a small town like Flat Skunk? It's in the air, right along with the scent of polecat.

"They gave her a shot of something."

"No, I mean the baby! Is the baby all right? One of the nurses came running out looking very upset. Tell me!"

Russell had grabbed my shoulders. The calm facade I was used to seeing had dropped away. This man looked panic-stricken.

"I don't know, Russell. No one would tell me anything. All I know is they wanted me out of there fast." I began peeling off the big pajamas, then yanked the funny hat from my head. I wadded the whole ensemble into a ball, looked around for a proper receptacle, then tucked it into my backpack.

"Shit!" Russell said, as he glanced behind me. I turned around. A couple holding hands had entered the waiting room. They appeared to be in their late thirties, early forties. They were looking hopefully at Russell.

Russell rolled his eyes. "Great. That's all I need."

He took a deep breath and headed over to greet the couple, once again assuming his usual air of confidence, warmth, and intelligence. I watched as he talked with them, unable to read their lips but clearly able to understand their reactions. The woman's once-smiling face twisted. Tears streamed down her cheeks. The man wrapped his arm tightly around his wife.

I had a feeling this was the adopting couple, and Russell, as their attorney, had the unfortunate job of relaying the possibility of bad news. Russell's back was to me, but I moved closer so I could read the couple's lips more clearly.

". . . and if there's something wrong . . . sure you can get us another one . . ."

I could see Russell nodding his head vigorously.

". . . how long . . . don't think I can wait another few weeks . . ."

More head nodding. Russell's arms reaching out to touch their arms.

". . . how can you guarantee us like that . . ."

Even more head nodding, hands now gripping their shoulders.

". . . how much more . . . used all our savings . . ."

At this point, Russell glanced around and caught me staring. He turned back to the grieving couple and slowly led them out of the room, and out of my prying eyes.

I sat down in the waiting room, wondering what exactly was going on. There was certainly nothing illegal about Russell's connection in all this. He was an attorney. He must be handling the adoption. It probably explained why Devon called for him after the delivery.

But something had gone wrong. Devon's baby didn't appear to be perfect. And this expectant couple didn't seem to want an unhealthy infant.

Was Russell offering some kind of alternative?

I stood up, wanting to ask a nurse about Devon, when Russell reappeared.

I turned to face him. "Russell, are you handling the adoption for Devon Bodie?"

"Connor, it's not polite to listen in on other people's conversations."

"I wasn't listening. Exactly."

"You'd make a great attorney." He started to move away. I held him by the arm.

"Russell, what happens if there's something wrong with Devon's baby? Does that mean the adoption is off?"

"Connor, I can't answer your questions. I have my client's confidentiality to protect. You know that."

"But that couple seemed to think another baby—"

"Connor, this is none of your business. What I do is not illegal. I provide a service for pregnant minors and childless couples. I think it's one of the most important and rewarding jobs a person can do. But I can't discuss it with you further—"

"Then you'll discuss it with me!"

It was Sonora. She had seemingly appeared out of nowhere. And she wasn't a happy grandmother.

Sonora!" Russell reached out both hands in sympathy.

Sonora ignored them, keeping her own arms folded tightly across her chest. Her eyes glistened with pain and anger. "What's wrong with the baby?"

Russell helplessly turned up both palms. "Listen, Sonora, I'm sure it's nothing—"

"You're the one who did this! You're responsible for my daughter's pregnancy. And you're the cause of whatever's wrong with her baby!" Sonora's face was distorted, making her difficult to read, but I caught most of it. Her finger punctured the air as she spoke.

A crowd gathered.

"Sonora?" The sheriff appeared beside her. He took her by the shoulder, but she wrenched free. He raised his hands in a gesture of surrender. "Calm down, now. Everything's going to be all right."

"All right?" She looked like an angry cat as she spoke. "All right? My teenage daughter, who should be out with her friends listening to music and doing her hair, has just given birth to her first baby at the age of seventeen! Now I hear there's something wrong with the baby and no one wants to talk about it. How can anything be all right? I want to see my daughter!"

I stood transfixed, watching the speakers like a spectator at a tennis match, trying to guess who would speak next. Multiple conversations were almost always impossible for me to follow. I caught up with Russell halfway through his sentence.

". . . your jeans."

Her jeans? I looked at her clothes. What did her pants have to do with this?

". . . dare you! I was . . . I was . . ." Sonora burst into tears. The sheriff led her over to a waiting-room chair and tried to calm her down. Russell left the room. I waved the curious crowd away, then joined a raging Sonora and an overwhelmed sheriff.

"He's contemptible! That man is . . . he's a blood-sucking parasite, living off other people's misery and greed." Sonora pulled a tissue from her purse and wiped her running nose.

All heads turned as Devon's doctor appeared at the door, his face expressionless. "Sheriff? Could I see you a moment?"

Sonora started to get up, but Sheriff Mercer gently settled her back down. "I'll handle this. C.W., stay with her."

I nodded, as Sonora sat back. When Sheriff Mercer left with the doctor, I turned to her, and placed my hand on her knee in comfort. The nubby silk fabric of her slacks felt rough beneath my fingertips.

The pants reminded me of the word "jeans."

"Are you all right? Can I get you a drink of water or something?"

Sonora shook her head and muttered something I didn't understand. I glanced down at her pants again. Jeans. Genes!

"Sonora, this afternoon, when we talked, you didn't tell me everything, did you?"

She said nothing. I wondered if she heard me. Maybe I was talking too softly.

"About . . . that night, I mean." Still she said nothing. "What really happened?"

She looked at me blankly.

"I don't know what you're talking about. I told you—"

"Devon isn't Caleb's daughter. Genetically, she's not a Bodie at all, is she? You got pregnant with someone else's child."

She bit her lip as the tears began cascading down her face. She buried her head in her hands and shook for several seconds. I dug around for some tissues in my backpack. When the sobs subsided, she took the proffered tissue, wiped her eyes gently so as not to smear her makeup, and blew her nose. She seemed to deflate, sinking back into the seat as she exhaled a deep breath.

"Sonora, I know about the birth certificate and medical report. The blood types don't match. You want to tell me what really happened? It may help the baby."

Sonora took a deep breath and blew it out between her lips as if it were smoke. "I . . . wasn't raped, exactly. I was . . . involved with someone at the time. And I got pregnant. The boy . . . told me his parents would never allow him to marry me. They had great plans for him that didn't include the girl with alcoholic parents. But he had a plan."

"Which included making up the story about Caleb?"

She nodded.

"Because Caleb couldn't defend himself."

She nodded again.

"Just like he can't defend himself against these murder charges now."

She grabbed my hand and squeezed hard. "I had nothing to do with that! Please! You can't tell anyone what you've found out. Especially not about Devon. She thinks Esken was her father and I want to keep it that way."

"But her medical history doesn't match. And now it's apparently affected her baby. She has a right to know what her genetic background is."

Sonora turned away, not wanting to hear anything

more. It was a trick I used myself. Unfortunately for her, she could still hear me, and I didn't stop talking.

"Sonora, you've got to tell the doctor the truth. Maybe he can do something for the baby."

She shook her head violently. Her hair blew around her head.

I looked up and saw the doctor and Sheriff Mercer in the doorway. Sonora sensed my distraction and followed my gaze.

The doctor relaxed his frown. "The baby was born too early. She has a condition called respiratory distress syndrome. Her lungs weren't fully developed, but it's treatable. We'll have to keep her here, do some tests. We're doing everything we can to help her."

As Sonora stood to question the doctor on the details, I headed over to Devon's room to see if I could get in. Twaina Bryson stood across the hall opposite Devon's door, sucking on what looked like a large candy.

"Hi, Twaina," I said softly. "How are you doing?"

Twaina pulled her hand from her mouth and rested it on her tummy, giving the abdomen a light massage. She didn't look well. I hoped she wasn't another poisoning victim.

"Are you feeling all right?"

She shrugged, without making eye contact, and chewed her candy.

"Devon's going to be fine. And the doctor's working with the baby. I'm sure everything is going to be all right."

She nodded listlessly and stroked her stomach in a light, circular pattern.

"So when are you due?"

Stunned, she looked me in the eyes for the first time.

"You're pregnant too, aren't you? Are the Tums helping?"

She dropped her hand from her abdomen and straightened up, trying to pull in her stomach. The loose grunge clothes covered her figure well, but the slight swelling was unmistakable. She was probably about four to five months along. Was pregnancy among teenagers in this town becoming epidemic?

I had to know what was going on. Twaina wasn't responding to my gentle probes. It looked like I'd have to get out the forceps and pull the information out of her.

"Are you going to give up your baby for adoption, too?"

Her eyes narrowed.

"Who's handling it for you?"

"That's confidential," she said, and turned to look down the hall, as if to dismiss me. I had expected "None of your business." Now where had I heard the word "confidential" recently?

"How much is Russell paying you?"

She whirled around. "That's none of your frigging business, lady!"

"Enough to buy a new car and some cool CDs and maybe a new stereo system?" I suggested.

She glared at me, her eyes dark embers. "Enough to get away from my obsessive mother and this backward town. Enough to live on my own, in the city, the way I want. So butt the hell out!" With that, she stomped off down the hospital hallway and disappeared around a corner.

I spent the next few minutes looking for Russell, but he had apparently vanished. I gave up and headed for the car, which I had hastily parked outside the emergency room after following Devon there in the ambulance. I was trying to make sense of it, but it wasn't much of a leap figuring out what had been going on.

Russell Jacks was a baby broker. Worse, I had a feeling he was somehow recruiting vulnerable teenage girls into becoming pregnant with promises of money, escape, and lifestyle changes. Maybe teenagers didn't think having babies was such a big deal these days. True, medical science had improved their mortality rates; their lives were rarely at risk. And young women seemed to bounce back quickly.

But what about the psychological scars, the emotional

reactions they weren't prepared for, the changes I was sure they went through with such a monumental event?

The financial payoff must seem enormous compensation to the immature adolescent with little life experience, earning minimum wage at the local fast-food restaurant. And there was always the added bonus of pissing off the parents and getting all that extra attention.

But what did any of this have to do with the death of Devon's grandmother?

I backed the car out of the parking space. With a last look at the Mother Lode Memorial Hospital, I caught a glimpse of a large figure, covered in a coat and woodsman's cap, lumbering through the emergency door. I considered returning to the hospital, then shook my head, put the car in gear, and drove out of the lot, headed for Russell's law office.

It couldn't have been Caleb Bodie.

Russell was on the phone when I burst in. Startled, he turned away so I couldn't lip-read his side of the conversation. I saw a lot of head shaking and hand gesturing as I sat down in the chair opposite him. It looked like a vigorous conversation, but lacked meaning for me.

After a few minutes he hung up the phone and faced me. Folding his hands, he set them on the desk and sat up stiffly.

Some hearies think deaf people are abrupt, even a little rude, but I think it's just that we don't beat around the bush. We use language to get to the point.

"You're a baby broker, aren't you, Russell?"

The smile faded. He didn't move, but his knuckles turned white as he tried to keep his folded hands under control. The forced smile never left his lips.

"Connor, what on earth are you talking about?"

"Devon. And Twaina. And God knows who else. You arranged for the adoptions of their babies. You pair up young pregnant teens and desperate infertile couples and arrange the deal. You probably charge the couples outrageous sums of money, playing on their desperation, and then offer sizable payoffs to the girls, while pocketing a substantial fee for yourself."

He looked dumbfounded. "Have you gone crazy?"

"You sell babies."

He recovered quickly and forced a smile with a slight edge to it. "Connor, do you know what libel means? It means a person cannot make false accusations unless he— or she—is prepared to be sued for defamation of character. It means—"

"Cut the crap, Russell. Your bullshit legal jargon doesn't mean a thing to me. You're selling babies, and that's illegal."

"I'm afraid you're wrong there, Connor. Nothing I'm doing is illegal. Everything is precisely within the letter of the law. I should know. It's my profession—not yours, by the way. Your profession appears to be butting into other people's business. And that's going to cost you your business, your reputation, and your bank account, when I get through with you in court."

"Don't bother threatening me, Russell. You're in deep shit and we both know it. You used Devon, and it won't take long for her to figure that out."

"You don't know what you're talking about, Connor. It's time you left."

I ignored him and his phony grin. The thought of this man exploiting young girls like he had infuriated me.

"Wonder what the sheriff will think about the coincidence that so many of the young girls in town are getting pregnant. Is it the water? Or maybe the Nugget Café coffee? No, that was poison. My mistake. Still, I think he'll find a connection somewhere."

Russell dropped the smile and stood up. "You're way over the line, Connor. Now get out of my office before I call Sheriff Mercer."

I remained seated. In fact, I sat back, with my hands folded over my chest, trying not to show the rage building inside. I wanted to stay calm, not lose control. "By the way, Russell, how did the girls get pregnant in the first place? Did you have something to do with that, too? Bet it won't take long to determine, with all that DNA testing we've got now."

He flushed but tried to remain composed. "I told you. I've done nothing wrong. In fact, just the opposite. I've made a lot of people happy, and I'm proud of what I do. Couples who can't conceive are overjoyed to finally have a child. Young girls who find themselves pregnant are relieved to find a home for their offspring and to have their bills covered. And the babies get a good home, from a loving, financially stable couple, mature enough to be good parents. I'd say I'm doing society a favor."

Offspring? I stood up slowly.

"Russell, I don't like men taking advantage of young girls—it's one of my pet peeves, you know, like child abuse. The way you do business is despicable. I'll find out exactly what's going on with these girls, and then I'll find out how all this ties in with Sparkle and Esken's deaths. Because I'm certain there's a connection."

Smoke him out, I thought, just before I slammed the door behind me. I'd lit the match; I just had to be careful that I wasn't the one to get burned.

I needed a walk to clear my head. After going through the birth experience with Devon, I felt as if I'd practically had the baby myself. Then talking with Sonora, and confronting Russell, I was more confused than ever.

I pulled on my sweatshirt and took a few side streets, walking heavily, as deaf people sometimes do, occasionally glancing at the clapboard homes that line the historic residential area of Flat Skunk. Unlike the tract homes being built on the outskirts of the town, each home in Skunk is unique, but there are still common traits. Dogs and cats run free between fences. Old dingy furniture sits propped on the porches, too ragged to keep inside, and too sentimental to throw away. Rusting vehicles with missing parts languish in the sun. And satellite dishes grow like giant mushrooms in nearly every yard.

What was I not seeing? I was sure everything was right there in front of me, except for the damn page from the Bodie family tree. Was the information still hidden somewhere? Or had it burned in one of the two buildings that had mysteriously gone up in flames?

Thirty minutes later, I found myself approaching Main Street again. I peeled off my sweatshirt from the heat of the walk and felt a light breeze cool my face and arms. Inhaling, I smelled the lingering smoke of the museum fire that laced the air before I spotted the gutted structure. There wasn't much left of the place, and the yellow "Do Not Cross" warning tape stuck out against the charred ruins like gold veins in a black mine.

Ducking under the tape, I approached the building cautiously. I wasn't planning to go inside, knowing the ruin could collapse at any minute, but I was curious to see the place where I'd been trapped only a few hours earlier.

When I peeked in, I saw I wasn't alone.

Sonora knelt over a charred pile, poking at the ash with a stick. I watched her dig around in the refuse, looking for something. Even in the dim light, I could see she'd been crying. Dark streaks etched her face. Caused by ash particles that dusted the interior of the damaged building? Or makeup streaked from tears?

I must have made a noise. She stood up and whirled around, the stick held out in front like a sword.

"Oh, it's you. Don't come creeping up on me like that. You startled me."

I stood at what had once been the front door, peering in. "You shouldn't be in here, Sonora. It's dangerous. The whole place could come crashing down on you at any time. Come on out."

She ignored me for a few minutes, then dropped the stick, and headed slowly toward me.

We stood, staring at the building, saying nothing. Finally I turned to Sonora.

"What were you looking for in there?"

"Nothing." She shrugged. "Just curious. As much as my mother-in-law might have thought otherwise, I hated to see the place destroyed."

"Was it something from the genealogy report that Aubrey was working on?"

She paled, and the streaks of black stood out prominently on her face. "I don't know what you're talking about."

"Of course you do. And for some reason you thought it might be here. But I beat you to it."

She looked at me sharply; her eyes widened. "You found it! Let me see it!"

I pulled the folded paper from my backpack and she snatched it from my hand. Scanning the front, she didn't seem to find what she was looking for.

"Turn it over," I said.

She did. She read the words, "Blood Type?" then stared back into the blackened building for a moment. Catching herself, she met my gaze and thrust the note back at me, then checked her watch. I noticed a slight tightening of the jaw as she spoke.

"This is nothing. We're both wasting our time. I've got to go see my daughter." Without so much as "Have a nice day," she left.

But she didn't head for the hospital. She pulled her car out, drove a few yards, then swung the car over and stopped in front of another building.

Naturally I followed her.

She seemed in such a hurry as she got out of the car. I didn't worry too much about being spotted, but I kept my distance. I had a hunch where she was headed and in a few seconds, I knew my hunch was correct.

Russell's law office.

I was about to catch up when she stopped abruptly, midstep, and turned around. For a moment I thought she'd seen me, but she didn't appear to be looking for her shadow. She seemed deep in thought. Quickly I ducked out of sight before she spotted me. She retraced her steps to the sidewalk, then veered onto another path.

She was headed for the library.

What was going through her mind? I wondered, as I sneaked up to the library building after she'd gone inside. The door was closed, but peeking through the glass plate, I could see her talking with someone at the desk. When Sonora moved, I caught a glimpse of Twaina Bryson, who helped out Aubrey after school and on weekends. Twaina was pointing to a filing cabinet.

Sonora pulled out one of the drawers, riffled through the files, and extracted a folder. I had no doubt which one it was. I tried to see her reaction as she discovered the folder was empty. As she set it down on the open drawer, I could almost see the wheels in her head turning.

She stuffed the folder back into the drawer, slammed it shut, and headed for the door. I ducked behind the side of the building, my heart pounding, holding my breath.

The door swung open. I could tell by her hurried step that Sonora was a woman possessed. She headed down the Main Street sidewalk again, quickening her pace, almost running. This time I was right—she was headed for Russell's office.

And I was right behind her.

While Sonora made her way to the door, I slipped around to the side of the office, to play the peeping Tom. The building had a high foundation, common to Flat Skunk structures, and I had to stand on a garbage can to see in. Precariously balanced with a grip on the dusty windowsill, I spotted Sonora just as she pushed open the door to Russell's inner office. From my vantage point, I had a full view of the room.

Russell wasn't there. I peeked over the rim of the windowsill, hoping she wouldn't catch me, as I watched her tear violently through his filing cabinet. As she dug out the papers, she flung them in the air, littering the place with sheets of documents, letters, forms, and photocopies.

Not until she tried to pull open Russell's bottom drawer did the frenzy end. The drawer must have been locked. Sonora yanked at it twice, then grabbed a gold letter opener lying on Russell's desk. She went to work on the lock, not gently and carefully, but as if she were digging into a rock-hard vein with a pickax.

In a few moments, she had the wood around the lock nearly destroyed. With a kick, she forced the drawer open, pulled out a multipaged document, and began scanning the pages.

That's when I lost my balance and hit the ground, cutting my chin on the edge of the garbage can lid as I nose-dived into the bushes. Shit! Something or someone had knocked the garbage can out from under me.

"What do you think you're doing?"

Russell had his arms crossed over his chest and he glared as he spoke. "I knew it wouldn't be long before you did something stupid—and illegal. I'm calling Sheriff Mercer."

I pushed myself up from the cold ground, wiped off the dirt, dabbed at my bleeding chin, and tried to glare back at him.

"Russell, someone's broken into your office. I was just trying to see who it was."

He gave me one of those "Yeah, sure" looks.

I shrugged. "Okay, if you don't believe me, look for yourself." I nodded toward the window, dabbing at my chin with my palm.

Russell moved closer. He righted the garbage can, then hoisted himself up.

"Shit!" He jumped to the ground. As he ran for the front door, I hobbled behind him, favoring the leg that hadn't been bruised and scraped as badly as the other. I caught him in midsentence.

"What the hell are you doing here, Sonora? I'm calling the sheriff. He can take you both to jail. This is breaking and entering, theft, destruction of private prop—"

"Shut up, Russell. I found the wills. Both of them. You're in deep shit."

Russell stopped cold. No doubt he was trying to come up with more legal jargon to control the situation. But Sonora was not about to be controlled. He took a step toward her, his hands raised in a "calm down" gesture. Apparently he wanted those wills. I wondered if there were extra copies.

When he started to reach for the papers, Sonora grabbed the letter opener again. It was gold-plated, ornate, and engraved, but I couldn't read the inscription. It was also sharp enough to open just about anything, from a hardwood drawer to a soft abdomen.

She had it aimed directly for Russell's gut.

"Sonora, don't!" I said, quickly. "Put it down and let's call Sheriff Mercer."

Sonora glared at me. I opened my hand and reached out for the letter opener. She swung it at me fiercely, slicing the blade across my palm. I pulled back, stung and bleeding.

In the commotion, Russell made a dash for the documents on his desk.

Sonora lunged at him.

Russell didn't see it coming. He was too busy trying to get the document.

But I did. All I could do was give her a shove as she tried to plunge the letter opener into Russell's stomach. The blade deflected, cutting him across his waist. Sonora lost her balance in the follow-through and tumbled to the floor.

Russell looked stunned, unable to comprehend the fact that someone had just stabbed him. He touched his side where the letter opener had struck; a dark bloodstain was spreading onto his white shirt. He pulled his hand back to reveal bloody fingertips.

"My God! You've gone crazy!" Russell stared down at Sonora in disbelief. The fall had forced her grip open, causing the weapon to slide a few inches away from her hand. She picked herself up from the floor. Within seconds she had the letter opener tightly in her grasp again.

I glanced at Russell, who had turned gray and was perspiring profusely. He held his hand pressed to his waist; blood seeped through his fingers. With his other hand, he reached out for support from the desk.

Before I could think, Sonora came at him again, running on rage and adrenaline. This time an unexpected shove from me was not going to stop her. It was time for brains, not brawn.

"Sonora! Stop!"

The words distracted her only momentarily. I could see her knuckles turn white as she gripped the letter opener tighter.

"Think of Devon! Think of your new grandchild!"

Sonora glanced at me for a second, then returned her attention to Russell.

"They need you! This coward isn't worth the energy. He'll go to jail for what he's done."

She blinked rapidly; nothing else moved.

Russell seemed near collapse from the loss of blood. I had a feeling he was going into shock. He'd soon be completely defenseless against her.

"Sonora! You don't want to kill anyone else!"

She swung the blade in my direction, looking confused for a moment as to which one of us she most wanted to hurt.

"Maybe you had a reason for killing Sparkle. And Esken. I don't know. The courts will decide that. But don't make it any worse than it already is."

Sonora stood frozen to the spot, the letter opener now aimed directly for my chest. But her look of hatred had vanished.

"You think . . ." She glanced back at Russell, then again at me. "You think *I killed* my mother-in-law! *And* my own husband?"

She seemed genuinely stunned at the implication.

"I just . . ." I started to cover my accusations, thinking they might backfire, and make her more violent.

"I didn't kill them! I didn't kill anyone. Don't you understand? Russell is responsible for everything. Everything! He has to pay for what he's done!"

Russell now lay slumped on the floor, resting his head against the side of the desk, his hand uselessly covering his wound. His breathing came slow and shallow, and his face looked sickly and discolored. He tried to shake his head.

"I . . . I . . . didn't . . ."

Sonora swung around viciously. "You did! You killed Sparkle because of the will. I know you. You didn't want me to get any of that money because you were jealous of my inheritance. And you killed Esken because . . . because . . ." She was floundering now, trying to justify her need to finish Russell.

"No . . ." he puffed as he spoke. I could hardly read his lips, they moved so little. ". . . no . . ."

While Sonora continued to rant, I thought about calling for help. I reached for the phone but Sonora swung the lethal opener at me. Instead, I knelt down beside Russell to see what I could do about the bleeding, and tried to make him more comfortable. In propping him up, I felt something hard in his pocket. On the pretense of assisting him, I discreetly removed the object and slipped it behind his back.

I'd never used a cell phone in my life, but I'd watched plenty of hearies use them. It looked to me like you just pulled up the antenna, flipped open the receiver, and punched in the numbers. And then you talked. While pretending to give Russell more support, I peeked behind him and fumbled with the phone. Sonora still stood over him, hurling accusations, venting it all before she took that final step.

I inched the phone's antenna up between my fingers, felt for the opening, and released the lid. Peering behind him like a devoted nurse trying to see to my patient's every need, I surreptitiously glanced at the numbers.

Russell was coughing now. I had no idea if a cell phone made noise, but I decided to join him in the coughing jag, to cover the sound just in case. Between the two of us, we might make enough noise to disguise any beeping noises. Sonora looked at us both as if we were crazy, not congested.

I punched on the power, then the numbers, 911, then "send," coughing with each punch, then stuffed the phone under the desk, leaving it open. Mentally crossing my fingers, I hoped someone would hear the commotion, trace the call, and send the sheriff.

Just as I finished the task, I noticed Sonora watching me curiously.

"I said, what the hell are you doing?"

Apparently she'd been talking to me and I hadn't heard her. I had to distract her before she lost total control.

"I was coughing. Something stuck in my throat." I pounded my chest for effect. "Sonora, this man is seriously wounded. We've got to get him to a hospital."

"He won't need a hospital. He'll need a morgue. Now get away from him."

Russell's eyes widened at the threat. I didn't move.

"Sonora, how do you know Russell killed Sparkle and Esken?"

"Because I know him. Because he cares only about himself. And he won't let anything get in the way of his so-called 'perfect' plans." She focused on Russell and snarled, "Isn't that right, darling?"

Darling?

"You know nothing about his scams and lies, Connor. Nothing. There's not one true bone in his body. Tell her, Russell. Tell her what you did to me. Go on."

Russell's eyes were closed now. "I . . ." He tried to speak but his breathing was so weak, the word barely formed on his lips.

"I'll tell you what he did. He told me he loved me. He promised to marry me. Then he got me pregnant."

I caught my breath.

Russell winced. Was it at the pain—or the memory?

"I was seventeen years old, the same age as my daughter. He told me he couldn't marry me because his parents wouldn't send him to law school and it would mess up all his perfect plans. That's when he said he had an idea. Why didn't I find someone rich to marry, then I could divorce the man later, get his money, and marry Russell."

I thought about the Bodie brothers.

"Well, why not the 'dummy,' he said? The retard who couldn't talk. I was supposed to tell his mother he raped me and then she'd have to pay me tons of money to keep quiet. Only Sparkle had a better idea. Instead of paying me off, she coerced Esken into taking the vows, by holding his inheritance over his head. And Russell thought it was a great idea! I'd get even more money when she died. Old Sparkle was on her last legs anyway, he said. She wouldn't last much longer."

But she'd held on for quite some time. Nearly two decades, in fact. Even at the end she had to be helped along.

"So I was supposed to give birth to our baby, wasn't I, Russell darling? But something went wrong." She paused, and seemed to weaken a bit as she continued. "I lost the baby."

"You had a miscarriage?"

She nodded, biting her lip.

"But . . . but Devon . . ." And then it all came together.

"Russell told me he'd take care of everything. He said I needed to have a baby to insure the inheritance; otherwise, Sparkle would probably have the marriage annulled. And we'd get nothing."

"So Russell got you a baby."

Tears filled Sonora's eyes. She nodded and wiped her nose with her hand. "He told me to fake the pregnancy. I wasn't sleeping with Esken, so he never saw my body. I pretended to go to checkups in Whiskey Slide, but of course, that was just part of the ruse. In the meantime, Russell started looking for an unwed teenager giving birth about the right time."

"A replacement baby. Devon."

"He arranged for me to go away a month before the baby was due, to see my 'sister' on the East Coast. Instead, I went to a motel in Sacramento and waited for him to bring me a baby. Then I went back home to the Bodies, claiming I'd had the baby early. They had no reason to doubt me. After all, I'd been 'pregnant' for months!"

"So that's when you started your black-market baby business!" I glared at Russell. "You've been doing this for seventeen years!"

"And I've been waiting—for *seventeen years*!"

"So who's Devon's father? And mother, for that matter?"

Sonora reared up, her face twisted with anger. "*I'm* her mother! Me! I'm the one who raised her and cared for her and—" the anger turned to a rush of tears. "And loved her."

"Russell?"

He shook his head. He either couldn't speak or didn't have an answer to my question about Devon's parenthood.

"And that's why Devon's birth certificate was altered," I said, more to myself. Then speaking to Sonora, I asked, "Did Russell finish off Sparkle so you two could finally get the inheritance?"

"Of course he did! Only problem was, he knew I wasn't going to share any of that money with him, not after seventeen years of hell with that woman and her crazy sons."

Russell seemed to come alive at that last statement. He coughed again, opened his eyes, and tried to speak. "I . . . didn't kill her. I didn't kill anyone. I bring lives together . . . I don't take them away. I . . . I'm not a murderer." He sputtered and the tension left his body once again.

Time was running out. Where was the sheriff?

Suddenly Sonora's eyes flashed. She began scanning the room. "What's that noise?"

I didn't move. I hoped it was Sheriff Mercer. Or someone. Anyone.

"Where's it coming from? Godammit, move!"

But instead of heading for the door, Sonora shoved Russell aside and began rooting under the desk. Within seconds she found the cell phone. She flipped the top closed.

"You pathetic man! You thought calling the police would prolong your life? It's only going to shorten it." She raised the letter opener.

I held up a hand. "Wait! What about the will? Does Russell have it?"

Sonora paused for a moment. "I have it. I have both of them. The original and the one he fabricated that cut me out."

Russell coughed again. "I didn't falsify it. Sparkle really did change the will. It . . . had something to do with . . . the genealogy chart she was having done. She found out about Devon from the work Aubrey was doing for her. She . . . knew Devon couldn't have been Caleb's or even Esken's baby, because of the Rh factor. She also knew you wouldn't use the money to preserve the town. She wanted it to go to the museum foundation and the Clampers."

The museum—which was now a pile of cinders.

I looked into Sonora's eyes, and wondered for a moment if she could have murdered Sparkle after all. It was apparent she was capable of killing Russell. She was a heartbeat away from doing it.

Sonora's head reared up. She spat as she screamed the words, "You liar! God, I hate you!"

She brought the glistening blade down. I swung my arm out and blocked its path. As she cut through my flesh, I felt the searing pain. I lunged at her and rolled, my other arm flailing, my legs kicking.

It took the sheriff, his deputy, and Dan Smith to pull me off of her.

"How did you know where I was?" I asked Dan, after
he and the sheriff had untangled me from Sonora. I made
it to Russell's swivel chair, breathing heavily and holding
Dan's shirt on my sliced arm. Sonora, defeated and sobbing,
sat slumped against a wall, cuffed. The EMTs huddled
over Russell; their bodies and equipment blocked my view
of him.

"Did nine-one-one trace the call?" I asked between
puffs.

Dan shook his head. "Can't trace cell phones. But Rebecca heard voices and realized something serious was up.
She alerted Sheriff Mercer and had him listen in. He recognized your voice; you have a unique accent, you know.
Sonora's voice was a little distorted, since she was mostly
screaming, and Russell was difficult to hear, but when you
started talking about the will, the sheriff figured you were
all at the law office."

How nice that I wasn't the one who had difficulty hearing, for a change. "Dan, how did *you* get here?"

"I saw the sheriff jump in his car with the lights and

sirens. I asked him what was up and he yelled out something about there being trouble at Russell's office. I figured you were involved, so I followed along on foot."

"Wipe that smile off your face. Don't think you rescued me or anything. I had everything under control."

"God forbid I should rescue Connor Westphal."

As the sheriff questioned Sonora in the corner, the paramedics hoisted Russell onto a stretcher and headed for the hospital.

"You better go, too," Dan said. "Let them have a look at that arm."

I nodded, and Dan volunteered to take me in the Chevy. I especially wanted to see Devon while I was there. I didn't know exactly what I was going to say—that her mother was being held under "temporary restraint" at the sheriff's office for attempted murder? I'd think of something.

After the gashes in my arm and palm were cleaned, stitched, and bandaged, and the cut on my chin from the garbage can fall had been Mercurochromed, I found Dan in the waiting room around eight, reading a dog-eared copy of *Modern Maturity*.

"Planning to retire?" I asked.

"It was either this or *Humpty Dumpty Magazine*." Dan tossed the magazine on a side table that was littered with identical copies of the same periodical.

"I need to make one more stop before we leave. Do you mind?"

"Nah. I'll go get something in the cafeteria. Want anything? I hear they've got a butterscotch pudding that's to die for."

I gagged and waved him off, telling him I'd meet him there in a few minutes. "Order me a piña colada and a steak."

Women in labor were all over the maternity ward when I entered. Must be a full moon, I thought, remembering an old wives' tale from my great-grandmother Sierra Westphal's pioneer diary. There was a sign on Devon's door that read: "Do Not Disturb." I wondered what that meant. But before I could push the door open, a nurse stopped me.

"I'm sorry, you can't go in there."

"Why not?"

"Doctor's orders."

That old roadblock. Can't argue with doctor's orders. Kind of like arguing with pregnant women. They both get away with murder.

Pregnant women.

I glanced around and found the rest room. Once inside a stall, I pulled out the hospital scrubs I'd stuffed in my backpack. I slipped on the green pajamas over my clothes, then stuffed the backpack under the shirt and into the pants. The elastic waistband kept the pack from falling down. The effect was perfect. I headed back for Devon's room, waddling like an overfed duck and rubbing my pregnant-looking pillow puff as I moved.

Suddenly I was invisible to the nurses on the ward. I pushed open Devon's door without interference, and slipped in.

Devon looked pale and sleepy, but her sunken eyes were open. I pulled the backpack out from under my shirt and dropped it to the floor, then slipped out of the pajamas. The moment she saw me she turned away. I stepped in slowly, wishing I'd brought a handful of teen magazines and gummy worms to offer her. But the gifts probably wouldn't have helped her mood.

"Hi, Devon."

She turned back to face me, tears welling up in her eyes.

"She's going to be okay," Devon said, as if to reassure herself, not me. For a moment I thought she meant her mother. Then I realized she meant the baby. I nodded.

"That's great news."

"She's got to stay in intensive care a while, but they said I could see her. She's got some kind of breathing problem, but the doctor said she'll be all right."

Devon closed her eyes, the tears rolling down her cheeks. The drops veered sideways, then disappeared into the pillowcase. She sniffed and wiped her nose with the arm hooked up to an IV. I grabbed a handful of tissues from the table and offered them to her.

"Is there anything you need?" I asked, after she had composed herself.

"Where's my mother?"

I hadn't been looking forward to telling her about Sonora, but she had a right to know. She had a right to know a lot of things. I explained, briefly, what had happened, but I didn't mention her adoption.

There were no tears this time, only a gentle nodding of her head, as if she expected to hear the story I had just told her.

"You know, I don't blame her really. Russell is a total jerk. All this time I thought he was such a good guy, helping people who couldn't have babies, helping teenagers start new lives. To think he was . . . he was—"

She bit her lip and turned away again, not wanting me to see the hurt and anger in her face.

"You knew, then."

She turned back and nearly spat the words: "What? That he didn't have the guts to marry my mother when he got her pregnant? That he made her accuse a defenseless man in order to get the family's money? That he actually 'bought' me to replace . . ." For a moment, she couldn't continue. "God, he was scheming for money from the get-go."

"When did you find out?"

Devon wiped her nose before speaking. "A few days ago. I was having second thoughts about giving up my baby. I started having these feelings for it, you know. So, I went to Russell to ask how I could pay back the money he'd already given me, if I decided to keep the baby. He had a fit."

I brushed a wisp of damp hair away from her cheek, then found myself smoothing the loose tendrils around her forehead.

"What did he say?"

"He said if I kept the baby, he'd tell everyone the truth: that I wasn't really a Bodie, I was adopted. I'd get nothing from my grandmother. He thought his threats would convince me to give up my baby. He even threatened to tell my dad—Esken—that he wasn't my real father."

Devon wasn't crying now. There was hatred in her eyes. Her hands gripped the white hospital sheets tightly, as if she were holding on to keep from falling out of the bed.

"It must have been a shock when you found out your parents weren't biological."

"Oh, it was. At first I didn't believe him. Then he showed me the birth certificate that had been forged, and my real health forms."

"So he tried to blackmail you?"

She nodded. "I wasn't the only one he was blackmailing into doing what he wanted."

"You mean Twaina?"

Devon looked surprised but said nothing.

"Devon, I'm sorry to ask you this, but did Sonora try to kill Sparkle when she found out about the new will?"

Devon tried to sit up. "No! No, she never did anything like this before! She's not a violent person. At least, she wasn't . . . until now."

"You're sure she didn't try to stop Sparkle from—"

"No! I told you!" She was leaning on one elbow now, her face livid.

I could tell she had something more to say. I decided to push it, and hoped the nurses didn't come running in and throw me out.

"How can you be so sure, Devon?"

"Because!" She lay back down, seemingly exhausted. "Because . . ."

And then I knew. Only a simpleminded person would try to kill someone by giving her an overdose of all the medications on hand. Or a young, inexperienced kid.

"You're the one who tried to kill your grandmother?"

"I . . . I wasn't trying to *kill* her, exactly. I just wanted to, you know, slow her down. So she couldn't make that new will and destroy my family. I thought if I gave her a bunch of medications, it would make her sick, and she wouldn't be in good enough health to make the changes and leave my mother with nothing."

"So you gave her drugs."

Devon tensed, her face flushed. "Medications! I just

gave her a little extra, in her food and her drinks, so she'd be sick. I didn't plan to kill her. I just needed time to figure out what to do. I was panicked, don't you see?"

"But she almost died, Devon!"

Devon teared up again. "I know, I know! I really thought I'd killed her by accident. I prayed for a miracle to keep her alive. I was so relieved when she woke up! When she didn't die, I thought my prayers had been answered. I swore I'd make changes in my life. Beginning with the baby."

"But somebody went to the hospital and tried again to kill Sparkle. That time it worked."

Devon looked horrified. "I didn't do it! I couldn't kill anyone deliberately like that. What I did was an accident, I swear!"

"Did you tell anyone that you gave your grandmother those medications?"

She lay still, staring at the ceiling. I followed her gaze. She was staring at a decal of a bird that someone had placed overhead for patients to look at while they lay in bed.

"Devon? Did you tell your mother?"

Devon bit her lip.

"Do you think Sonora might have—"

"Killed Sparkle?" She met my eyes, her face pleading. "No. She couldn't have. She wouldn't. Maybe she's not my biological mother, but she's still my mother and I love her. Yes, I thought she might be accused of it when they found the note for the will and saw the changes Sparkle was going to make. That's when I had to do something."

"Like what?"

"Like trap the murderer, don't you understand yet? I knew who it was, but I had to prove it. When my . . ." she hesitated saying the word, then went on. "When my father—Esken—was murdered, I knew my mother would be next. But I needed evidence, otherwise the killer would never be arrested."

"You think it's Russell?"

"I *know* it's Russell. Don't you see? He's the one who killed my grandmother by smothering her in the hospital.

He gave my father an overdose of insulin. And tried to kill Aubrey after he found out all that genealogy stuff."

"But why?"

"Because! Because Russell knew about the new will, disinheriting us. And he wanted Sparkle dead before she could sign that new will. Otherwise he didn't have a chance of getting anything. He probably planned to blackmail my mother into giving him half the inheritance."

"How did you find out about the will?"

"Sparkle wrote herself a note. I saw it in her room."

I thought about the note I'd seen in the box hidden under Sparkle's bed. It had read what I thought was "churchill," written in blue ink, the ink found on Sparkle's finger. So it had meant "change will" not "churchill."

The ink.

"Do you have any proof that Russell—"

I had suddenly lost her attention. Something in the doorway had distracted her.

Caleb!"

The deaf man gave no visible response to my greeting. He stood in the doorway of Devon's hospital room, filling it with his bulk. His wide eyes came to rest on Devon lying in her bed. I glanced at Devon and thought I caught her smiling at Caleb. He stepped inside the door.

I wondered how he had gotten past the militant nurses.

Devon lifted a hand in greeting. Caleb moved in slowly and crossed to the other side of the bed. In his hand he held a wadded ball of paper, which he placed on the bed next to Devon. She carefully opened it. A tiny gold nugget the size of a pea fell into her hands. I watched her react in disbelief as she scanned the words on the paper.

I knew Caleb couldn't read, but he must have known the paper was important. By Devon's reaction, I knew it was too. As she laid it on her lap, I slowly took the paper from her hand and read it.

It was the deed to the Bodie Mine. And a copy of Sparkle's will.

Devon gently reached out for Caleb's hand, then lay

back down and closed her eyes. The door opened suddenly and Nurse Ratched's evil twin sister stood glaring.

"What are you people doing in here? Can't you read?"

I was tempted to say something, but held my tongue. I took a frightened-looking Caleb by the hand, and we slipped past her, the deed and will still in my other hand.

Suddenly remembering Dan, I led Caleb to the cafeteria, where I found him reading a copy of the daily *Mother Lode Monitor* over a cup of coffee.

Caleb followed me reluctantly to the table and I gestured for him to sit down next to me. Wide-eyed, his eyes darting around the room, he sat, kneading his fingers as if they were dough.

"I don't think he likes hospitals," I said, stealing a sip of Dan's coffee. It tasted bitter next to my usual mocha. Maybe, like me, Caleb had been to too many hospitals over the years.

"Where'd you find him?"

I filled him in, but I couldn't explain why Caleb had risked coming to see Devon. Did he have no idea of the trouble he was in?

I no doubt held the answer in my hand. I withdrew the copy of the deed and read the contents out loud to Dan. According to the document, Evan Lee Bodie had taken over the mine that originally belonged to the murdered Bennegar Jacks—Russell's great-grandfather. On the back of the deed were the dates showing when Bennegar had taken possession of the mine. Remembering the newspaper article the sheriff and I had found in the burned-out house, I knew what that meant.

"This mine originally belonged to the Jacks family. Is it possible Russell Jacks killed Sparkle and Esken Bodie to get even in some way? Maybe he planned to take over the mine for his tourist business."

I glanced at Caleb. He was tense, alert, and, I thought, ready to flee at the first sign of trouble.

"It's okay," I said, patting his leg. He patted mine back, a little more forcefully than I would have liked. The guy was definitely on edge.

"We better get you out of here. Dan—"

But before I could ask Dan to take Caleb to my office, Caleb reached for my backpack and dug inside. Withdrawing a pen, he began to write something on the back of a napkin. I watched him put together lines using his "splintered writing." A special education teacher in Whiskey Slide once explained for an article I was writing that some kids simply copy letters of the alphabet without really knowing they have meaning. It was as if they were doing a performance, most likely to please their desperate parents, but didn't have a clue what they were doing.

I had to strain to make out the symbols. At first I thought it was a drawing of a lollipop. But as he added more detail, crude letters arranged themselves into a familiar word.

"QUIET."

I frowned at him, not understanding. Bringing a finger to my lips, I made the universal gesture for "shhh."

He repeated the sign and nodded.

"I . . . don't understand . . ." I shrugged my shoulders in an exaggerated attempt to express my lack of comprehension.

"Shhh . . ." He made the gesture again, his finger pressed to his puckered lips.

I looked down at the word he'd drawn more than written.

"QUIET."

What on earth could that word mean to him? Were people always telling him to be quiet? How did he know how to write it? I thought about the scrawled designs in the cave, but they weren't the same style. Whoever had written the word in the cave, I was convinced, had not been Caleb.

Russell? He could have sneaked into the hospital room, finished off Sparkle, and made it look like Caleb. Then he could have killed Esken in the cave, after Esken found out the truth, and again made it look like Caleb. He could even have poisoned Aubrey, when Aubrey found out too much from the genealogy chart.

Dan pulled me from my thoughts with a nod toward Caleb, who was gesturing another "Shhh."

I nodded, then pulled him up. "Dan, would you mind taking Caleb to my office for a little while. I need to stop at the library and check something. I promise I'll be right there."

Dan agreed, after giving me a knowing look. We headed out of the cafeteria, down the elevator to the exit. I held open the door for Dan and Caleb, and watched Caleb shuffle out, glancing back to be sure I was following.

I drove back to Flat Skunk favoring my good arm. At least I could still drive the automatic. I dropped the guys off, racing to the library before it closed. The place was only open one night a week. Twaina Bryson was sorting through books when I entered. With little enthusiasm, she handed over the file of old microfiche for early issues of the *Union Democrat,* and in a matter of minutes I found the article and date I was searching for.

Old man Bodie had been initially suspected of killing Jacks, but nothing had been proved, and the mine had gone to the Bodies, leaving the Jacks family penniless.

I headed back to the hospital.

The candy striper informed me of Russell's room number. When I entered, he was sitting up, eating some yellowish pudding I figured was the butterscotch. Holly Bryson stood with her back to me. I could tell by her body language she was upset with Russell. But to look at his face, it was difficult to tell if he was even responding to her. His recovery appeared so remarkable, I almost forgot how weak he'd been at the office.

Holly Bryson must have heard me enter. She turned around, acknowledging me briefly, then gave Russell a quick last glance.

"We'll discuss it later," Russell said, dismissively.

"You bet we will. All three of us." With that, she pushed past me and out the door. I could guess what the two of them had been discussing to cause her to be so upset.

"Did I interrupt something?"

Russell's demeanor grew cool. He returned his attention to his pudding. "No, she just stopped by to wish me well. I can't say the same for you, can I?"

As Russell played with the spoon in his mouth, I thought about Holly Bryson. She, too, had a reason to kill Russell, much like Sonora, with her daughter in the same predicament. But would she have had a reason to get rid of Sparkle, and then Esken? I supposed the discovery of that second will would have been very beneficial to the museum. Holly was certainly passionate about preserving Flat Skunk's heritage. The museum would probably close without the financial support of the Bodie wealth.

But why try to poison Aubrey? Now, with the newspaper article, I kept coming back to Russell.

I moved closer, hoping to distract Russell from his pudding. Clothed in hospital-issue pajamas, he'd left the shirt open at the chest, revealing a large white bandage at his side. Apart from the wound, he looked to be in good condition. His color was bright, his hair was combed, and his appetite was certainly back.

"Russell, you look so much better. How're you doing?"

"Better than I was back at the office. I guess I should thank you for helping me. Sonora probably would have killed me if you hadn't tried to stop her." His cold exterior was beginning to warm up.

"She was pretty upset. Guess she won't be bothering you for a while. Sheriff's got her locked up now."

"Thank God. You know, I actually feel sorry for her. She must be crazy. That's the only explanation. Why would she kill her mother-in-law and her husband, and try to kill Aubrey and me, if she weren't mentally unbalanced? Probably carrying around all those secrets for so many years, and having no one to blame but herself."

I nodded in tentative agreement. The sight of Russell, sitting there in false sympathy, disgusted me, but I knew I wouldn't get anywhere if I antagonized him. He was relieved about something. Best to make him think I had come to my senses and was on his side.

"You really think Sonora killed them?"

"You don't?"

"There are some loose ends that I'm still concerned about."

"Like what?"

"Like the genealogy chart. It doesn't sound as if she knew about the new will."

"She knew. She was just pretending so she could get away with trying to kill me."

I nodded noncommittally again. "What about Sparkle's death at the hospital? Sonora was there in plain sight. Wouldn't it have been foolish to sneak in and finish the job with everyone knowing she was there?"

"Not to me. The more obvious you are, the more you seem above suspicion. Great trick, but I saw through it."

"And what about Esken at the cave? She could have killed him any time. Why then? Why there?"

Russell took another spoonful of pudding and savored it as if it were *crème brûlée*. "I don't know. Because no one would see her there, I guess."

"I don't think so. It seems overly complicated for her to lure him there, kill him, do those drawings, and get out."

"Maybe she put Caleb up to it. After all, the sheriff said it was his drawing on the wall in there."

"Maybe. But he's not exactly easy to communicate with. It would have taken a great deal of effort to instruct him on the details."

Russell held his pudding-filled spoon in midair. "Connor, what are you trying to say?"

"Nothing. I'm just thinking out loud."

He placed the spoon back in the plastic cup without eating the prepared bite. "You still think I did it, don't you! You still think I killed Sparkle Bodie, then Esken, and then tried to kill Aubrey. My God."

"No, of course not, I mean, well . . . I suppose you could have poisoned Aubrey at the café. You did have the opportunity. And you certainly had the motive."

Russell punched a button and a red light on the wall began blinking. He glared at me and I took a step back. Time was about up.

"Russell, if you did do it, Sheriff Mercer will do a thorough investigation and something will turn up to incriminate you. You—"

The nurse appeared in the doorway. "Is something wrong, Mr. Jacks—" she started to say, then saw his flushed face and distorted features. I'm sure she thought he was worse, but I knew that look for what it was: rage.

"I'm afraid you'll have to leave, miss," she said, pulling out the blood pressure cuff. I backed up.

"I just have to ask one more question."

The nurse applied the cuff and pumped the bulb. "Not now, miss. You'll have to go."

"But it's very important—"

She whirled around. "Quiet, please! I'm trying to listen to his blood pressure. Now leave or I'll call security. This man needs quiet!"

I stepped backward through the door and out into the hallway.

Quiet.

I closed the door to Russell's room and stood in the hall-way, contemplating my next move. After weighing my op-tions, I decided to delay returning to Caleb at my office. Dan was with him; he could wait—I hoped. My next hospi-tal visit could not.

I entered the elevator and rode to the third floor where patients from intensive care were housed. I located room 311, tiptoed past the sleeping guard, and pushed the door open slowly.

"Aubrey?"

Aubrey lay on his bed, looking pale and weak. He turned his head slowly toward me and forced a small smile.

"Hi, Connor." His lips barely moved when he spoke.

"How are you doing?" I stood close to read him more clearly. He said something and I had to ask him to repeat it.

"I said, I'm doing okay. Doctors said it was a close one."

I shuddered. "Sheriff Mercer have any idea who tried to poison you yet?"

Aubrey blinked slowly and gave a single shake of his head.

"He'll get whoever did this. Don't worry." The words felt weak on my lips, but I didn't know what else to say.

"I heard—" Aubrey coughed, patted his chest a few times, and began again. It looked like it hurt to speak. "I heard there's been some more trouble."

"Shhh," I gestured to Aubrey. "You shouldn't talk. How about if I do most of the talking and you just rest." He nodded and gave another weak attempt at a smile, while I proceeded to explain the latest events. He listened calmly, taking it all in.

"Sonora is in jail?" he said, surprised. "And Russell is here at Memorial? Wow, a lot has happened since I got here, hasn't it?" He was beginning to look a little more alive.

A nurse popped in to check on Aubrey, take his blood pressure, monitor his IV, and give him some medication. I waited patiently while she went through her routine. Aubrey seemed to perk up even more at her attention, but as soon as she left, he wilted back into the bed.

"It seems like they're treating you well. Look at all the flowers, and cards, and balloons."

Aubrey glanced around at the gifts and tokens of sympathy. They seemed to give him momentary pleasure. I hated to bring him back to dark reality, but I was there for a purpose. Caleb's life was at stake.

"Aubrey, do you have any idea who might have done this to you?"

Aubrey frowned. "The sheriff asked me the same thing, Connor. But I just don't know. I mean, what did I ever do?"

"What about the genealogy research you were doing for the Bodies? Obviously you found something in there that upset them. And now Sparkle and Esken are dead. Whatever it was must still be important to someone."

Aubrey met my eyes with a glimmer of recognition. "You don't think . . . Russell . . . ?"

"Do you think he had a reason to want that information? Was it enough to cause him to murder two people—and try to kill you?"

Aubrey thought for a moment, taking shallow breaths.

"I suppose, but I don't know what it was . . . I mean . . . if I'd had more time to think about it, maybe there was a date that didn't quite jibe, or maybe there was a long-lost cousin, a black sheep in the family, that no one wanted identified."

"What about illegitimacy? Or a falsified birth certificate?"

Aubrey's eyes darkened. He chewed on his lip, then said, "Yes, I suppose that could have been it. You're referring to Devon."

"You knew."

He nodded solemnly.

"Aubrey, Sonora tried to find the file at the library, but your work is still missing. Can you remember anything in there that might tell us more?"

Aubrey's eyes started to close. It was obvious he was fighting to stay awake.

"I don't . . . know. I didn't pay close attention . . . while I worked . . ." His eyelids were still.

"Aubrey?"

No answer. He was out cold.

It was dark by the time I left the hospital. I drove the Chevy to my office, trying to piece together the bits of information I'd gathered, but I was still in the dark. Caleb's problem weighted heavily on me.

I hurried up the stairs of the hotel and tried Dan's door. No answer. Locked. I turned on my office light. Caleb and Dan were nowhere in sight.

I was about to panic when Dan burst in.

"Dan! You nearly gave me a heart attack. Would you stop bursting in on me like that?"

Dan stood there grinning as if he enjoyed seeing me nearly wet my pants.

"Where's Caleb?" I pushed past him and darted into Dan's now-open office door.

There he was, sitting on Dan's chair behind the desk, opening a pizza box.

"You went out for pizza?" I looked at Dan in disbelief. Caleb's face darkened. My frantic demeanor probably frightened him. I forced a smile and gave him a reassuring wave. He gave a tentative wave back, as if trying to size up the situation.

I turned to Dan, who was leaning on the doorjamb, his large arms folded across his black T-shirt. "Want some?" he asked.

I shook my head. "Thanks for taking care of him, Dan. Does anyone know he's here?"

Dan pulled up a chair, spun it around backward, and sat down. "Nope. It's just me and my buddy, eating some pizza, talking about old times." He held up a thumb to Caleb, which Caleb promptly imitated.

"Best buds, huh? Can you ask him what the hell has been going on around here then?"

"That's your job. I got about as far as finding out what he wanted to drink and then things got kind of murky after that."

I sighed and pulled up a chair, the three of us forming a triangle. Dan made another offer of a slice, and I suddenly realized I was starving. I made the sign for pizza to Caleb—index and middle fingers slashing the Z sign of "Zorro"—and helped myself. Dan got us each a Sierra Nevada from his tiny office refrigerator.

"Do you think that's a good idea, giving him beer?" I asked, twisting open the cap in record time.

"He's over twenty-one. One beer won't hurt him."

Caleb knew what to do with the beer. After twisting off the cap, he downed several large gulps, then set the bottle on the desk and gave what looked like a hearty burp. I always wonder what a burp sounds like, but I can only imagine. I know it makes everyone giggle, so it must be a funny noise. Dan gave him the thumbs-up sign again.

"Dan, I want him to stay here tonight, while I sort things out. Could you keep an eye on him for me?"

"I don't especially relish harboring a fugitive, Connor."

"He didn't do it, Dan, and you know it."

"I was sort of hoping to sleep with you tonight, not him. I kinda liked your Shake-Awake gizmo. Turns me on, you know?"

"Dan, a pizza turns you on. I really need you to do this for me."

"Yeah, yeah, okay. But you owe me."

"I promise to buy you your own bed shaker if you help me out."

"I don't want you to *buy* me a bed shaker."

"Oh? What *do* you want?"

"I want you to *be* my bed shaker."

I gave him my sexiest smile. It looked like things were going to be back to normal soon. "When this is all over, I've got something really special in mind for you, big boy."

Dan's face lit up. I don't think it was just the beer that gave him that flush. "Oh, yeah? Something stimulating? Mechanical? That vibrates?"

"As a matter of fact, all three."

I waved them both off and headed home to my empty bed, wondering how much a pager would cost.

It didn't take me long to get ready for sleep. I was too tired to floss, too lazy to change out of my T-shirt, and too fuzzy to begin the latest Janet Evanovich mystery. It was all I could do to feed Casper leftover macaroni salad and some doggy "chocolates," and give her a good brushing. After she'd curled up in her favorite spot at the foot of my bed, I slipped off my jeans, careful of my recent bruises and stitched-up slashes, and extricated myself from my bra. I set the Shake-Awake alarm for seven A.M. After all that exercise, I barely had the energy to unfold the sofabed and crawl in.

The next thing I knew, I was about to be taken by the leader of a motorcycle gang when I realized my lips were wet.

Dan?

I sat up, feeling someone's breath on my face. Casper? Before I could reach for the light, my blanket fell over me like an ocean wave. Disoriented, I tried to pull it off, thinking I was just tangled up. But the blanket held firm.

Someone was there.

Whoever it was had me trapped like a netted animal in my own blanket.

I flailed around under the constricting cover, trying to free myself, but strong arms held their grasp. The intruder lay down on top of me, trying to flatten my body on the bed as I fought the constraint. I could feel a strong pressure on my smothered face; I tried to draw in a gasp of air.

Frantically, I wiggled back and forth, trying to get loose. If I could just get my legs free, I could kick the intruder and have a chance of getting away. But my legs, now in pain from the pressure on my bruises, were trapped beneath the weight of the other body.

Again I struggled for breath. It was difficult getting air through the thickness and pressure of the blanket. Gasping, I tried to push the body off, but my arms were pinned. I tried rolling from side to side, and managed to grab a short breath.

Think, Connor! All you've got to do is get an arm free.

As I rocked back and forth, I tried to remember what was nearby that I could use as a possible weapon if I ever freed myself. Each time I rolled, I inched my arm toward the edge of the bed. Closer, closer, each breath harder, shallower.

Finally! My arm slipped out from the cover. Waving frantically, I tried to make contact with the end table. I hit my wrist on the corner, then felt my way around until I grabbed hold of something. It was hard and square with sharp corners.

With all my strength, I brought the object down hard, hoping to hit the assailant in a vulnerable spot.

Contact! I could feel the instant release of the blanket over my face. I threw off the covers, the object fused to my hand. In the glow of the electronic numbers, I could see it was covered in blood.

Without hesitating another moment, I began slamming the Shake-Awake alarm against the head of the figure who now lay in a fetal position on the floor. I brought the thing down again and again in a panicked frenzy. I had to force myself to stop when Casper leapt up on the bed in distress, her head snapping wildly.

I lowered the alarm, reached over, and switched on the light to see whose head it was I'd turned into a bloody pulp.

Then I called the sheriff.

Aubrey Horne lay bloody and barely conscious on the floor of my bedroom, curled up like a baby. While I still had the advantage, I grabbed the sheets off my bed and began wrapping them around Aubrey's body, from his feet to his neck, until he looked like a B-movie version of *The Mummy*.

While Casper continued to snap her teeth and wag her tail furiously, I called the sheriff back and told him to send an ambulance. As I dialed Dan's number, Aubrey's eyes began to flutter. I hoped the body bandage would do its job and keep him incapacitated and at bay. Thank God Dan had bought that secondhand TTY.

The red letters of my TTY lit up the small screen. "Connor? What's up? GA."

I typed back quickly, forgoing the hearing style of typing for the standard all-caps. "DAN CAN U COME OVER. IVE GOT A PROBLEM. SHERIFF IS ON HIS WAY. BRING CALEB. GA."

"Connor, what's going on? Are you all right? GA."

"DONT HAVE TIME TO EXPLAIN. PLS HURRY. GA SK."

I switched off the machine, removed the receiver from the coupler, and returned my attention to Aubrey. His mouth kept opening and closing like a goldfish. Rolling his bloody head back and forth, he appeared to be in pain. No wonder. My Shake-Awake alarm was covered with blood.

I turned Aubrey over so that I could see his face better, in case he said something important. Still hovering, I sat back on my haunches and checked the mummy wrap for weak spots. Finding a loose end at his feet, I tied it off with an extra knot.

I was perched there, watching him like a mother hawk, when the front door light began to flash. I dashed to the door and let in Sheriff Mercer.

"What's this all about, C.W.?"

I led him to my back room, behind the diner's kitchen.

"Holy shit!" he said. "Aubrey?" The sheriff glanced at me as if hoping for some kind of confirmation.

I nodded.

As he knelt beside the mummy, the sheriff examined the bound librarian. I had to lean over to read the sheriff's lips when he spoke.

"C.W., you wanna tell me what's going on? This man was nearly poisoned to death. He should be in the hospital. What's he doin' here?"

"Aubrey, do you want to tell Sheriff Mercer, or shall I?"

Aubrey's eyes flickered open. He spoke in short bursts. "Sheriff . . . help me. She's gone nuts. Tried to kill me . . . with some kind of brick or something. I—"

I cut him off. "Aubrey, tell Sheriff Mercer why you came creeping into my room in the middle of the night, when you were supposed to be on your deathbed at the hospital."

Aubrey rolled his head back and forth. In human bondage, it was about all he could move. "I . . . I don't know how I got here. I remember being in the hospital, and then someone dropped me off here and . . ."

"And what, Aubrey?" I asked, urging him on.

"I . . . tried to wake up Connor, Sheriff . . . to get her help . . . but she didn't answer the door—"

"So you broke in!"

"She . . . must have thought I was a burglar or something, 'cause she started whaling on me with that brick. . . . Help me, Sheriff. I need to get back to the hospital . . . I'm bleeding to death here."

"The EMTs are on their way." The sheriff began to untie Aubrey's feet. I touched his arm to stop him.

"I don't think you want to do that yet, Sheriff. Aubrey has more to say. The truth this time, right, Aubrey? The truth about how you sneaked into the hospital that day and smothered Sparkle Bodie. How you stole Esken's insulin, and after you read up on it in that medical book, lured Esken to the cave and gave him a fatal overdose of his own medication—"

"Sheriff! I didn't do any of that. . . . Can't you see, I'm the victim here. Caleb was the one . . . He tried to kill me after he murdered Sparkle in that hospital room, and Esken in the cave. He may act retarded . . . but he knew I was working on the genealogy chart. And he knew I had found out something about the Bodies . . . that could cause problems."

"It wasn't the Bodie secrets that interested you, Aubrey. It was the Bodie Mine. You found the secrets in there, didn't you?"

"I don't know what you're talking about. . . . Sheriff, get me away from her before she tries to kill me ag—"

He stopped short, his eyes bulging with fear. I whirled around to see the object of his attention.

Caleb Bodie stood in the doorway, with Dan behind him. Caleb appeared agitated, one hand rubbing the side of his pants. The other hand was pointing at Aubrey. It reminded me of the picture he'd drawn.

"Get him away from me! He'll try to kill me again!" Aubrey tried to back away from Caleb. Encased in my bedding, he looked like a fat, white, wiggling worm.

The sheriff stood. "Caleb Bodie, you're under arrest for the murder of—"

"Sheriff! No! It wasn't Caleb. Don't you understand? Caleb, show him." I made a gesture of pulling something from a pocket, hoping he'd understand.

Caleb reached into his own pocket and pulled out a balled-up paper. He tried to hand it to me, but I pointed toward Sheriff Mercer. Caleb shifted hesitantly toward the sheriff, who took the paper, looking puzzled.

"C.W., what is this?" He unfolded the wrinkled paper and pulled out a small glittering rock about the size of a marble. "Holy shit! This is the real McCoy. Where'd it come from?"

"That's mine!" Aubrey called out, rolling his body in an attempt to sit up. "Give it to me!"

"This?" The sheriff held up the nugget of pure gold.

I shook my head. "No, the paper."

The sheriff smoothed out the paper Caleb had shown Devon in her hospital room.

"Careful!" I said quickly. "It's the only one."

The sheriff held the document up to the light, squinted, and shook his head. "Well, I'll be damned. This is the original will. With Sparkle's signature on it."

I nodded. "I think you'll find that the new will was not actually signed by Sparkle Bodie. It's a forgery, signed by Aubrey. This is her only will."

The sheriff leaned against the couch bed, rereading the document. "Says here Esken, Sonora, and Caleb get everything. They haven't been disinherited after all. Where did Caleb get this?"

"Aubrey had it. He stole it from the library file."

"But why? What difference does it make to him?"

I sat down next to the sheriff, facing him. "Here's my guess. After Aubrey started doing research on the Bodie family, he got the idea to falsify Sparkle's will and disinherit the family. Somehow he knew that Caleb had found a vein of gold in the abandoned Bodie Mine. Aubrey must have followed Caleb to the spot, then thought about either killing him or getting him out of the way somehow, so he could secretly mine the gold that was there for himself."

Caleb reached back into his pocket and pulled out a felt

pen. As he glanced around the room for a piece of paper, Dan sensed his need. He pulled a sheet of computer paper from my printer and handed it to Caleb. Caleb sat down on the floor near Aubrey and began to draw.

The sheriff returned his gaze to me. "C.W., what's going on? None of this makes any sense. That place was mined to death years ago."

"I think you're wrong, Sheriff. There's still plenty of gold in that mine. But with all those twisting caverns, and dead ends, and shaky ground, the bulk of it went overlooked for years—until Caleb found a vein."

"But if he found gold, why didn't he tell Sparkle?"

"He didn't know its value."

"But why would Aubrey kill Sparkle? Why not just sneak in there and take the gold without anyone knowing?"

"Insurance. Aubrey figured if Sparkle was dead, Caleb and Esken would inherit the mine, and Caleb would eventually show Esken the gold. So he thought of a way to change that. If Caleb, being an uncommunicative eccentric, was accused of murdering his mother and then his brother, he wouldn't be able to defend himself. If he was convicted, he wouldn't be eligible to inherit his mother's estate, including the mine."

Sheriff Mercer was unconvinced. "But the money, according to the new falsified will, would go to the Clampers. They may have a wild streak in them, but they're sincere about wanting to preserve Flat Skunk's heritage. Granted they would have bought a kegger or two, but they would have used most of the money for the museum, just as she instructed. Aubrey wouldn't have gotten any of it. There was no reason—"

The sheriff stopped talking when Caleb put down his marker and held out the paper for me to see. I took it from him, then showed it to the sheriff. He studied it for a few moments, looked at Caleb, and began to nod.

The drawing clearly showed a man smothering a figure on a bed. As Caleb lifted his finger toward Aubrey, tears filled his eyes.

Aubrey's eyes grew large again. "Sheriff, this is crazy! I

wouldn't have benefited from the new will. . . . Like you said, the Clampers would have gotten everything, including the mine . . . which happens to be worthless."

"Actually, you would have benefited, Aubrey," I said. "You belong to the historical society and the Clampers. In fact, you were to be the next Big Poobah, or whatever they're called. You would have been in charge of making sure that the Bodie Mine wasn't turned into some kind of amusement park for weekend tourists. Because if it was, the gold would surely be discovered then. This way you could mine it at your leisure—without the threat of discovery by the Bodies."

The sheriff stood up. I could seen his mind processing the information as I watched his lips. "So you paid a little visit to Sparkle. Either you had her sign her name so you could copy it, or you somehow got her to sign the new will herself. And that new will left everything to the Clampers—with you as director. Then you hurried along Sparkle's death."

"No! You've got it all wrong—I was never near that hospital room! Caleb's trying to take the blame off himself and accuse me!"

I shook my head. "Caleb's not capable of that kind of guile, Aubrey. He's not retarded. He just thinks differently. Only someone who knew about the will would have sneaked into Sparkle's room and smothered her. Unfortunately, Caleb saw you do it. But you weren't worried, 'cause you thought he couldn't tell anyone. He was distraught, acting a little crazy, which made him look guilty. And you thought you'd get away with it."

Dan stepped forward and I turned to see him say something. I'd almost forgotten he was there. "But you didn't expect Esken to become suspicious, did you, Aubrey? When he did, you had to do something about him, too. So you lured him to the mine and killed him. And set it up to look like Caleb did it."

"So the attempt on your life—the poisoning—" the sheriff began.

"Was faked." Dan finished his sentence.

I nodded. "Easy to do. Read about dosages in a pharmaceutical book from the resource section of the library, then ingest just enough to make yourself sick without actually killing yourself. Cause a scene in a public place so everyone will see you've been poisoned, and get yourself to the hospital in time to pump it out."

Dan looked down at Aubrey, who had grown still. "And while you're in the hospital, you've got the perfect alibi for committing another murder."

I shuddered at the implication. He meant mine.

Dan continued. "That put him above suspicion when it came time to get rid of Connor, who was becoming a bit of a nuisance. I suppose you planned to make it look like Caleb did that one, too."

Caleb held out another drawing, this time handing it to the sheriff.

Sheriff Mercer looked at it, then shook his head. He reached over for the felt pen and added something, then gave it back to Caleb. Caleb smiled as he studied the drawing. I took it from his hands and shared it with Dan.

A tall figure stood behind a number of vertical lines, the eyes closed, the mouth turned down. It was obviously meant to represent Caleb behind bars.

But Sheriff Mercer had added a little more detail. Now the figure looked just like a mummy.

The ambulance took Aubrey to the hospital, with the sheriff right behind them. There was blood all over my sofabed sheets, so I threw them in the washing machine, while Dan made us Raspberry Zinger herbal tea. I'm not much of a tea drinker—I don't see the point. You drink coffee for the buzz, juice for the vitamins, milk for the stamina, and beer for the decompression. What the hell do you drink tea for? But it was Dan's idea and I wanted to indulge him.

After the sheriff had read Aubrey his rights, the EMTs took the bloody man back to the hospital, this time in custody. Caleb was put up at the Mark Twain Slept Here Inn—thanks to my friend, innkeeper Beau Pascal—until arrangements could be made for placing him in an assisted-care housing program. I'd put in a TTY call to Lindan Barde at the Silence Is Golden Deaf Club in the morning, to see about getting Caleb some kind of basic supervised work. It was time to get him involved with the deaf community and find out what improvements could be made with his communication skills—and the quality of his life.

I sat down on the freshly made bed, trying to picture Caleb at the Deaf Club. Maybe it was time for me to get involved there, too, I thought, as I sipped my tea.

"Not bad." I scooted back to rest against the pillows, pulling my clean T-shirt over my knees. Dan unbuckled his belt, slipped off his jeans and T-shirt, and stretched out next to me while I held his steaming mug. After the close call only an hour ago, I welcomed his company. Casper tried to squeeze in between the two of us, but after a brief stare-down, Dan convinced her to lie down at the foot of the bed.

"Thank you," he signed, bringing his fingertips out from his lips, after I handed him his tea.

I smiled and replied with the sign for "You're welcome," a hand curving down in front of my face.

"It's my own recipe. I added a special ingredient." He continued, using speech. He kissed his fingertips, then spread his fingers open. Another one of those Italian signs.

I took another sip. "Cognac?"

He shook his head.

I took another sip. "Brandy?"

"Nope."

One more. I was starting to feel a little dizzy. "Oh, no. Not—"

He nodded.

Nothing like a mug of Raspberry Zinger with a shot of Sierra Nevada beer.

"Good," I said, grimacing.

"So what do you think will happen to Caleb?" Dan said, after a lip-smacking sip of his own doctored tea.

"I'm sure they'll find him a place to live as independently as he can. And some kind of community work, I hope. The money from his inheritance will cover the expenses for the rest of his life."

"What about Sonora?"

"I don't know. She tried to kill Russell. I suppose she'll be prosecuted for that," I said.

"Well, I'm glad you're all right. Pretty smart of you to club that guy with your Shake-Awake alarm. Although I'm going to miss the thing. Guess we'll have to invent our own Shake-Awake alarm, huh?" He rocked the bed, nearly causing me to spill my tea.

"There are still a few loose ends."

"Like what?"

I set the mug down where the alarm had once been.

"Well, who started the fire at the Bodie's home?"

"Don't know, but I'll bet you have a hunch."

"I'm guessing it was Aubrey. He wanted to destroy everything that might have caused complications with the will."

"I'll go along with that. Think he did the same thing to the museum?"

I nodded. "But that time I think he was out to destroy me."

"Did you ever figure out who smashed Esken's car window?"

"I'm sure it was Aubrey again. Probably trying to make it look like Caleb using his brute strength."

"But wasn't he in the hospital getting his stomach pumped then?"

"I guess he sneaked out. He figured no one would suspect him, since he'd just had his stomach pumped."

"Any idea how Caleb managed to write the word 'Quiet' if he can't really write?"

"It's that splintered writing again. He saw the sign so many times at both the library and the hospital, it looked like a drawing to him. He really just 'drew' the word as he remembered connecting it to Aubrey. He has a good mind, you know."

"And I suppose he gets credit for helping you escape from that cave-in at the mine. I don't get to be the hero anymore?"

I smiled. "You're still my hero. But I'm sure it was Caleb who led me out. He knows the mines like the back of his hand. It's funny how things seem so simple, yet underneath they're much more complicated."

"You referring to me?" Dan set his own mug down, then rested his hand on my abdomen.

I laughed. "No, I was referring to the goings-on in Flat Skunk."

"You mean, the way all this happened because of underlying greed?"

"I guess it was greed. Aubrey wanted all the gold in the mine for himself. Sonora married into the Bodie family for the money. Russell arranged adoptions to people who would pay anything for a baby. Young girls thought they were making easy money. At least Russell will be out of commission for awhile, now that he's on his way to prison. Bogus claims and gold fever—they never seem to disappear around here."

"I wonder how Devon is going to make out."

"Sonora loves her very much. That much is clear. I'm sure they'll work things out, and raise that baby together."

Dan moved his hand in a circle on my stomach as he spoke, and it brought me back to the memory of Devon's once pregnant abdomen. I wondered how she was doing. And Twaina. And Amy Allen.

I hesitated before I asked the next question. "Have you . . . heard from your ex-wife?"

"Yeah. Even she was in it for the money. The baby wasn't mine. The test proved that. When I confronted her about it, she confessed she hoped it would bring her a regular paycheck—mine. I feel sorry for her, you know. But thank God she's gone back to New York."

"She left?"

Dan nodded.

"Who was the father?"

"She wouldn't say. I offered to help out a little, until she gets a job, but she said she'd manage fine without me." His hand came to a stop. "You all right?"

I nodded.

"She was never a threat to you."

"I know," I lied. "I just don't like the way she tried to manipulate you."

"She didn't. I knew she was up to something."

"At least something good came out of all this."

"Oh yeah? What's that?" The hand began to move again, upward, this time more slowly.

"Del Rey got a citation from the Clampers for Outstanding Mortician of the Year."

"You mean for not embalming a body that wasn't dead yet?"

"I'd say that was worth a plaque, wouldn't you?"

Dan's hand moved to the hot zone on my chest. He leaned over and kissed me, lightly at first, teasing, then he held on. Tongues were involved, and the suction was strong enough to leave me with collagen lips. After a few minutes, he pulled back.

"I forgot to tell you. The Clampers are coming by tomorrow."

I blinked, pressed my swollen lips together, then asked, "Why?"

"Del Rey isn't the only one in this town who's being honored."

"What do you mean?"

"We're getting a plaque from the good old boys of E. Clampus Vitus."

"Why? You mean the diner? Because it's a local landmark?"

"Not exactly. Actually, the plaque is going right there." He pointed to the wall above my head.

Still puzzled, I frowned, wishing he'd use those lips for something besides rambling on incoherently. "What are you talking about, Dan?"

He grinned, flashing white teeth between his still rosy lips. "They're commemorating this sofabed."

With that, he reached over, turned off the end table light, and I couldn't read another word on his lips.

Didn't matter. The body language was clear. And I kept those lips pretty busy for the next few minutes. Then I went for the gold.

ABOUT THE AUTHOR

Penny Warner has sold over twenty-five books, including four books in the Connor Westphal mystery series from Bantam: *Dead Body Language* (1997), *Sign of Foul Play* (1998), *Right to Remain Silent* (November, 1998) and *Quiet Undertaking* (1999). Warner has a Master's Degree in Special Education/Deaf, and teaches child development, sign language, special education, and mystery writing at the local colleges. She lives in Danville, CA, with her husband of twenty-eight years, and has two kids in college.

If you enjoyed Penny Warner's third Connor Westphal mystery, *Right to Remain Silent*, you won't want to miss any of the books in this exciting series. Look for *Dead Body Language* and *Sign of Foul Play* in your favorite bookstore, and keep a sharp eye out for:

QUIET UNDERTAKING

**The next mystery
featuring Connor Westphal
on sale in Fall 1999.**